THE WILD WIND

SHEENA KALAYIL was born in Zambia in 1970 where her parents were teachers seconded from Kerala, India. She arrived in the UK aged eighteen and, after graduating, worked all over the world. She has a doctorate in Linguistics and teaches at the University of Manchester. Her debut novel, *The Bureau of Second Chances*, won the Writers' Guild Best First Novel Award, and was shortlisted for an Edward Stanford Travel Writing Award – Fiction with a Sense of Place. Her next novel, *The Inheritance*, explored the aftermath of an ill-fated love affair between a lecturer and his student. She lives near Manchester with her husband and two daughters.

The Wild Wind

Sheena Kalayil

Polygon

First published in Great Britain in 2019 by
Polygon, an imprint of Birlinn Ltd.

Birlinn Ltd
West Newington House
10 Newington Road
Edinburgh
EH9 1QS

www.polygonbooks.co.uk

ISBN 978 1 84697 491 5
eBook ISBN 978 1 78885 221 0

British Library Cataloguing-in-Publication Data
A catalogue record for this book is available on
request from the British Library.

Typeset by Biblichor Ltd, Edinburgh

Printed and bound by CPI Group (UK) Ltd, Croydon, CR0 4YY

I heard their young hearts crying
Loveward above the glancing oar
And heard the prairie grasses sighing:
No more, return no more!

O hearts, O sighing grasses,
Vainly your loveblown bannerets mourn!
No more will the wild wind that passes
Return, no more return.

– 'Watching the Needleboats at San Sabba',
James Joyce

For B.K. and S.K., for the growing-up years

Prologue

MY grandfather worked as a groundsman in the Thattek-kad Bird Sanctuary in the Western Ghats, a job with security but which had little monetary return. One blessing, there were five sons and only one daughter, my mother, who would need marrying off. Another, the family were given a house set in the sanctuary, within the forest, among the birds. When we stayed there, on our returns to India, I would tape-record the calls of the hoopoes, sketch the pelicans that breakfasted with us, collect bits of bark and leaves for my scrap-books, compile inventories of nests. These activities enchanted me, whereas they had been the norm for my mother, all through her childhood. She had grown up swimming with her brothers in the river that cut through the hills, with full rein of the sprawling forest, so immersed as to be unaware of the luscious, lush natural beauty of the environs.

I remember one hot afternoon when my mother and I were in the water, in one of the secluded lakes that the river fed. My father was sitting on the banks – he could not swim – and my mother was calling out, mocking him. She was wearing an old nylon slip; it was not the custom, at least then, for women in Kerala to wear a Western-style swimming costume, and the wet cloth must have hindered her efforts in the water, but seemed not to. I swam with her, competently enough, but not like her: ducking under and up, her hair sleek and black against her head, as lissom and lithe as a water creature. When, on her instruction, she and I crept towards my father, grabbed his feet, and then pulled him into the lake, I remember – as he floundered, helpless, on his back in the shallow water – how she swam away, as if to show him both her prowess and how she could leave him high and dry if she wished. And then later, as my mother hid behind a tree, in her underwear, wringing out her slip, my father approached her stealthily to take his revenge. He slipped up suddenly from behind her, and tipped her over his shoulder in a fireman's lift. I watched, wide-eyed, as, my mother bumping against him, he ran back to the water to throw her unceremoniously back into the lake. The sight of my father manhandling my mother, of my mother soaring through the air – her bare legs exposed and splayed – upset me; I was only about six years old. I burst into tears, and my parents, mortified, hurried to kneel in front of me, to console me, even as they were both still helpless with laughter. I remember the sight and feel of my mother, half-naked and wet, her hair plastered against her body, holding me tight against her golden skin; and behind her, my father, his arms encircling us both. All of us shaking like jelly, as my parents tried to regain their composure while I cried hot tears of confusion. But then, not long after, it seemed that my fears that my father's careless antics would harm her were confirmed: my mother fell ill, was not herself, was given a sabbatical from her teaching duties, in order to convalesce. She spent most days in her nightdress, greeting me when I returned from school as if all was normal, but I could see she had not stirred from the bedroom during the day. For many months, perhaps even a year, she was not the mother I knew. But by the time I was eight, nine, she had returned. She regained her energy, moved around the house and beyond with her usual supple grace. She had always had that harmony with her body. When she was in her teens, she learned to dance, as most girls her age were expected to. But she excelled, performed so frequently that eventually my grandfather demanded that she stop; prospective husbands would not look kindly on the fact that she had shown so much of herself in public. My father, thankfully, was not intimidated by my mother's loveliness, her tomboyish childhood running free with her brothers. He had grown up in Ernakulam, the youngest of a family of four children, then stayed with an uncle in Mattancherry when his parents died. He had left Kerala to study in the north of India, as foreign a territory as if he had moved to another planet. And then he did just that. Plucked his young wife away from the familiar surroundings, left Kerala and took her to Africa.

Then began a life of shuttling between two countries, two continents: from heat and dust, to warmth and quiet. In Zambia, we lived far from the sea, and my parents talked wistfully of it. Back in India, they thought of the open land with nostalgia. We would travel first into the Ghats, to Kothamangalam, so my mother could visit with her parents, both paysans, people of the land, who looked on our arrival with bewilderment rather than welcome. And then on to my father's uncle's home in Mattancherry, for a flurry of shopping, of attending weddings delayed for our return, for First Communions and baptisms. It was from there, braving the annoyance our absence would cause, that my father would kidnap me for a day.

He had made it our tradition to travel further south, to the backwaters in Alleppey, to watch the snake boat races. In the intense humidity of the monsoon season, our clothes would be sticking to our backs within minutes of arriving on the banks of the great lake. My father would place me on his shoulders, my legs dangling down on either side of his neck, and I would clutch at his chin, terrified at being so high, but rigid with excitement. From my vantage point, I had an uninterrupted view of the grey water and the long dark canoes, with their raised prows like snakes' heads, the oars moving in a precise rhythm, the rowers as dark as the wood they sat in. Just as I would draw the birds in the sanctuary, my task was always to draw the boats, later, on the train back to Ernakulam. And after all this time, I still have the prized sketchbook from my young years, with page after page of hieroglyphic-like gashes – the soaring heads, the long dark tails – one of the strongest, tangible reminders I have of my father, and of what we enjoyed together.

On returning to Zambia, a change. The landscape was less exuberant, more subdued. The soil was a dusty, humble brown. Here, solitary trees dotted the horizon. The sun was different. Not heavy and blurred, but crisp, dry. Long roads, surrounded on either side by open grassland, space, sky, air. It was as if the land was meant to be looked at and loved, not obscured by a mass of people and a thousand coconut trees. Here, it was the openness that was the beauty, under the eyes of the stars and the sun. And under the sun, we lived in a small pink bungalow, up on a hill, set back from the narrow strip of road, backing onto open bushland and scatterings of trees. A bungalow flanked by mulberry bushes and flame trees, with a front yard of acacia trees and a patchwork of aloes, set in the grounds of Roma Girls' Secondary School, located on the fringes of Lusaka. Ours was one of eight staff bungalows which stood in a row. Two held South Africans who kept to themselves, one an Irishwoman, another remained empty, and four held families from Kerala: transplanted, as were we, from that slender state into that modest campus. The bricks of our bungalow – rose-pink, a shade which deepened in the dusk – were the palest of the whole row, an aberration that made our home stand out from the others; the front door was blue. Opposite our front yard were the steps leading down to the netball courts. And beyond, low school buildings dotted around a pleasantly green space. Down the hill and through gates, a long thoroughfare began, which fed into the dusty central artery of the city, Cairo Road. Once there, I remember a bustle, shops, and the handsome presidential palace.

I know now that we were living in the middle of something much larger. But a child's view of the past is faulty, ephemeral.

Thinking about the city, the overwhelming memory I have is of the smell of the inside of my father's car, a book that would keep me company while I waited, the sound of the door being unlocked, and my father returning with a parcel from the post office, a bag of shopping. A glimpse of road signs, the taste of ice-cream, the musty smell of a cinema. Back at Roma: the walk from my house to Aravind's, Bobby's back door, the space between the houses and the incline of the hill on the east where a clump of trees offered a hiding place from the adults. The school library with its dark parquet floors; the smell of polish and incense in the small chapel. It was a universe for a child. For my parents, it was a scanty, claustrophobic flyspeck.

I returned home to the bungalow from my school in the city at lunchtimes, but the girls at Roma continued their classes into the afternoon. Until the bell rang to signal the end of their school day, I was obliged to stay indoors. I was to finish any homework I had and take charge of my baby brother, at that time seventeen months old. This entailed coaxing him into his afternoon nap by rocking his cot, usually done with my big toe from my position sprawled on my parents' bed, a book in my hands. While he slept, I could enjoy my freedom, although the bungalow did not offer much space in which to roam. The living room was separated from the dining area by a low stone wall, and on which sat the television. Two doors, one from the living area, one from the dining area, led to our bedrooms. The kitchen stood in one corner at the end, and the bathroom in the other. From the living-room door we walked onto our terracotta-tiled veranda, then into our yard; but all that was out of reach for me until my parents returned. When my baby brother woke up, we would keep each other company. I would lift him out of the cot to change him, manipulate the large safety pin that invariably pricked my finger, and then place him on a rug in the living room with his box of toys. There, my brother would patiently build a tower with his bricks. Then, when the fancy took him, he would knock them down, watch them tumble with fascination, and start again. My role was to ensure that his tower did not fall too early in the process; a testy toddler would then be on my hands. When I grew bored, I would leave him and take up my position by the window, from which there was a view of the garden, the road and the school below. Occasionally, I would glance over and see that he was watching me, his gaze steady, his tiny limbs tensed in expectation. If our eyes met, he often screwed his face up; it was an opportunity to cry. But if I turned away in time, he would whimper, forgoing a protest.

I was looking out of the window – on my knees and leaning against the back of the sofa, my palms laid flat on the window-sill – the afternoon when Ezekiel fell to the floor, clutching his chest. I had been staring at a trail of ants on the other side of the glass, two of which carried a crumb each, held aloft, I imagined, as an offering for their queen. In the next room, my brother was beginning to make the snuffling sounds that heralded the end of his afternoon nap. As I spun around, I saw behind me Ezekiel. He groaned as he lay there, his face creased in agony; his lean arms were wrapped around his body. He gasped, rolled to his side. 'Get your mother,' he whispered. When I didn't move, he shouted, 'Your mother!'

I fled. I ran out the door, across our front yard, across the strip of tar that we called a road, down the steps, across the netball courts, and down the next set of steps to the science laboratories. I ran up and down the covered walkway until I could hear her voice. Outside her door, I paused, tried to steady my breathing. I had been instructed never to disturb my parents when they were giving classes; this was the first time I had done so. I peeped through the window and saw rows of girls, sitting at lab benches. Some with their hair cut into halos around their heads, others wearing fine cornrows. The dark green of their uniforms reflected on their skin, so that they appeared almost navy in colour. Rows of navy girls, in green dresses. One looked across and caught sight of me; she giggled and nudged her friend, who waggled her fingers at me. Before long, a dozen faces were turned towards me.

The door opened and my mother stood before me, resplendent in her pristine white lab coat, the folds of her sari peeking from the bottom, her feet in the smart heels she wore for work. As always, her face was dominated by her eyes. Large, with edges that curved slightly upwards, framed by her long eyelashes, and punctuated by her eyebrows arching above like wings.

'You left Danny alone?'

My baby brother. My blood chilled, and I felt the skin on my scalp tighten.

'It's Ezekiel,' I whispered. 'I think he's having a heart attack.'

Now my mother's eyes flared wide open, and she took a sharp intake of breath, a hand flying to her throat. Her reaction both startled and scared me, and I yelped in response, so that for a few seconds we were mirror images, open-mouthed, staring aghast at each other. Then she opened the door to the lab. 'I have to go, girls, sorry,' she said. 'Please copy the notes on the board and . . .' But she turned away without finishing her sentence and walked briskly down the walkway, then broke into a jog, holding up her sari so that it swished against her calves. Up we trotted, up the steps, past the netball courts, up the second set of steps, across the road, up the short path to our door, by now our breath ragged, my mother not looking to see if I was keeping up. I cantered beside her, my two plaits bouncing off my shoulders. By now, the urgency I had felt had dissipated, to be replaced by a twinge of unease, for my mother's agitation frightened me more than Ezekiel's fall. I remembered how his voice had been strong. How he had been a little aloof through the afternoon, not his usual companionable

7

self. As if he had been plotting. Now, I fretted for myself, for I had broken the code of conduct my parents had demanded: I had abandoned my baby brother.

When we stepped into the living room I saw with relief that Ezekiel was still on the floor; I had not imagined his collapse. At that moment I hoped he was, in fact, dead, but on hearing our steps I saw his body move. He shifted to lie on his side, turned to watch us approach.

'Madam . . .' he began. His voice was soft, but even I could discern a slyness, a satisfaction.

My mother stared at him, her cheeks flushed from her exertions, her chest beneath her lab coat rising and falling, her hand again at her throat. And I realised then that all through our rush home she had been full of fear: not for Danny, but for Ezekiel. He seemed to realise the same, because as if to assure her of his wellbeing, with a quick, fluid movement, he sat up. My jaw dropped. I saw his eyes slide towards me guiltily as he slowly stood up. His ploy was revealed; he had wished to speak to my mother alone, without the presence of my father.

Now my mother moved; she stepped around him and walked across the living room to her bedroom. I saw her leaning over the cot and I trailed behind, peered around her. Danny was awake, playing contentedly with one of his teething rings. When he glimpsed my mother, he made a slurping sound of surprise. My mother reached into the cot, adjusted his bib, threw me a quick glance, and then turned to Ezekiel. Behind us, Danny began to wail.

'Madam . . .' Ezekiel began again. 'I need money, madam. I need an advance.'

His voice was now barely audible above Danny's cries. He cleared his throat. I stared from him to her, my head turning from one to the other. My mother's lips were pressed tightly shut. Ezekiel was looking down at his feet, his hands clasped in front of him. His eyes slithered from left to right, and he raised his hand as if to scratch his head, before letting it drop.

'Ezekiel? Is it for your medication?'

He became suddenly animated, as if the suggestion offended him, and he shook his head vigorously. 'No, not for medicine,' he said. 'Just my girlfriend is troubling me.'

At that moment, Danny stopped crying abruptly and Ezekiel's words echoed in our small house. I looked at my mother; she looked dumbfounded. I could not but sympathise; much as I was fond of him, I had never regarded Ezekiel as girlfriend material. Eventually, he raised his head and gave my mother a slow, sheepish smile. That did it for him.

'Please leave, Ezekiel,' she said.

He did not persist, did not protest, but moved immediately towards the door. When he had pressed down the door handle, he turned back, gave me another small, apologetic smile. His shirt sloped off his shoulders, he stood with one shoulder higher than the other, his whole demeanour oozing untrustworthiness and indolence.

'Bye bye, Sissy,' he said.

Then he was gone.

My mother turned to me, 'Don't open the door. I'll be back soon.'

'Mama . . .'

But she did not wait. The door closed behind her, and there was silence. I ran to the window from which I could just make out Ezekiel sauntering down the road to the left, with his uneven, lethargic gait, as if taking a leisurely stroll, as if nothing of import had taken place, and just ahead of me, my mother disappearing down the steps to the netball courts.

My brother was now sucking his teething ring furiously, making little grunting noises. We were alone again. I walked over to his cot. He looked compact, busily rolling from side to side, his bottom oversized in proportion to his tiny body, his

9

tiny fists. It would not be long until my parents returned. My mother with her books and lab coat folded into the basket she used; my father carrying a set of essays against his chest. Often, they would meet at the steps by the netball courts and walk the last few hundred yards together; a chance for them to start their catch-up on the day. As soon as they arrived, my duties were over; I could pass the reins for my brother's safe-keeping over to them. I would dart out the door, into the light of the afternoon, to meet my friends. That day, however, I knew I would not be allowed to escape so quickly. My mother would have relayed the news to my father; there would be a discussion, not only of Ezekiel's deception, but of my incompetence and gullibility. Indeed, when they opened the door that afternoon, they were in mid-flow, so intent on their conversation that they continued even as they walked into the house. I willed myself not to hope, but there was a flutter in my chest; surely my father would not be angry with me.

'I never wanted to have him . . .'

'But we need someone . . .'

'He shouldn't be left alone with the children!'

'We need him,' my father repeated. 'Perhaps we can let him make one silly mistake.'

My mother's eyes flashed, and she deposited her basket to one side, then turned her back to him, kicking off her shoes and throwing her plait over her shoulder with a furious swipe. There was a silence and then: hello, mol. This was directed at me, as if my father had just noticed me. He patted my head, and I felt my stomach unclench. He did not look angry, only amused.

'Hello, Papa.'

'You had an adventure?'

I glanced at my mother, and before I could reply, he said, 'Doesn't Mama look beautiful in her lab coat?' and pinched her cheek.

My mother slapped his hand away, but her mouth had softened. She came towards me, tugged at my plaits, then headed for the bedroom, reaching behind herself to catch the end of the palloo of her sari and tuck it in at her waist. She bent down, her long plait falling to one side, as in one graceful movement she straightened up, Danny now on her hip. My brother shoved his fist inside her blouse and she pulled his hand to her mouth. Then she tilted her head at me, raised her eyebrows at my father and moved to the kitchen. I turned my gaze from my mother to my father. I saw that he was looking down at me, a frown line appearing on his forehead.

'Any appointments to keep?'

I shook my head.

'No important meetings to attend?'

He opened his arms out, his palms facing me. His expression was serious, but I knew he was teasing. I was usually out of the door in seconds after my parents came home. I did not like to arrive too late for my rendezvous with the boys at the other end of the road. There was a risk that my playmates would move on without me, but it was clear that my father expected me to stay. He held out his hand and I took it, and we sat down on the sofa. I snuggled next to him, my legs folded under me, then reached up to finger the thin gold chain tucked in his shirt, the cross dangling at its end. This he wore, he insisted on telling me, out of my mother's earshot, because it was a memento from his late father, not for any superstitious beliefs. I leant against him, as if settling in for a story, but knowing that I was only delaying a more serious discussion. His sideburns tickled my forehead, and his hands were gently curved around my elbows.

'Did Ezekiel scare you?' he asked.

The question troubled me. Now my father's voice sounded solemn, his words more portentous than Ezekiel's ludicrous performance deserved. I thought back. Yes, when I had run out of the house I had been mobilised into action by fear. But my nerves had calmed by the time I had reached the laboratories, I had already begun to have doubts. And not once did any concern for Danny feature in these. I had simply obeyed Ezekiel, just as I would obey a command from my parents, without paying any heed to the implications. I had left my baby brother alone, something I had been ordered never to do. Perhaps I had a chance to mitigate my actions. I felt my head slowly dip down, then up again. My father smiled slightly, but a ripple of sadness moved through his eyes. Whether he was thinking of Ezekiel and his now more tenuous future, or whether he could sense that I was being less than truthful, I could not tell. He patted me on my forearm, kissed me on the forehead. For a moment, I had a close-up view of the open neck of his shirt, the black hair on his chest, the gold cross. Then he cleared his throat and reminded me of my obligations: my baby brother was precious, vulnerable. Yes, I was young to be given this responsibility but, at a few months short of twelve, not that young. And what choice did we have? My mother had been required to return to her teaching duties: the crèche run by the novices in the convent closed after lunch when they had their religious instruction, and when I, fortuitously, returned from my school in town. We each, in our small family, had our contribution to make. Then he smiled, opened his arms wide as if signalling the end of his lecture and freeing me from his embrace, and I slid off the sofa, scampered to the door and out into the sun, grateful that the rebuke had been brief.

But for some reason that day, no doubt because of the strange events of the afternoon, I had not run full tilt to the end of the road. I stopped just after leaving our house, and turned around. I saw that my father was standing at the window, watching me, as if he knew that he had only delayed – not erased – the effect that Ezekiel's departure would have on my family. The reflection of the trees on the glass meant that my father's form was not clear; rather, I saw a shadowy shape wearing a familiar white shirt. He was tall by the window, his head near the top, and as I waited, holding my breath, I saw a movement, a flash as he waved me on. And for years and years later, despite my knowledge that this day in my memory occurred weeks, perhaps even months before the actual event, it was that day which I regarded as our farewell.

Part One

I

WHEN, in the year I was to turn eighteen, I took the train from Philadelphia to a small town an hour away, neither that school campus in Africa nor my parents were in my thoughts. Worries about my own future consumed me. I had no idea what I wanted to do with my life. I knew I loved books, and that I would like to work with them. Beyond that, my ambitions were vague at best, murky at worst. I was in the middle of college applications, and was attending an interview at a small liberal arts institution, one into which I felt I was unlikely to be admitted, and even if I did have such luck, one for which I would need to win a scholarship. But I hankered after an intimate, intellectual ambience, and I had sat the national tests and received excellent scores; in effect, the world was my oyster. I feared, however, that, despite my academic credentials, the interviewer would find me an awkward bumpkin. All through the train ride I rehearsed the answers to the questions I expected to be asked. I had not made this journey before and enjoyed the view as the train chugged rather than sped through the landscape. Next stop but one, miss, said the conductor as he punched my ticket. I got off at a quiet, sleepy station and made my way on foot to the college.

I had arrived with an hour to spare, intending to while away the time absorbing the atmosphere. I wandered among the criss-cross of paths under the stately trees; the green of the lawns was just becoming visible through the melting snow. The college buildings, covered in ivy budding into leaf, exuded elegance and learning. Every student I passed looked not only erudite and enlightened, but self-assured, as if they belonged. As the minutes counted down to the time of my interview, I was having grave misgivings; that the buildings and walkways, the lectures and seminars, the professors and their acolytes would chew me up and spit me out. It was with some trepidation, then, that I knocked on the door I had been directed to, but the professor with whom I had the appointment was gracious and welcoming. I had been required to submit a photograph with my application and therefore no more than a quiver of an eyelid betrayed his reaction to my appearance. He showed me around the department before settling me in his office so that we could talk.

I had imagined a scenario not dissimilar to a job interview, with the professor sitting across a desk, a list of questions in front of him, but we settled in the armchairs positioned in front of the floor-to-ceiling late Georgian window that overlooked the lawn and trees in front of the college building. He had arranged a tray with coffee pot, jar of sugar and milk jug, and he poured out two cups of coffee while we conversed. The essence of the interview, it appeared, was to determine whether I could comport myself in a fireside chat, and I felt both disappointed and faintly ridiculous. I would guess he was not much more than forty; he had done well to secure a position in such rarefied surroundings. His accent was anchored in the East Coast, but harked back to the subcontinent, and it was clear from his name – Professor Sanjay Tharoor – that he was Indian. And so it was not a real surprise when he said after an hour or so – it was clear the question had been weighing on him – that I looked Indian but my name didn't. I said: my stepfather has adopted me. I was Olikara before that.

Olikara? He looked puzzled, then beamed. Well, then you must be Malayalee! When I hesitated, he added: like me. I'm Malayalee! He looked me over with renewed interest; he appeared delighted with the discovery, adding, you don't look like a Keralite.

Then he cleared his throat self-consciously; perhaps he was worried that I would interpret his comment as a verdict on the scars on my face and neck, scarring which, he would not know, extended to below my shoulder. I smiled to reassure him, and he responded with a grateful duck of the head. He asked: Malayalam parayamo?

I shook my head, dredging up some words, surprising myself. My mother and I had long stopped speaking to each other in Malayalam.

Manassilayam. Pakshe . . . I don't speak much.

No matter, no matter, he replied, switching back to English. Olikara, he repeated in wonder.

He appeared to make an effort to resume his bookish tone of earlier. We talked a little more about the projects I had done at school and the courses on offer, about the books I had read when I had prepped for the interview. And then he glanced at his watch. Any questions?

I shook my head and stood up, and it was only when we were at the door that he said: it's been nice to meet a fellow Malayalee. If you don't mind, could I ask where your family is from?

I told him that my mother came from Kothamangalam but hadn't visited for many years, not since we had left Zambia nearly six years ago. And that my father was from Ernakulam but had lived latterly in Mattancherry, on the peninsula across from the city.

Yes, yes, he said, smiling, I know Mattancherry well. When I was a student, my friends and I often took the ferry across.

And he asked where the house was exactly. He might even know the street. Was it near the hospital?

I told him that I couldn't remember. And then, for some reason, I continued, told him that I had not seen my father in those same six years and that I had no idea where he was, that my mother did not talk of him.

He stilled, his hand remaining on the doorknob, but then he dropped it, and stood looking at me.

I'm sorry to hear that, he said.

I shrugged, but something must have shown on my face because he did not move, just stood motionless, looking at his shoes.

That must be difficult for you, he said eventually, and I did not reply, only noticed as if I had avoided looking at it before, the photo in a heavy frame on his desk, taken in a studio; of the professor with his arm around a woman in a heavy silk sari, one small boy standing next to her, the other on her lap.

Sissy. Let me do one thing, he spoke suddenly into the silence. Let me make some enquiries. Can I do that?

Sure, I mumbled, and I continued in the same nonchalant vein as he went back to his desk to take notes. My father would have left Zambia when? Sometime in early September 1978 I would say, I replied. And he studied where? Not sure where in Kerala, a college in Ernakulam I think, but I know he also studied in Aligarh. But he had a degree in history? That's what he taught but I'm not sure that's what he studied. And your parents married when? January 1966, I said. And they divorced when? I shook my head.

No matter, no matter, he said briskly, smiling, but his eyes were troubled; my story was certainly strange and unsettling. It helps that your father used his tharavad, you know, his family name, he said. It's not common in the Syrian Christian community, is it? I shrugged again, and his smile grew wider as if to mask his discomfort. I'll make some enquiries, he said, leading me back to the door, and I'll be in touch – as if we were not talking of my father, but a prime real-estate opportunity.

I returned to Philadelphia and my mother did not mention the interview. She was not disinterested, more anxious that I would suffer a slight or disappointment if I aimed too high. Furthermore, I wore evidence of what had happened on my person, as if a physical rebuke: a continual, living, breathing reminder. She talked at length while I helped her prepare dinner, unusual for her. She asked about the train journey, commented on the sunshine that we were enjoying, and passed on some news she had heard about a high-school friend whose mother she had bumped into in the supermarket. She must have been waiting for me to interrupt, to supply her with a debrief of my day at the college. But I offered nothing, not wishing to be drawn into any discussion which would reveal the coincidence that the professor I had met was from Kerala, had ascertained that I was as well, and had then offered to seek out my father. And indeed, as the days passed I questioned the wisdom of telling a stranger about those most intimate aspects of our lives.

I received two letters from the college in the month that followed. I was offered admission and some financial assistance, but by then I was no longer sure I wanted to study there. I had moved on from the idea of post-colonial literature and was now tempted by Italian Studies, something as far removed from anything I had considered before, or which had been considered for me. And why not? The opportunity of spending a year in Rome was enticing. For this, the state college, charging lower fees and, at three hours away allowing me more independence, would be perfectly acceptable. The other letter I received was from Professor Tharoor.

Haverford, April 10 1984
Dear Sissy

It was a pleasure meeting you a few weeks ago, not only because you are a fellow Keralite, but because I enjoyed hearing your views on the works of Rushdie and Naipaul. You certainly showed me a new perspective! It is not often that I make notes of a discussion I have had with a prospective student, but your comments have led me to a new direction for something I am working on. I would be happy to elaborate when we next meet, and I certainly hope to meet you again.

Regarding the other matter, I can tell you that a George Olikara was registered as a guarantor in a court case against one Raju Kumaresan, in 1978, at the High Courts in Ernakulam. The case extended to three weeks but Kumaresan lost and was imprisoned. After that, I have no information on George Olikara, but I can give you some context to the whole affair. Kumaresan was a former Communist Party activist, who later became a journalist. In fact, I am familiar with some of the articles he wrote and some friends I contacted remember his reports as well. He was stationed for a time in Madras, and later in Bangalore, before he was posted back to Ernakulam. It was on his return to Kerala that he became involved in exposing the corruption in the Communist Party of India (Marxist). Most significantly, in July 1978, he wrote a report alleging intimidation and racketeering among the inner circle of the Party. This was a very risky decision on his part and it comes as no surprise that a few months after the publication of his report, Kumaresan was put on trial for money-laundering.

As far as I can gather, Kumaresan comes from a very ordinary background. He has an elderly mother in Trivandrum and two sisters: all illiterate. It is very possible that your father was one of the few people he could rely on. I'm happy also to let you know that Kumaresan secured an early release and left the prison three years later. However, there is no mention of any involvement by George Olikara from that period.

I hope that this information fills some gaps in your knowledge. Please keep in touch, and if you should accept the offer the college has made, I would like you to come and have dinner with my family.

Warm regards

Sanjay

On reading this letter I did not feel much. I read it with interest, certainly, but also with some annoyance at this reminder of the huge hole inside me, one which I was avoiding contemplating, determined as I was to forge ahead and build my own life. The revelations from Professor Tharoor did not ignite a burning desire in me to track my father down, locate this hero, this loyal friend that it transpired he was. But the other name, Raju Kumaresan, stayed with me and embedded itself in me, so that over the months that followed I whispered it, doodled it, dreamed it. It was as if I would rather invest myself in *this* man than trouble myself over the *other* man, my father. I did not speak of it to my mother; she accepted my revised study plans without comment. I did not show her the letter, but neither did I discard it. For, much as I tried to dispel any feelings of curiosity or of intrigue, one question persisted, repeated itself in my head. If his friend had been sent to jail, then his work was done, even if he had been unsuccessful, ultimately. Why then, had he not returned?

2

THE story of Ezekiel's fall from grace did not hold the head-lines in our circle for very long. Not long after, there came news of a plane, shot down near the border with Rhodesia: the first time – this fact conveyed with some relish by one of the men – that a civilian aircraft had been downed in such a way, in the history of aviation. As another said: it had fallen out of the sky like a dead bird. I turned these words over and over in my head; it was an immense image for a child. With the boys once, I had witnessed their pride in using the catapults they had fashioned to hit a bird that had been sitting on a low branch of a tree. It was a fluke, but its effect was instant. I had always imagined a bird would flutter to the ground, its wings outstretched, a breeze in its feathers. This bird fell straight and undignified in a dark ball to land with a thump, to the whoops and cheers from the boys. I had run away in fright, willing to endure their scorn, unwilling to be party to whatever they plotted with the dead body.

I had worried that my gullibility and Ezekiel's dismissal would dominate my parents' concerns, but in the evenings my father gathered with the menfolk, to stand in a circle to smoke and talk of this terrible event: the fate of the plane and the provenance of the incident. Amidst all these late-night ensem-bles, a few days after Ezekiel left, Grace came to our bungalow. She didn't knock but called softly from outside the back door: bwana, bwana, it is Grace. I was carrying a stack of plates to the kitchen sink; my mother was in the bathroom with my baby brother. When we heard her voice, my father opened the back door and stepped out onto the small porch. The only light came from the dim bulbs we had hanging up, unshaded, in the dining area. I peeked at Grace from behind my father.

'Go, mol. Finish clearing up,' he said to me, his hand gently pushing me back into the house. I heard their two voices as I shuffled to and from the dining table to the kitchen. Neither sounded angry; rather they seemed to be commiserating on a shared disappointment. Often, they made the same noise together, a kind of hum; two parents sharing their disappointment over their errant progeny. When she was taking her leave, through the sliver of space between my father's body and the door-frame, I caught a glimpse of Grace, as always wearing her red knitted hat. She saw me and raised her hand, gave me a small smile. I felt a surge of relief and chirruped a goodbye: she did not blame me.

Although I cannot be sure whether she did or not. What I *can* be sure of is that it was innate to Grace to be courteous and deport herself with decorum, even while she might have seen me as a nuisance, a silly girl who had played some part in her son losing his job. Ezekiel would become a burden to her again. I knew that he lived in her modest dwelling with its corrugated iron roof, in the settlement outside the school gates. I knew that in that block, aside from the small attached bathroom, there was only one room, divided into areas by a criss-cross network of rope and cloth. I knew this because a year ago, or more, I had visited with my father. Grace had been unwell, and he had offered to buy her medicine in town and deliver it to her. That evening, seeing Grace in the small pool of dim light, I remembered how she had looked smaller in her own home, her head uncovered.

It was Grace who had first worked for us, coming every other weekday. We were not the best family to work for, because we did not have much work for anyone. At the time there were only three of us; the small space only required a few twists of a dust-cloth, a swipe with a mop and polish. Any competent cleaner could be finished in an hour at most. My mother enjoyed cooking; Grace was only asked to chop a few vegetables in advance. Washing and ironing the clothes were the most onerous tasks; with no washing machines on the campus, the task had to be done outside, and by hand. When Danny was just over a year old, we went back to India to show him off. There he was passed around like a sweetmeat, cooed over and tickled, while I was left alone to reunite with my cousins as if the interim years had been minutes. My parents were in between contracts, and as always there arose the question: should we go back or should we stay? In the end we left again, but on returning to Roma, we discovered that Grace had found a better, full-time position. There was a new American family, who had moved into a large four-bedroom house a few miles away. Mr Cooper had been seconded for a year, to head up a development agency. He made frequent trips to war-torn Mozambique; Mrs Cooper volunteered at an adult education centre; and there were two daughters. The family needed a cook, a cleaner and a caretaker, and she could even live on the premises if she wished. No one expected Grace to refuse the opportunity. And it was then that she had, as if by sleight of hand, suggested her youngest son, Ezekiel.

The first day he came to the house, he bore a letter of introduction from his mother. It was a Saturday, and we had arrived back from India the previous night. Our suitcases, bulging with spices and new clothes, still lay open and unpacked on the floor in my parents' bedroom. My father had read the letter, standing at the back door. I was inside the house, looking past my father to the young man on the step who held himself in such a way as if he had one leg shorter than the other.

My father said after a long silence, 'So you are Grace's son?'

The young man nodded.

'But I've not seen you before,' my father said.

'I have been away, sir.'

'Away?' my father asked.

'Yes, sir. I was living in Livingstone. With my father.'

'And you haven't found a job?'

'No one will give me a job.'

'I see.' My father turned and caught sight of me. 'Leave us, mol,' he said and waited until I went into my bedroom.

It was only later at night that I heard my parents' discussions: epileptic seizures, but Grace gave assurances that the condition was under control. My mother's voice: unconvinced, disturbed. She had known a girl in college with epilepsy. What if something happens when we are not here? My father's: he is Grace's son and that is the best recommendation we can get.

My father gave his assent and so Ezekiel arrived for his duties a few days later. He was half an hour late. My mother was waiting for him, exasperated, with her lab coat and basket ready. I watched from my bedroom window as he took the pile of clothes to be washed to the small paved area near the outside tap. Then he sat on his haunches, not moving, staring at some space in front of him, for a long time. The minutes ticked by and still he had not moved. I glanced at Danny in his cot and then I opened the back door and stepped tentatively outside. When I was standing a few feet away from him, he looked around and smiled, his mouth lurching to one side on his face: his distinctive crooked smile. He was lean, almost thin, but his teeth were white and straight, and the smile was genuine. We stared at each other for some time. Then he said, 'Let me begin.' He scattered some grains of soap powder into the bottom of the tin bucket and then ran the tap; the soap suds began to bubble up to the surface.

I stayed with him, sitting cross-legged on the grass, and thus we began our friendship, based on my skill at relating amusing anecdotes from my day and Ezekiel's patient, pliant companionship. So how was school? was always his opener when I appeared and crouched down beside him. Followed by: and what did you study today? I regaled him with the minutiae of a convent school education. Ezekiel rarely spoke, and I never asked him questions. He must have found my company appealing in some way, or he may have simply tuned me out as he wrung and rinsed, at times whistling through his teeth. When he started hanging the clothes up on the line, I would hold the basket of pegs for him. It felt like a long, languorous relationship, but it was only for three or four months at most. It had not even been Ezekiel who had taught me my few words of Nyanja, that had been Grace. Perhaps I grew fond of him simply because he seemed so much more content with my company than my usual playmates, Bobby and Aravind.

They were the sons of our neighbours, and their parents were friends, or surrogate older siblings, to mine. There was a gathering that weekend, the week after Ezekiel's departure, a regular occurrence for which there was an informal rota. By lunchtime we were walking along the road to another bungalow, my mother carrying the plate of appams she had made, Danny on my father's arm. The women moved inside, into the kitchen, to finish preparing the food. The men settled outside in a semi-circle of chairs, a crate of beer to one side, and immediately reprised their discussions of the plane, of the people who had died, of the inevitable consequences, for consequences there would be, surely. I stayed with the boys, outside, away from the men, under the trees.

I was the youngest, just as my parents were the youngest, and the only other girl, Reeba, who was sixteen, shunned our company and remained with the women. Aravind, Bobby and I set up with the cricket ball and bat in the patch between Bobby's house and the house of the two male teachers from South Africa who kept to themselves. The older brothers would join us later but for now they were gathered further away, faces shadowed with dark growth, intent on sharing their packet of cigarettes without the adults noticing. Aravind's brother, Rahul – who was leaving in a few months to go to medical college in Bombay – was my favourite. I had found him sleeping in our living room, the morning after Danny was born. He had stayed overnight when my parents had left for the hospital and we had had breakfast together, after which he had helped me brush my hair. Now, as he passed by, he pulled my ponytail, which always cheered me; he noticed me. But he was gone in a flash and I was left with Bobby and Aravind. The story of my escapade had lent me some valour with the boys. I had already described my flight, my descent down the hill and down the steps to the nether areas of the school, the science laboratories. My insurgence into this zone was at first the garner of some attention, but my fame didn't last long, and that afternoon I could sense that they were only tolerating my presence.

The door to the house beside us opened, and Miss Munroe, the English teacher from Dublin, emerged, in black Capri pants and fitted white blouse. I saw my father get to his feet and walk over to her, take the suitcase from her hand and carry it down to her car. There, they stood talking for a few minutes. Miss Munroe laughed at something my father said as he stowed away her suitcase in the boot, before she slipped into the car and drove away. She had been invited to the gathering, but I knew the adults were relieved when she declined. Her absence allowed them to lapse into Malayalam; no need for translations into English for Miss Munroe's benefit. And on her side, I was sure she found being shunted into the kitchen with the womenfolk tiresome, when she always laughed loudest and longest with the men. It was fortuitous that she had offered to housesit for a friend over the weekend, a house complete with manicured lawn and swimming pool. It was a regular arrangement, and one which I suspected relieved the boredom of the rest of Miss Munroe's days on campus, surrounded by families with domestic commitments.

As my father walked back to the group of men, my mother came out of the house, proffering Danny to him. And as he took Danny, I saw my father stroke her cheek and my mother smile at him in return. I watched as my father swung Danny up and down, watched as my baby brother cackled.

There was a yell, and I saw the cricket ball soaring towards me, but I fumbled, dropped it, and then had to pick it up and pass it clumsily back to Aravind, embarrassed. An easy catch but I had mistimed. As I walked back to my position, I realised that my ineptitude had sparked an argument, and before long the boys were having a heated discussion about me.

'Let her play a few more minutes,' Aravind was saying.

'She can't bat and she can't catch.' Bobby was almost spitting with disgust.

Both boys spoke as if oblivious of me, standing metres away from them. I knew that their argument was less about me and more about the rivalry that was growing between them; only months apart in age, they were competing for the same places on the cricket team, the football team, the science prize, at the boys' high school they both attended in Lusaka. Their frustration with each other needed to be deflected; I was conveniently at hand.

'Are you ready, Sissy?' Aravind asked.

I nodded, and he bowled – too low, too slow – and Bobby made an easy swing. The ball hurtled towards me, smacking me on the chest.

I squealed in pain, tears blurring my vision.

'Look what you did, you idiot!' I heard Aravind shout.

'She's all right.'

'You've hurt her!'

'She's just play-acting.'

'No, I'm not!' I managed to protest.

'Why are you here anyway?' he continued, voicing what I had long waited to hear: that I was outstaying my welcome.

'Don't listen to him, Sissy.'

'I mean, why do we have to baby-sit you?' Before I could retort, Bobby continued, his voice a sharp falsetto, his words striking me like another blow: *'Oh no! Ezekiel's having a heart attack! Oh no! Ezekiel saw my tits!'*

Aravind gasped, and I turned away to run, then crouched down, my head on my knees, my hands over my ears. The cricket ball had indeed smacked me in the chest, and had been hurtful enough, leaving a circular, throbbing, intense pain, but one which was wholly real. The jibe, the ugly words and their sentiment, seemed to invade from another world, one which I felt unready for. I could not stop myself glancing down at my chest, where I could see the soft swellings pushing through my top; the boys had noticed even if my mother had not. My shoulders shook, and they must have seen my tears splashing onto the ground. They were silent for some time and I heard some footsteps approach.

'What's going on?' Rahul's voice. I felt a hand on my shoulder. 'Sissy?'

He was so kind, his voice was so gentle, but he was not a playmate. He would be leaving soon, and then I would be left alone with Bobby and Aravind.

I croaked, 'It was an accident. I'm fine.'

'Are you sure?'

I tried to rally myself, raised my head, and smiled, nodded, and I could see in the corner of my eye Bobby throw me a grateful look.

Rahul straightened up and said as he moved away, 'Learn some control, you little prick.'

Aravind stifled a laugh, and Bobby reddened.

When Rahul rejoined the older boys, Aravind approached, patted me awkwardly on the shoulder. I kept my eyes on my feet, still curled up in a ball, unwilling now to unfold myself and reveal my frame. There was some semaphoring I could sense, then Bobby knelt down next to me. 'Sorry, Sissy, I shouldn't have said that.'

We stayed like that for some moments; they did not rush me and I began to feel warmed by their patience. I wiped my eyes and dared to look up at them. Two faces, both concerned. We resumed our game but none of us could ignore the constraint that had settled between us. Soon after, we were called into the house where we filed by the women, plates in hand, while they spooned the several curries onto our plates. I did not return to my playmates, but instead sat on the grass next to my father, who did not query my presence. The sun was hot, and my head felt heavy. I did not enjoy the food, and after I had played with it for many minutes my father told me to take my plate back inside.

Things might have appeared to return to normal in the days that followed, but Bobby's words did not leave me. They had lent a sinister aspect to my fondness for Ezekiel, one that I had hitherto never imagined. I regretted boasting about my tale; it was my version of events that had been Ezekiel's undoing. My small left breast, hardly a breast yet but a reminder that there was another stage to my life around the corner, throbbed and ached, and would remain bruised for some days after. Days when we saw no more of Ezekiel; when he might have fallen away from others' thoughts, if not from mine.

3

THE arrival of the American family, who had headhunted Grace, was serendipitous for my parents. Ally, two years above me, would be attending the International School in town, but the younger daughter, two years below me, Mary-Anne, would be attending my school. If my father dropped me at their house, then I could be ferried to and fro, saving my parents the journey. The Coopers happily obliged. They arranged playdates during which I entertained the girls with stories of our chaotic visits to India which, delighted by the opportunity to display my skills as a raconteur, I embellished with details of domesticated elephants and wayward cousins. I became popular with the American girls; their family became indispensable to mine.

They lived in a sprawling bungalow set in a beautiful garden, with a small orchard to one side, a hammock and a barbecue to the other, and a patio with pots of herbs. The girls each had a bedroom of their own, coordinated in a colour of their choice. Ally had chosen yellow, Mary-Anne green. They had curtains made of thick patterned material which skimmed the polished wooden floors, shelves full of books and comics, packs of felt-tip pens and stickers, wardrobes with rows of neatly hung and folded clothes. They had reading lamps and quilted bed-covers, fluffy rugs. Staying in their house was like walking into the pages of the stories I read. The only reminder of reality was spotting Grace in the kitchen, in her smart uniform. She always broke off her work to greet me: ah, Sissy, and how is your mother?

Their home was a hub for a constant stream of visitors: journalists, researchers, logisticians and activists. Most were American, a few were Zambians; there was one particularly intellectual-looking scholar from Ghana whom everyone called 'Professor'. All held a driving passion for the region, for ensuring its future and solving its ills, and an equal passion for home comforts, good food and drink. The fridge in the house was tightly stocked with bottles of beer and colas; the guest room's bed linen was always on the washing line, being readied for the next arrival. These men treated Mrs Cooper with courtesy and familiarity – why, that's kind of you, Cindy – but Ally would whisper: my mom hates having all these guests. Mrs Cooper, on sufferance of her husband's posting to Africa, had taken a year's sabbatical from her career as a law lecturer, and was not fond of the role of chatelaine.

We were in the back garden one afternoon – Ally in the hammock, Mary-Anne and I with our skipping ropes – when a fair-haired man in glasses, younger than most of the other men, emerged from the kitchen and came up to us.

'Hello, everyone.'

The sisters chimed their greetings with casual familiarity; he was obviously one of the more regular visitors.

He stopped in front of me. 'Hey there. You live in Roma, don't you?'

When I nodded, he continued: 'I'm a friend of Fee Munroe. Do you know her?'

'She's our neighbour.'

'Oh right. You must be one of the Olikaras.'

The Olikaras. I had not thought of us as such, but the reference endowed my family with a literary air I quite liked.

He held out his hand to me and I took it. Then, 'What's your name?'

'Priscilla.' I hesitated, adding, 'But everyone calls me Sissy.'

'I see.' He appeared to weigh up this information. 'So, can I call you Sissy?'

I nodded again, and he smiled. 'Well, there you go.' He released my hand.

As I turned back to my skipping rope, he laughed. 'Don't you want to know what *my* name is?'

Mary-Anne was giggling at my gaucheness and I felt my face grow warm. 'Yes, please.'

'I'm Charlie,' he said. 'Charlie Lawrence.'

'Pleased to meet you.'

He laughed again for some reason. 'Well, it's been a pleasure meeting you, Sissy Olikara.'

I was spared the need for another response when Mr Cooper appeared at the back door calling him back, 'Charlie, have you got a minute?' I could escape, but we met again a few days later when I was in the front yard of our house with Danny. Mr Lawrence came out of Miss Munroe's house, and as if we were long-standing friends called out to me, 'Hello there, Sissy. How are you doing?'

They all had that easy, beguiling way with them – all the adults who frequented the Coopers' house – a combination of light-heartedness and depth. And while I had always seen a great affection between my parents, as there was between Mr and Mrs Cooper, this couple also spoke with each other, at length, in serious tones: at the table, while they cleared things away, even after dinner, in Mr Cooper's study. 'You've got to really think on that, Sam,' Mrs Cooper would often say. 'Really think on that.' Mr Cooper would nod, gravely, before replying, 'I know that's not the way you see it, Cindy, but do you agree that it's the best of a few very poor options?' Alongside their gravitas, in appearance they were an arresting couple. Mr Cooper was tall, bearded, with longish brown hair. He was good-looking; my mother had said so to my father when we had driven back after our first meeting. Mrs Cooper with her wavy, blonde bob was nearly as tall – just as good-looking, as my father had countered. The couple were as carefully matched in appearance, manner and intellect as if their parents had arranged their marriage.

A few weeks had passed since Ezekiel's departure, when my father arrived at the Coopers' house to collect me. The girls were readying themselves for a visit into town, and so I said my goodbyes and ran out. I saw my father with Mr Cooper, both men leaning against my father's car, and as I approached, they did not notice me. They were deep in conversation and they were talking about Ezekiel.

'I wanted to help him' – this from my father – 'but what choice did he leave me with?'

Mr Cooper was nodding his head in sympathy as my father continued: 'I would give him another chance, actually, but Laila doesn't want him to work for us again. She says she never did, although I'm not sure that's true.' Then he chuckled. 'She blames me . . .'

Mr Cooper laughed. 'I don't think anyone could have predicted that he'd pull a stunt like that.'

'Perhaps you could point that out to my wife at your next convenience.'

Mr Cooper laughed again and my father grinned. 'She didn't talk to me for three days once when she was angry about something. At least this time it was only for one night.'

'Well, George,' Mr Cooper was smiling, 'sounds like you got off lightly.' Then he became serious, sighed and shook his head. 'He's very unreliable. Ezekiel, that is. I arranged for him to help out at our canteen in town? He didn't turn up on the first day.'

They both looked ahead, as if they were watching the event unfold.

'That's a pity.'

'And the problem is, people don't like having him around. They believe he'll bring them bad luck. And he looks awful at the moment. He's lost weight and seems to be getting sick all the time . . .'

They fell silent for a long time before Mr Cooper spoke again. 'There's still this stigma associated with epilepsy. There's a lot of ignorance about it. Even an intelligent woman like Grace can be surprisingly superstitious.'

'It's the same in India.'

'Well, probably in some parts of the States, too, to be honest.' By now his voice was so low I had to strain my ears to hear. 'I think she's been turning to the local witchdoctor. Charlie Lawrence knows him. The man's a charlatan . . .'

Mr Cooper broke off when he spied me, and the men ended their conversation. We took our leave, and driving back home, I asked my father, 'Why were you talking about Ezekiel?'

He glanced at me. 'What did you hear?'

'Has something happened?'

My father turned away to look out the windscreen. He was silent for a few minutes and then he said, 'His mother is worried about him.' Then, 'Just as sometimes Mama and I worry about you playing with those boys.'

I stayed very still, held my breath.

He waited a few moments before continuing, 'Miss Munroe spoke to me today. She says she thinks they were peeping through her windows yesterday.'

Relief flooded through me. Yesterday, I had spent the whole afternoon with Reeba and her mother, helping them pack for a wedding in India.

'Do you know how disrespectful that is, Sissy?' my father asked.

I met his gaze. I could feel how huge my eyes were, I could feel the prickle of tears under my eyelids. 'I wasn't with them yesterday, Papa.'

'I know,' he said, 'but you are with them nearly every other day.'

I didn't answer, but felt suddenly mutinous at the inquisition. I looked out of the window and there was a long silence until he said, 'Here, take it.'

It was another one of our traditions, and I hoped that it spelled the end of his displeasure. I reached over and held the steering wheel while he reached into his trouser pocket and pulled out his cigarettes. Then, with a hand resting lightly on the wheel, he lit one and blew smoke out of his window.

'Those boys are older than you, Sissy. They're fourteen, fifteen. They'll be interested in different things from you.'

It was strange to hear him talk of 'those boys' when he knew their fathers so well, but I said nothing.

'Now, I know you don't have any girls your age at Roma. It's nice for you to play with the Coopers, isn't it?'

'Yes, Papa.'

'Well, you can still play with Bobby and Aravind. But maybe not every day, okay? Let's see if you can find something to do at home, okay?'

And true enough, the next day, my mother asked whether I could help her make Danny a small tent with some banana leaves that afternoon, after his nap? Her motives were obvious: she and my father wanted to distract me from playing with 'those boys'. But I acquiesced, happy with the thought of spending time with her, while having a certain knowledge of my parents; they would not be able to keep it up, and eventually I would regain my freedom. The school would be celebrating its fifteenth anniversary in a few weeks, and with preparations for the event entering full swing, my parents had been relieved of their afternoon classes. My mother and I made our plans, and my father took the opportunity to drive back into Lusaka to check our post box and buy some supplies. Danny went down for his nap, and my mother and I lay on our sides, facing each other, on the bed in my parents' room. She had a magazine borrowed from Miss Munroe in her hands and

I had my book; my feet were burrowed in the folds of her skirt. Since Danny's birth, any moments alone with my mother were rare, and I found myself feeling extraordinarily content. If I had been a cat I would have purred.

She had taken off her sari and was lying in her under-garments: in the sari-blouse that ended just below her breasts and the sari-skirt that fell to her ankles. The drawstring of the skirt was tied just below her navel, and her hip curving upwards from her narrow waist made a pleasing silhouette. At the time, my mother would have been not quite thirty-four years old, young to have a child of my age. Without the sari wrapped around her, she appeared even younger, her limbs longer and even more slender. As we read I lowered my book and stole glances at her; her eyes did not seem to move as she looked at each page, the pupils barely moving from side to side, but she turned the pages. She must have felt my gaze because she raised her eyes.

'Not reading?' she said in a low voice. The muted light, my mother's warm body beneath my feet, her gentle tone and the glint in her eye all lent a deliciously clandestine mood to our company.

'What's in the magazine?' I responded, in a similar hushed voice.

'All the things that women are supposed to be interested in.' She smiled. 'Cooking and clothes. And stories.'

'What are the stories about?'

She laughed and tapped me on the head with the magazine. 'Love, mostly,' she said. She watched me, a smile on her lips. 'You know, husbands and wives.'

'When will Miss Munroe get married?'

She raised her eyebrows. 'Maybe she wants to wait and meet the right man,' she said. 'That's what happens sometimes. Or sometimes your parents choose for you.'

I nestled against her arm. I had heard the story before. 'Did Pappan choose for you?'

She nodded, her smile was wide now, and she opened her mouth to speak, but then we heard a soft knock on the bedroom door.

'Madam.'

It was Jonah.

With Ezekiel gone, my parents had struggled with the commitments of their teaching and the housekeeping until, ever the facilitator, Grace arranged for Jonah to work for us. Jonah, a recent arrival in Roma, already did odd jobs around the school, and was attending night classes at the college a few miles away. He could help three afternoons a week, to supplement his income, an arrangement which suited us well. On the first of such afternoons, he had arrived while my parents were still teaching. He greeted me and promptly started on his chores with an efficiency and conscientiousness which enabled him to finish much earlier than Ezekiel ever did. He then sat down on the veranda and pulled out some of his books, alternately reading and making notes, to await my parents. I watched his back from my seat at the dining table, munching on a snack.

Now I watched my mother sit up, pick up a lungi that lay folded on the chair next to her. She tucked it around her like a half-sari, to cover her blouse and bare midriff, and opened the door.

Jonah stood outside, tall and broad-shouldered. 'Madam, the tap in the kitchen is broken. And water is wasting.' He had a deep, slow voice, but his words were clear. 'Shall I fix it?'

My mother hesitated. I saw her hand go to her neck. 'Do you know how to?'

'I need some tools.'

'I'm not sure if we have any.'

My mother seemed timid; her voice was higher than normal. I noticed that Jonah was straight-backed and strong-jawed, unlike Ezekiel.

'I will ask.'

'Ask?'

'Moses.'

So Jonah knew Moses, and Grace knew Jonah, and Ezekiel must know them all, I was thinking.

My mother nodded. 'Thank you, Jonah.'

We heard him leave the house, and my mother crept back to the bed. We stared at each other, our eyes fixed on each other, not speaking. It was as if we were both holding our breath, Jonah's intrusion taking on a much larger significance. When he returned a few minutes later, we could hear some creaks and bangs in the kitchen.

'He's very good, isn't he?' my mother whispered.

'Not a mundun like Ezekiel,' I whispered back.

She burst out laughing, then caught herself. 'No, Sissy,' she said, but her shoulders were still shaking. She grabbed my hand and made me give myself a pretend slap on the cheek. 'No, you mustn't say things like that.'

I had a fleeting sense of betrayal over how I had described Ezekiel – a numbskull – but mostly I felt very pleased with the wit I had demonstrated.

Danny woke up, and we took him through to the living-room. While my mother settled him on his play-mat, I went into the kitchen.

Jonah was clearing up, putting some tools back into a box. He looked at me, smiling. 'It is all right now,' he said.

There was satisfaction in his voice. The tap had been bothering him, even though we had got used to the leak. I saw my mother had moved outside, and was looking at the pile of his books on the veranda. She picked one up and flipped through it. Jonah came back into the living room, and stopped when he saw her.

'Are these yours, Jonah?'

'Yes, madam.'

'You're studying chemistry?'

'I am taking an exam at the end of the year.'

'Only chemistry?'

'And mathematics, madam.'

My mother's eyes skimmed over the page, before she turned to the next. 'You didn't finish this question, Jonah?' She walked over, her finger holding the page, then, placing it against her chest, she opened his book for him to see.

'I did not understand that section.'

She closed the book and brushed some strands of hair away from her face. 'Before you leave today I'll help you with this.'

'Thank you, madam.'

'Or maybe I should ask you first if you want some help?'

'I want some help,' he said simply.

'We can sit here,' she pointed to the dining table, 'when you are ready.' And then she looked up and smiled at him, with that smile I had only ever seen her use with my father. He did not return it, only bowed slightly, silently took the book as she handed it to him. Then, as she turned away and bent to pick up Danny, I saw his eyes, briefly, travel down her plait.

He moved to the back door. 'I will give the tools back, madam.'

'Can I go as well, Mama?' I asked.

My mother turned, Danny's fists tucked into her blouse. 'Okay. Say thank you, remember.'

I walked out the door with Jonah. If it had been Ezekiel I would have immediately asked him how he knew Moses. I would have asked him what section of his book he did not understand. I might even have bragged that I could also help him with his studies. But this was Jonah, and we walked in a dignified silence down the path and then along the road. He took long strides, but when I fell behind I noticed that he slowed down, took shorter steps. We could have walked up the short driveway to the front door, but Jonah pushed aside the branches of the mulberry bush and motioned for me to go ahead, to the side, where we found Moses working in the garden, and who greeted me with a cheerful smile before addressing Jonah in Nyanja. I listened to the men, enjoying the music of their voices. I did not understand what they were saying but I could tell that they were talking of other things, beyond the campus, of the world that began at its boundary. The fragrance from the mulberry bush, the guava tree and the clothes hanging outside on the nearby line wafted around us, and we stood in the soft late-afternoon light. I remember that it was the first time of many to come that I had Jonah by my side, and I remember that I found that situation pleasing.

4

A FEW days later, Mrs Cooper drove me all the way home, and then produced a bag of books and clothes from near her feet. Hand-me-downs from the American girls, which my mother gushed over, Danny on her hip. The Coopers were going back to the States for just over a fortnight, to attend the wedding of Mrs Cooper's sister, and had had a clear-out. 'Laila, I don't know how you manage,' Mrs Cooper was saying. 'With the baby and going back to work and all.' 'These nuns don't understand,' my mother replied in a mischievous voice, leaning into the car. Mrs Cooper honked with laughter, and I saw Ally roll her eyes in irritation.

The Cooper hand-me-downs were welcome, but the Cooper absence was not. That evening my parents mulled over the practicalities of taking me to school. Before Danny had arrived, it had not seemed so difficult for my father to leave the house with me an hour earlier. Now the mornings were more chaotic; my mother had an exam class which had an early morning revision spot, and my father had more extracurricular duties helping the deputy.

'Rahul can take Sissy,' my father said. 'I'll ask tomorrow.'

'They won't like it . . .'

'He's free now. It's not so difficult for him.'

'Sometimes I wonder if it's all worth it,' I heard my mother interrupt. Her voice was tired. 'Enikku vayya. If we were back home, we wouldn't have all these problems.'

'True. We'd have other problems.' I could hear my father smiling. 'Like your family, for example.'

But my parents' worries about taking me to school while the Coopers were away proved unfounded. The morning of the first Monday, I woke up with a fever and a throat that felt raw and swollen. I had had tonsillitis before, but this episode proved to be the most severe. The first two days when my mother and father left for their classes, promising to come back and check up on me in the mid-morning break, I could only grunt from beneath the bedcovers. In the silence that surrounded me, my feverish sleep would be so deep that it felt like seconds had elapsed before I heard someone moving in the room, and one of my parents would enter, feel my forehead, make me drink some water. The nurse in the school infirmary had given us the antibiotics I needed, but by the time I had recovered enough to take note of the goings on around me, nearly a week had passed. Thursday morning, when my parents left the house, I finally left the bed, pottered around the living-room. It looked different; it was bathed in morning light and I was the only person in it. I sat by the window for some time and then went into my parents' room. Their bed was neatly made, and Danny's blanket was folded at the foot of his cot. Next to their bed, on the little table on my mother's side, I saw an aerogramme.

I had always loved the idea of writing words and then folding them inside themselves, along the dotted lines, sealing the edges. By doing so, the words were concealed, kept safe, until someone slid a ruler into the slit, made a clean cut, to open, unfold and liberate them. In our house, it was often I who was given this task; my mother knew I loved doing it. But I had not seen this aerogramme. It must have been collected from our post box in town by my father when I was too ill to take notice. The address of the sender – written in English, in a neat, precise hand – showed the name of my mother's cousin, now married and living in Madras. The letter began: *Dear Lailamma*. Inside, in blue ink, were the comfortingly curly loops and swirls of Malayalam. I recognised the letters that formed my name, which I knew how to write, a few more, but not many. It was a script that was so familiar to me, yet one which remained mysterious. Interspersed among the softness of the Malayalam were the alternating spikes and curves of a few English words. These I read carefully: cinema, haircut, business, Delhi.

I took the aerogramme with me to my room and lay on my bed. I held it above my face so that the light from behind filtered through and the words written on the other side threw their shadows on the words facing me. I read out the English words in a low voice, imagining my aunt saying them as she bent over the paper, writing her letter. With her dark skin and curly hair, she looked unlike my mother, bearing a greater resemblance to my grandfather, Pappan. But I knew they were close; they were the same age and had shared a room for some years in adolescence. The aerogramme fluttered closer to my face as my hand drooped. I dreamt I was back in the bird sanctuary, the river in front of us and the sun a molten ball in the sky. My mother's cousin was sitting next to me, holding my hand. I looked up and saw on the other side of the river Ezekiel, wearing his crooked smile and a worn grey shirt.

I woke to a scraping sound outside. The aerogramme lay on my face, like a blue sheet. I pushed it aside and struggled to a sitting position. I went through to the living room, and from the window facing the road, at the end of our front yard, I saw two men with a ladder. They were putting up what looked like bunting; the school was being decorated for the anniversary celebrations. There was a long trail of red string, holding what looked like multi-coloured flags, but closer inspection revealed that they were alternating pictures of the president and the emblem of the school. One man held the ladder while the other climbed to the top, fixed the line to a lamp-post, then the ladder was dragged a few metres down the road, and the process was repeated. When the men were directly opposite our bungalow I realised that the younger one, who was climbing up and down the ladder, was Jonah.

I opened the door and went out onto the veranda. The older man looked back at the sound of the door closing, then turned away, but not before he saw me wave. I saw them exchange some words, and then Jonah waved at me. He climbed up the ladder and then down again. It was only when he saw me still standing there that he said something to his companion. He came up the path to our veranda, walking with his now-familiar long strides and easy athletic grace.

'Muli bwanji, Sissy,' he said. He smiled, a wide smile, as if he was genuinely pleased to see me.

'Ndilo bwino, but . . . I haven't been well,' I replied, the extent of my Nyanja having been depleted.

'I know, Sissy. Every afternoon you have been asleep.'

He looked down at me, still smiling. We had never spoken like this before, facing each other, and I found I felt a little shy. He stood before me with his hands clasped together, as if we were accustomed to each other's company.

'Are you feeling better?'

'I've missed school all week,' I said, and to my chagrin, saying the words made me feel the loneliness of my days, the silence inside the house, and the long hours that stretched before me. I knew the American girls were back home and not giving me a second thought. I knew that Bobby and Aravind would have been enjoying each other's company without me. My dispensable existence seemed, suddenly, to overwhelm me. My eyes welled up with tears. Jonah continued to smile, but I could see that his eyes had darkened, and he tilted his head in sympathy.

'Ah, don't be sad, Sissy.'

Then he pointed back to where his companion stood waiting, the ladder resting against his shoulder. 'Do you see?'

I nodded, tried to smile, brushed my tears away with the back of my hand.

'It will be a big party!' Jonah grinned. 'Singing, dancing.'

I nodded again.

'You will feel better then and so you will enjoy.'

My head was beginning to throb. We fell silent. With no story to relate about my school day, my head feeling heavy and my throat beginning to scratch, I couldn't think what to say.

'You need to rest, Sissy. Go inside and lie down now.'

He spoke with an authority that held an intimacy which made me stare back at him. I was only accustomed to being spoken to like that by my parents. Then he walked across the veranda and opened the front door for me, waited until I was back inside, and closed it. I watched him walk back down to the road. It was a new, not unpleasant, sensation to have obeyed Jonah. Behind me I could hear the ladder scraping down the road to the next lamppost. I went back to my bed and drifted in and out of sleep.

When my parents returned later, they were relieved to see me awake and reading a book, my knees drawn up; even more when I repositioned myself in the living room, on the sofa. When Jonah arrived at the door he smiled his hello, before busying himself in the kitchen, then moving outside. He seemed more assured, as if he had moved up a few notches those days while I was sleeping. My father, in contrast, seemed disgruntled; I suspected he missed driving out of the campus to pick me up from the American girls' house, his chats with Mr Cooper. And my mother looked tired; she had been worried about me, and without my help, the afternoons had been fraught for her. Our bungalow seemed even smaller than ever; our lives seemed even more squeezed into that road, the campus.

While my father took Danny outside to keep him company as he dug in the garden and tended to his vegetable patch, I watched my mother clear some space at the dining table, and then Jonah re-entered, washed his hands in the kitchen sink, and sat down across from her. I noticed she did not use her teaching voice, even though she was correcting his work; it was gentler, as if she was being careful not to hurt his feelings. He asked an occasional question, and his voice in turn was respectful and tentative, as if he were afraid of revealing what he did not know. I enjoyed hearing their voices in the background, as I read my book. You know which is oxidation and which is reduction? And if there is no acid present, madam?

The light began to fade and my father came back inside, Danny on his arm. As he walked past, he squeezed my mother's shoulder. Jonah took this as a signal, and lowering his eyes, he stood up and gathered his books, then stepped outside. On the veranda, he bent down and picked up a bag he had left there.

'Sir,' he said to my father, 'I made this for the baby,' and he unfurled what he held, an ingenious small wooden cage, polished smooth and varnished, with ropes attached and trailing down. My mother's eyes were wide, and he smiled at her obvious surprise as my father grunted a thank-you, stealing a look at my mother.

'It will hang well there.' Jonah pointed to a branch of one of the trees in the front yard.

I saw my father put his arm around my mother's shoulder as if to stay her enthusiasm, and we all watched as Jonah went outside, slipped the ropes around the branch and knotted the ends expertly. He gave the swing a little nudge and it leapt forward encouragingly. My mother wriggled from my father's clasp, scooped up Danny, and skipped outside. I watched as Jonah helped her place my brother in his seat and give the swing another little push. Danny gripped the front bar and kicked his legs with delight.

'Jonah, it's wonderful!' My mother was looking up at him.

'Wait, I will make this tighter.' And he reached up to fiddle with the rope on the branch, in a gesture that was at once graceful and wholly masculine. Danny was bouncing up and down with glee, and both my mother and Jonah laughed at his antics. She touched his arm. 'Thank you so much.'

'It's nothing, madam.' He smiled down at her, clearly gratified by her reaction, and then he looked across the yard to me at the window and raised his hand. 'Bye bye, Sissy.' He called out, 'Tomorrow you will be even better.' Then, to my father: 'Sir.'

His attention touched me; he had not forgotten me. I raised myself on my knees and watched through the window as he kicked himself off on his bicycle and in a fluid, practised movement, his bag slung across his chest, glided away.

My father went out to push Danny, my mother came to sit next to me, and I asked, 'Is Jonah clever?'

She laughed. 'What a question.'

'Why are you helping him?'

She looked amused. 'Why do you ask?'

'You didn't help Ezekiel.'

The words arrived from somewhere I was unaware existed. She looked at me with a level gaze, and I thought for a moment she would stand up and move away, her lips pursed with annoyance.

She spoke finally: 'I never felt comfortable with Ezekiel . . . I know you thought of him as a friend—'

'He *was* a friend.'

She shook her head. 'Sissy . . .' She stopped, started again. 'It's unusual for a girl your age to be friends with a man Ezekiel's age.'

'But how old is Ezekiel?'

She smiled. 'To be honest, I don't know. Twenties? We can ask Papa, he might know.'

'And how old is Jonah?'

'I'm not sure.' She paused. 'Same age as Ezekiel, or perhaps a little older.'

I turned my face away. Jonah and Ezekiel: biblical names for ordinary men. They were the same age, and shared the same background, inhabited the same world. But I realised from where my discomfiture lay; my mother was picking and choosing in a way I did not like, even as I felt my loyalties to Ezekiel seeping away. I felt troubled, as if aware that very soon a small crack would appear in the bubble that was our lives. And that small fissure could not be sewn shut, but would fray and stretch, wider and wider. Until we fell through it, into the world, waiting for us, outside.

5

M Y father left not long after that day, the day of the swing. But of the circumstances surrounding his departure, I remember very little. He must have told me he was going away but I do not recall the conversation. My mother did not seem more vexed than usual. There was no stand-out row, my parents facing each other, eyes blazing. My thoughts were without a doubt elsewhere occupied. I was, at the time, upset by a growing sense of disconnection from the boys, and an incipient worry that the American girls, too, would begin to detach themselves from my company. I was unaware when a blue aerogramme arrived, unaware that it was opened and my father's decision made. Whatever news that rectangular blue sheet held had sent my father away.

Now, thinking back, while there was no set-piece event, I do remember snatches of conversation. But it is only my father's voice I can recall: it might be too late already. What do you mean? You're not alone, you're surrounded by friends. And one evening, after I had gone to bed, but then woken in the night to use the bathroom, I remember thinking that the dream I had been having was continuing, for there was a murmur of voices coming from the other side of the window. I opened the curtain a fraction to see my parents standing near the vegetable patch, facing each other. Even then, there was nothing distinctive about their body language to alert me to the ensuing separation. More memorable were the meetings my mother had to attend with the Mother Superior, in the days that followed. We had already had an extended stay in India to show Danny off. My father's sudden absence was, unsurprisingly, roundly condemned, and the Board of Governors initially called for his dismissal. However, after a long deliberation, they signed it off as unpaid leave. The tacit agreement was that my mother was too valuable to antagonise, being a chemistry teacher with exam classes and an excellent track record. Better to excuse one Olikara in the short term than sever ties with both Olikaras. The nuns became benevolent, offered to take charge of Danny in the afternoons until I could be properly returned from school. The Mother Superior gave her blessing – irrelevant, because by then my father had already gone.

Before that, however, we enjoyed our last airing as a family of four. A father, a mother and two children: a girl and a boy. Nondescript in many ways, but a unit and undeniably attached, with the father's arm around the mother's shoulder, the baby in the woman's arms, and the girl holding her father's other hand. Dressed for an occasion, too: the mother in a turquoise silk sari, her hair pulled into a bun at the back of her head, gold hoops at her ears. The father in a white shirt and tie. Even the baby boy was dressed up, in embroidered yellow shirt and shorts, his feet in matching yellow boots. And the older child, the girl, in a skirt-and-blouse combination, stitched for her on their last visit to India, in Mattancherry, a few months previously. It was the day of the school's anniversary celebration, and as Jonah had predicted, I was well enough to walk down to the netball courts at midday.

Ahead of us lay at least an hour of speeches, then a buffet lunch, followed by the entertainment – the singing and dancing that Jonah had mentioned. As we made our way to our seats in the marquee, I saw Bobby and Aravind standing at one end, both with their hair plastered down into neat side-partings. Aravind gave me a wave, and I smiled back weakly, trying to suppress the automatic gratitude I always felt at any acknowledgement from the boys. If I had been feeling better, this would have been a day of freedom, to be spent with my playmates, but I felt disinclined. I settled on my father's lap, as if I were years younger, but he did not remind me of this; my mother sat beside me with Danny. My outfit, although ridiculously over-dressy, I felt, in red and orange satin, was luxuriously soft against my legs, and I appreciated the way it caressed my body, still achy from the fever. The speeches began, the first by the bishop invited to oversee the day, who droned on, and behind me, his hand tapping against my leg, my father whispered: okay, mol? I turned my face so that it would brush against his sideburns, then reached across and took one of Danny's hands. He turned to me with delight then tipped himself into my lap. I pulled him close. We were a triple layer now: my father, myself and Danny. Beside us, my mother smelled sweetly of talcum powder. I saw my father's hand go to the back of her neck, to caress it briefly, his hand a dark mahogany against the gold of her skin. It was the last such moment I remember witnessing.

Out of the corner of my eye, I saw Bobby and Aravind leave the gathering and run down the steps away from the netball courts. I watched them until they were out of sight, then asked my father if I could take Danny for a walk. But I should not have left the comfort of my father's lap. As soon as I walked away, or rather was led by Danny – bent over him, his fingers twisted into mine, his hands held aloft while his feet marched, one in front of each other, a look of faint surprise on his face, as if he were being propelled by his limbs – I felt unsteady on my feet, my head in turns heavy and light. My tongue felt dry and over-large in my mouth, and it was only curiosity that spurred me on. If we positioned ourselves at the end of the netball courts, just before the hill which led down to the science laboratories and then on to the girls' dormitories, I would have a view of what Bobby and Aravind were doing. They were huddled together, and I saw

Aravind pull something from under his shirt, a pamphlet I thought at first, before realising it was a magazine. Both boys then leant over, their heads touching as they turned the pages, their backs to me, and I felt suddenly unwilling to remain in my crow's nest. I steered Danny away, thinking we could head back to the tent where I could get a drink, but when we reached the edge of the slope, I saw Jonah, by the small stand-alone storeroom that stood just below the brow of the hill. He was not alone. I recognised the young woman he was with, one of the cooks from the school kitchens.

She was leaning against the storeroom wall, her hands behind her back; Jonah had one forearm pressed against the wall above her head, so he was simultaneously pinning her in place and shielding her view with his body. He was wearing a long-sleeved dark green shirt over smart navy trousers, and the cook was wearing a fitted red dress, a white turban covering her hair. Against the terracotta wall they were both vivid splashes of colour. They spoke in low voices, their faces only inches apart, and they spoke fluently: Jonah did not have that reticence or stiffness as when he spoke with my parents, and as far as I could tell, he was in the middle of a long speech. His voice was gentle but there was a persuasive tone. I understood nothing, but his companion did; the cook's eyes never left his, and she punctuated Jonah's words with brief nods. Danny was motoring down the hill with furious intent, so I had to follow, and before I could change his course, we arrived in front of them. The cook's eyes slid behind Jonah to me, and she murmured something, straightened up, so that Jonah dropped his arm and turned around. He said something to the cook in Nyanja which I did not understand, then, 'Hello, Sissy.'

They looked down at me, smiling, but I could sense that they were both taken aback by our appearance. Jonah glanced again at his companion, gesturing to me. 'Musungwana wokongole,' before continuing. 'You look beautiful in your dress.' The cook nodded in confirmation and repeated in a surprisingly high voice, 'Very beautiful.'

'Thank you,' I said. And then I ventured, 'So do both of you.'

They laughed, and I saw the cook touch Jonah's arm briefly.

He bowed at me, his face serious but his eyes dancing. 'Thank you, Sissy. Are you better now?'

'I think so.'

He said a few more words to the cook and she clucked her tongue in sympathy.

'And how is this little man?' He bent down onto his haunches, held his hand out, and was rewarded with a smack on his palm by my delighted brother, who then pumped his tiny body up and down in the way that I knew meant he wanted to be picked up. I lifted Danny into my arms, and Jonah stood up at the same time so that he towered above me, looking down. There was nothing more to say. I raised my hand in a goodbye, and Jonah smiled as I turned away.

When we reached the top of the steps, I looked back and saw they had resumed their previous positions, although now the cook's hip was brushing against Jonah's. I felt a wave of fatigue all of a sudden, and so I set Danny down on a patch of grass. My throat was aching again, and I felt thirsty. The sun felt very hot, and my head throbbed. A shadow fell over us; it was my father. He pulled me up to my feet without a word, and I clung to him as he bent down and, more clumsily than in years before – for I had grown in the last months – picked me up so I could lay my head on his shoulder. Reaching to the side, he grabbed Danny's arm and swung him to his chest, and carried both of us back to the shade of the trees. Over his shoulder I saw Miss Munroe and Mr Lawrence sitting on the grass together, further away, watching us. The dancers were gathering, and after a few moments the drums started as, with a shout, the singing began.

Then, he left. And because it was only days after the anniversary celebrations these coincide in my thoughts as his send-off, engineered to bring us all together so that I could wander from one group of actors to another as if they were troubadours, travelling jesters gathered for the inauguration. For, while I remember that day primarily as a succession of sensations – the ache of my throat, the warmth of the sun on my skin, the harmonics of the songs – I can still recall concrete details of what we wore and what we said and what we ate.

And similarly, on the day of my father's departure I remember I was wearing one of my least favourite outfits – a green dress which rubbed against my skin like a sack for the very last time, as if his leaving allowed me the license to discard it. And just as I had been staring out of the window when Ezekiel fell to the floor, I was in the same position that afternoon. It was a Saturday. The sky was its usual clear, light blue; the trail of ants marched as busily as ever along our windowsill. All was as it had always been. The door to my parents' bedroom opened and he appeared, taking care to close it behind him quickly and noiselessly, without allowing me much of a view into the room, just as he had done those days – when I was younger, before Danny was born – when my mother was ill.

'Be good, Sissy, and help Mama, okay?'

He looked different: freshly-shaved, wearing his best shoes, with a suitcase in his hand, a jacket folded over his arm. Across the front yard I saw Miss Munroe in her car, behind the wheel, the engine running. Her demeanour was uncomfortable, strained, as if she were being forced to be party to something against her will. My father reached for the front-door handle, and then stopped as if remembering something. He came towards me, kissed me on the forehead, and stroked my cheek with his thumb. I felt the brush of his sideburns against my temple before he straightened up.

'Papa, my ankle hurts.'

A look of confusion passed over his features.

'It's been hurting since yesterday . . .'

Now there was another expression, frustration or impatience. He reached down and gripped my ankle briefly, squeezed it.

'It will be fine.'

'No, it's been hurting since . . .'

'Sissy,' now his tone was abrupt, 'it's nothing. Listen, be good and take care of Mama, okay?'

I watched from the window as he walked down the path, opened the back door of Miss Munroe's car to slide in his suitcase, then the front door to slide himself in. Miss Munroe seemed to wish to leave as quickly as possible; the tyres of her car screeched as, in a cloud of dust, they drove away. I stayed where I was, leaning against the back of the sofa for a long time, knowing, even then, that our farewell had been hasty and unsatisfying. When I finally moved away from the window I could see the pattern of the material of the sofa criss-crossing over my knees. There was a gulp, and I saw Danny shoving a wooden brick into his mouth. He was useless. I couldn't talk to him; he couldn't help me dampen the strange feeling rising inside my chest. Then he caught my eye, removed the brick, and gave me a wide toothless smile. I slid off the sofa and enfolded him in my arms. His head was damp and warm, his hands twisting into my plaits were sticky.

'Want a snack?' I whispered.

He hit me on the side of the head with his brick, a gentle bump, before replacing it between his gums. I walked into the kitchen and glanced at the small clock that we had never put on the wall but leant up against the fridge. It was only three o'clock in the afternoon.

And at that moment I felt as if I was learning about time. How there were endless minutes, hours in a day that stretched ahead of us before we arrived at the darkness when we could legitimately lie in our beds and close our eyes. Having spent so much time on my own, I was used to this. I knew my mother was less so. Aside from Miss Munroe, who occupied herself assiduously, perhaps to stem these exact same feelings, my mother had no one to talk to, no one to confide in. The Malayalee ladies were older than her and limited in their conversation. The Malayalee men enjoyed her company, and I knew they entertained her with their bravado, but their wives regarded these performances jealously. There was nothing around us, nothing to do, other than walk down to the bottom of our garden and up again, tend to the plants at the back, pick fruit off our trees.

I was surprised to have a vision flash before me of the street we always walked along in Kothamangalam, the street she will have walked along while she was growing up, with its stalls on either side, the large sari shop at the end, and the myriad opportunities to buy a snack, a coffee, clothes, books, plastic trinkets, gold ornaments, whenever we wanted. The air thick with the smell of fried snacks, jasmine, hair oil and talcum powder. The shouts in Malayalam, the persistent rickshaw drivers calling, the devotional songs from the temples, the namaz from the mosques, the chanting from the church. Here, there was nothing. It was a desert in comparison, and I felt something I would not recognise until much later: a sympathy for my mother, who rarely left the campus, and even then, only to go a few miles down the hill to the small church.

An hour later, my parents' bedroom door opened and my mother emerged for the first time that afternoon. She might have been crying, but I thought that she looked as if she had been sleeping; her face had that soft, just-awake look. She was dressed only in her sari blouse and underskirt; I spied her sari spilling off the end of the bed. She came into the living room, walking as if she was casually entering a stranger's house, giving me and Danny a distracted smile as if we were those strangers. I thought she might come and sit with us, or even go into the kitchen and make some decisions for dinner later, but she walked to the side-table on which our record-player, the type that played vinyl LPs, sat. I watched as she unplugged the player from the wall and, carrying it under her arm, gave me another small smile as she walked back into the bedroom and closed the door.

As I waited with bated breath, Danny beside me also staring at the door with open mouth, I heard the first notes of a song coming from behind the door, a record we had brought back from India the last time we were there.

Now I know what she would have been doing: observing the time-honoured tradition of playing sad songs to soothe your broken heart. She would have laid down on the bed again, tears streaked across her cheeks, her hands wrapped around her belly as her heart ached and her blood raged, wallowing in the songs and their aphorisms of love and life, wondering how my father could have left her as he did. For she will have already in those minutes missed him deeply. Not only for his helping hand and his strength – lifting the bucket of water from the barrel if the pump did not work, carrying Danny on his arm when my brother grew heavy with resistance, driving the car to and from the small grocery shop or into the city. She will have missed the man who was her first love and her first lover.

It is not easy for a child to imagine her parents as lovers, and I wonder why it was so easy for me. Perhaps because I was so young, and because of the way they were with each other; it was so innocent and unsullied, a natural extension of themselves. Perhaps I had witnessed something as a younger child when I shared their bedroom like Danny did now; something tender and loving, that did not perturb me but that had imprinted itself on my memory. An image of my mother lying next to my father, his hands on her form, which became a comforting assurance of the feelings they had for each other. I had heard them whispering late in the night, thinking I could not hear them. And I could hear sounds from their bedroom as they made love. My father's voice – muffled, as if buried in her hair – and the gentle, yielding responses that came from deep in my mother's throat. The footsteps after as my mother used the bathroom quietly, then to return to the bedroom where their voices intersected again. Their love, all aspects of it, was what cemented us together: when that was fractured, so were we.

At one stage in my life, a particularly bitter phase, I thought: she *let* it happen, she *let* him leave. Why does anyone let something happen if not because they *wanted* it to happen? But even in those moments, I could never cast her in so cold a light as to presume that my mother did not yearn for my father, miss him utterly, when I had seen all through my life until then how she melted at my father's touch or look; how her features became softer, as if in anticipation of when night would fall, and Danny and I would be tucked away.

That afternoon, her door remained closed, and through it we could hear only the plaintive, mawkish tones of the Malayalam love song as the light began to fade and the air became cool enough to close the windows. By then, Danny and I had exhausted each other's company; but somehow my baby brother had known not to test me, and he had been particularly pliant and good-natured. When it was dark enough to turn on the light in the living room and draw the curtains, I did so, then stood outside my mother's door. Again, all I could hear were the notes of the song. She must have played the same record four times by then. No other sound: of sobs, or cries of anger. Only when I had moved to the kitchen and opened the fridge to see with relief some eggs that I could boil for our supper and some vegetables to chop up for a salad, only after I had set a pan to boil and had found as well that we had two loaves of bread and a basket of fruit that my father must have bought in advance of his departure, did I see that Jonah was outside the window.

He was rolling the barrel that held the gallon of water we always stored in case of a water cut; rolling it a few feet to one side, then a few feet to the other, so that he zigzagged the barrel from where it stood at the edge of our plot to a spot just outside the back door. It was only a distance of a few metres, but it meant that we could reach for the water easily from the back step. I opened the door. He was wiping the barrel down, cleaning it as if it were a child. The music from my mother's bedroom wafted outside and I saw him glance quickly in that direction before he smiled at me. 'This will be easier for you. I will just fill it to the top in case. Get me the bucket, Sissy.'

I knew what he meant, and ran inside, found the metal pail under the kitchen sink and handed it to him, watched as he walked to the central tap between the houses at the rear, filled the vessel, then lifted it onto his shoulder and walked back, some water slurping out. After he had poured the water into the barrel, I held out the small towel I had retrieved for him.

'No, I don't need, Sissy,' he said, then, 'Are you well?'

He smiled again, but I noticed how his eyes held mine for a second longer than necessary, a shadow passing through them, before they glanced around me to the door of my mother's bedroom. As he turned to leave, I bleated a thank-you, then, after closing the door, rushed to the window to see him glide away on his bicycle. He would never have come if my father were here. He knew my father took note of how much water we stored, filled the barrel himself, although – I thought, my heart squeezing against my ribs with a flash of something, anger perhaps – without the effortless grace that Jonah had shown. So, they must know that my father had left this afternoon: Jonah and Moses and Grace. Ezekiel, too. Everyone knew.

At that moment my mother's bedroom door opened. She walked over to the back door, opened it and saw the barrel. She stared for some moments at it, or something else that I was not aware of, then stepped back inside, closed the door and locked it. She stood still for several moments, then glanced into the kitchen and saw the eggs I had removed from the fridge, the loaf of bread.

'French toast?' she said to me, and I nodded eagerly.

By the time we sat down, the three of us, to eat, it was past eight o'clock at night, and the meal was even more enjoyable for being so incongruous, a breakfast snack taken at dinner time. She did not ask after my feelings that evening for she knew I would not be able to express them yet, and she did not share hers. We did not speak; we were simply companions. We had survived the first five hours without my father; we would survive the many, many years hence.

Part Two

6

I WAS offered a place at Penn State, to major in Italian Studies. I longed to see the country and I did, spending two semesters in Rome, falling in love with the city. After I graduated, desperate to go to another big city, lose myself in its crowds, and of a mind to study further, I arrived in New York where I rented a room in an apartment on Nostrand Avenue, in Bedford-Stuyvesant. My landlady was a proud Brooklynite, who ran a cleaning service for the occupants of the grander brownstones in the more genteel Prospect Park. Her staff were all women, predominantly Haitian, and she operated her business more like a social development project, advising, or rather coercing, her 'ladies' to invest part of their earnings in English courses and book-keeping classes, with the intention of securing better jobs. You don't want to be cleaning houses in Bed-Stuy five years from now, was her refrain. She was an inspiration, and incredibly generous. It was through her that I added 'dog-walker' for her clients to my list of part-time jobs, which included proofreading for academic essays and tending a bar at weekends. The latter I applied for only on encouragement from my landlady, who upbraided me for my shyness: you got to face your fears, Sissy, put yourself out there and hold your head high. And after I did indeed face my fears, I admit I enjoyed the repartee and vibe of a late-night bar. Every other spare moment I spent buried in the library on Washington Square, reading through piles of journals and manuscripts.

During my final year on my degree I had explored the translations into Italian of late nineteenth and early twentieth-century novels in English. I had discovered, by chance, a rivalry that had grown between two Italians: Rossi and Montale. Both were commissioned later in the twentieth century to translate a short poem by James Joyce, and the differing receptions to their translations – the debate over whether maintaining the metrical verse or translating into free verse produced the most effective interpretation – echoed discussions on whether the translator's voice could ever mirror the author's voice, or whether translation into another language produced as different an artefact as adapting a novel into a film. All debates which were particularly germane to poetry. This, I felt, was my doctoral thesis in the making; still an embryonic idea, and needing further investigation. So that, by the time my proposal, a collection of sketchy arguments, was received and accepted, I had already spent many months in my hermetic routine of work and study, spending most nights with papers scattered around me in my room, my landlady occasionally banging on my door: Sissy, you still alive in there, baby?

By a twist of luck, three months later, my supervisor put my name forward to a writer who she knew and who had asked her to recommend a translator. His latest novel was to be published in Italy. It was a ruthlessly bare portrayal of a hapless and childless marriage between two unlikeable writers, a wry and cynical depiction of sexual desire and malice, which in his narrative were depicted as the same endeavour. I devoured his book over a day and night of non-stop reading, after which I mentioned to my supervisor that I was unsure whether I was the right person to undertake the translation. Wasn't I too young at only twenty-three? And – I had never translated a complete novel before – wasn't I too inexperienced? Neither would be a problem, she assured me. What counts is that you have an excellent feel for writing. But did I have the right temperament to work with the writer? I persisted. He might prefer a man, or someone whose life trajectory matched his more closely. To which she declared that I was exactly the right person because I was, in her words, so utterly removed from his world. She laughed at my anxieties. He doesn't bite, you know, although – she laughed again – he might try!

He lived in Brooklyn, too, in Clinton Hill, only a few blocks away from me, in one of the brownstones I walked past several times en route to my dog-walking assignations in Prospect Park, and we arranged to meet there, for our preliminary discussions.

He had brooding good looks, was bristling with confidence and unashamedly self-regarding. He was young, thirty-five years old – I knew that from his biography – but already considered a literary heavyweight. His latest novel was the first to undergo a translation into Italian, and this fact only magnified my trepidation. He was exactly the sort of man I found intimidating on account of finding him terribly attractive, and he made no effort to put me at ease, but stared at me with intensity, examining me closely, all of me, from head to toe. He was, in short, exactly the kind of writer I might have imagined writing the work I had just read, and it was only this thought that allowed me to have a laugh to myself, at his expense, and present myself with more assurance.

He made us coffee, we sat across from each other on bar stools at his breakfast bar. I had come unprepared, I realised too late, with only his novel and my research notes in my bag, and I cursed myself for not having a notepad and pen and a list of pertinent questions to hand. But I didn't, and so we made desultory conversation, until he began to probe into my doctorate. I delved into my bag, drew out the two translations of 'Needleboats', nervously pointing out my ground-breaking discovery of metric versus free verse, of how Rossi had chosen the words '*il vento gagliardo*' whereas Montale had insisted on '*il vento ribelle*', when he interrupted me, saying, read it out. I want to hear it in Italian.

69

I was taken unawares. It was not simply for semantic analysis that I had so connected with Joyce's poem. The poem's themes touched my heart so deeply that I was sure Joyce had observed me, then penned his poem and presented it: here you are, Sissy. But I felt I could not disoblige the writer, and so began, my voice disloyally quivering with nervousness: *Ho udito quei giovani cuori gridare/Spinti da Amore sul guizzante remo/L'erbe dei prati ho udito sospirare/Non torna, non torna più!* I did not continue because, as always, on reaching the end of the first stanza, with the words '*No return, return no more*' my eyes had filled with tears, and my voice was now not simply quivering but choking.

You get the picture, I mumbled, my face burning, and I tried to sip my coffee nonchalantly. He said nothing, and when my nerves had calmed, I managed to steer the conversation to his novel and my impressions of some of the scenes. Did he wish the characters' language here to be so formal – it would decide whether I used the second or third person – or was my interpretation misplaced?

He did not deign to give me a response but said: you seem to be invested so much in my novel it makes me wonder why you don't write your own.

I wouldn't know where to begin, I replied.

Well, start with yourself. Have you had any interesting things happen to you of late? His eyes travelled over me. I mean why on earth are you an Italian translator? You're Indian, right? And without waiting for a response, he continued: so immediately you have that whole diaspora thing going for you. That idea of returning. His tongue rolled over the last word, as if he was indexing my emotion earlier. Then he perused my face and shoulders, slowly, not flinching at my scarring, and I expected him to point and say: start with that, right there. There's your story.

I now eschewed the heavy make-up that I had worn like camouflage for a short period in my adolescence; it had only aggravated the skin and increased the irritation. I now embraced my scarring, which was, thankfully, as had been said many a time by a medical professional, not keloid, not that raised, could have been much worse. Take this young lady, Bill. Excellent outcome of a split-thickness graft we have here. Skin is nice and supple, take a look. I was paraded before medical students as a model of successful procedures. All through my adolescence I had also taken part in several clinical trials of non-invasive treatments for amelioration of the presentation of a facial trauma — silicon gels, cryotherapy, masks — all of which had made their small contribution to my recovery. But burns have a physiological and a psychological effect; while the surgeons who had overseen my care considered me 'healed', I still considered myself scarred. Our opinions, thus, diverged. Nothing could erase the fact that the scar tissue was a very delicate coral-coloured veil across one side of my face and neck, caressing one half of my collar bone. One of my counsellors told me that I had to develop a relationship with my scars as one would with a friend or lover. A perspective that we reached, and which helped me greatly, was to consider myself painted in half: on one side the golden-yellow caramel and clearly defined almond-shaped eye that pleased the viewer; on the other, a coral-pink, with a tougher texture. And an eye that functioned well enough but which, despite being the focus of the two operations I had undergone, did not close as easily; one that slightly unsettled the viewer. I looked, face-on, like an untidy yin-yang portrait, as if an artist had somehow downed his tools halfway through his work, in impatience. What I hadn't shared with my counsellor was the other overwhelming sense I had of myself, veils half-open and half-finished paintings aside: that I had had a rebirth at a younger age. I belonged now to a different tribe.

However, I was still a young woman, and I still wanted to be considered desirable, and it was not easy to allow the man in front of me to have his fill. Perhaps, rather than inspecting me, he was trying to provoke me into a reaction.

I remained silent, and eventually he let his eyes leave that side of my face and neck, then asked: what's with the name anyway? Have you anglicised it? Or is it your husband's? You don't have a ring on your finger.

My stepfather adopted me, I replied, and that particular combination of words chimed like a bell and I remembered my meeting with Professor Tharoor, all those years ago. The writer nodded – unsurprised, unmoved – continued to press me for a glimpse into my aspirations. His manner was partly unnerving, partly amusing; he seemed convinced I would have a future as a novelist.

That I had spent most of my childhood in Africa was not something I shared with many people; I was not going to spill out my life story to this man when I felt that I was embarking tentatively on a professional relationship. I was about to delve into the adventurous and colourful sex life his characters occupied; I was unsure whether I wanted to reveal more of myself. Certainly, while I knew that I found him attractive, I was beginning, as well, to feel a slight aversion to him, and I did not want that to develop. The fee I would be given for the translation and the kick-start this work would give to my career were welcome. But he touched a nerve, there is no doubt.

I had, until then, lived my life without looking right or left, not to my past, not to my future, bent on the present and ignoring any reminder that I might have been tainted elsewhere, might even be moving inexorably towards some kind of understanding, some kind of resolution. It was that very same evening, after leaving his apartment in one piece, dignity intact, thinking to myself that on balance, disregarding my tears over the poem, that I had managed quite well under the circumstances, that I took myself back to the library on Washington Square.

On the subway over the river I stood rather than sat, needing to feel my feet, hold myself up, rather than bow or bend. The young man beside me was wearing headphones, and moving his head in time to the beat of his music, engrossed. I was tempted to ask him what he was listening to, and this thought occupied me for the journey; from the movements of his head I tried to match him with a song. I would hum it to myself, in my head, and check if he kept the correct rhythm. His clothes and age singled him out as a hip-hop fan. My knowledge of the genre was limited, but eventually I found a match: 'Fight The Power', Public Enemy. Or, another ground-breaking discovery, Vivaldi's *Four Seasons*, depending on where I started. Perhaps he guessed my exploits because as we got off the train – we were both coincidentally descending at Washington Square – he glanced at me and gave me a grin. Such a light, unimportant, charming episode. But one that boosted my spirits, readied me for action, as I entered the library and ensconced myself not in my usual location, but in the archives, to find out more about the story of the plane.

I had to read through screeds of newsprint before I found an article, among scores that detailed the vestiges of the Rhodesian bush war, its entanglement with the civil war in Mozambique, and the attempts by the Zambian government to be a broker for peace in the region. There was only this one article, from the *Washington Post* foreign service, dated September 7, 1978, the date alone giving me a jolt. Joyce had written his poem, the one I had recited earlier, on that same day, sixty-five years earlier, and my father left us not long after, nearly twelve years ago.

Salisbury – A heat-seeking missile was responsible for the crash on Sunday of an Air Rhodesia passenger plane in which 38 of the 56 persons aboard were killed, confirms the Rhodesian government. They also report that ten of the survivors were killed on the ground by guerrillas.

Joshua Nkomo, co-leader of the Rhodesian Patriotic Front guerrillas, has claimed responsibility for shooting down the plane, but has denied that his men were responsible for killing any survivors. He insisted in a statement issued from his place of exile, Lusaka, that the plane was believed to be carrying war supplies.

Already a massive military operation to track down the guerrillas responsible for the crash is underway, and there is considerable speculation that it may target bases in neighbouring Zambia and Mozambique.

The white population of Rhodesia is baying for revenge, and in parliament Co-Minister of Transport William Irvine released a statement, clearly aimed at internal and external observers: 'The people of this country will not let those innocent [deaths] go unavenged. I can promise the leaders of the Patriotic Front that those who seek to ride the wind will reap the wild wind.'

I was startled by the final words, as if it were another sign that this newspaper article was meant to be read that day; that fate had deemed the time right for me to look back, connect my present to my past. The article goaded me with its tale, and I scanned through several screens, bracing myself for further revelations, but could find only this account. For it was a story that no one wanted to tell, it did not fit the narrative. A struggle for freedom required its actors to be pristine, noble, wronged, holding irrevocably the higher moral ground. If these men turned out to be capable of misdeeds, horrifying acts, in pursuit of their freedom, then did that make them less deserving? It embodied a moral dilemma, which I chewed over, all the while thinking I could do the same for him, search through piles of newspapers, go through a phone book, write hundreds of letters. I was a researcher, after all; I should be able to find my father, the loyal friend.

The direction of my thoughts set my heart beating as a series of images entered the library and swirled around me like wraiths: a vision of myself in a dark night, and my childlike, younger face, and alongside that, another face, which with its planes and hollows made me feel a surge of something, from my belly to my throat. Something: love, most likely.

I became morose, and for many minutes I sat quietly, reading over and over again the same article about the plane. There, I could hear the writer saying, there's your story, right there. But I knew even then that I had other stories. My scars, my lost father. Which of this triad, I could imagine him pondering, which had the greatest literary worth?

I eventually roused myself, pulled my thoughts out of the mire they were sinking into and left the library, to spend the evening with the writer's novel, making notes and a list of questions with which to arm myself for our next meeting. In fact, I did not meet him again, face to face, until a few weeks later, when my supervisor invited me for lunch in her home in Manhattan. When I arrived, I saw he was there, with a woman, and was that day in a gregarious, charming mood, kissing me on the cheek and throwing me a casual, how are you getting on? I had intended to share with him how I had spent the evening after our first meeting immersed in memories of my childhood, to tell him how strange it was that a poem written by an Irish writer in Trieste could have such a resonance in my life, describe the sinister echo in an old newspaper article and how embarrassed I had been by my show of emotion, but how I had explored as he had recommended, if not to write a novel then at least to understand my life story a little better. But the ambience was not conducive, and I worried that I would appear too intense, too solipsistic. A few weeks later, I completed the translation, sent it off and received my fee.

A few months after – it was by now late spring – I saw my mother. By chance or by design, my stepfather revealed that he had to be near New York for work and he could pick me up and drive me home for a visit, saving me a train fare. In the car, we shared our news: my mother was well, Danny was tied up with soccer camp. I gave an abridged version of my experience of translating the novel. My stepfather asked about my last research trip to Italy earlier in the year. He had visited Florence and Venice and Rome when backpacking around Europe as a young man, and was eager to reprise old haunts and loves. Then he took one hand from the steering wheel to grip mine. You look really well, Sissy, he said. A bit Italian, actually. Something's definitely rubbed off.

On returning to the house, I found my mother in the garden, tending to the anthuriums she grew in enviable quantities. My stepfather, after announcing my arrival with some fanfare, held back; it was clear she wanted to talk to me alone.

My mother was dressed in slim-cut jeans, a cream-coloured soft woollen sweater; she had discovered an elegant style which suited her new life as an American wife, a part-time administrator at the local college. I only ever saw her in a sari on the rare occasions she and my stepfather were invited to a party and he managed to convince her to wear one. She blamed the climate, although the summers in Philadelphia could be sweltering. Her hair was shorter now, just scraping her shoulders, and at that time was cut into a fringe which accentuated her heart-shaped face. She was still slight, youthful-looking; few would believe she had a full-grown daughter. We kissed, she hugged me. I was taller than her by half an inch. She touched my hair, fingered the necklace I was wearing: you look different. As always when her eyes skimmed my face, I saw her expression change – as if she was steeling herself or as if she was saying a prayer.

But I *was* different, she was right. I was exhausted by the undertaking of translating someone else's words into another language. I had found it consumed me, so that much as I was drained by the task I found I was enlivened by the task. I had found my métier. But it had taken a toll, and I wore my exhaustion on my sleeve, although literally, I wore sleeveless vests and ripped jeans designed to show my fragile frame, my slender limbs, as if to provoke the world: how can you expect me to endure such agony? None of this would I share with my mother, and I was not so self-absorbed that I did not notice a sadness in my mother's eyes, a greater effort on her part to smile and laugh at any comment I made.

What is it? I asked. Has something happened?

I got a phone call a few days ago, she said. From my brother.

She had long stopped referring to relatives by their names, but chose to preface them with 'my', as if by saying 'my brother' I would not feel as much attachment as if she had said Sibichayan, or even 'your uncle'; as if she wanted to assert that these people, they were attached to her alone.

My mother has died, she said.

I flushed. The news shocked me, and perhaps because the anger was always there, just below the surface, because it was so easy to feel a quick-fire hate for her, which would burn instantly to be replaced by a searing love, but which, nevertheless, flared brightly for a brief moment, I said, Ammachi?, calling my grandmother by the name my mother called her, and which I had done as a child.

It worked, whatever I had hoped to achieve, because my mother turned her face away, biting her lip, and I saw tears gather in her eyes, as if she realised that she had a match now, that I was no longer so young as to be a weak adversary.

She acknowledged all of this by saying simply, yes, Ammachi, mol. And then, turning to face me fully as if she knew that she had to punish herself in some way, she spoke with a generosity: do you remember her?

A little, I replied.

But by then any wish I had to punish had disappeared and I longed to talk of piazzas and vain novelists and hidden Etruscan gems.

Shall I help you with this? I asked, pointing to her flowers, and the bag of compost next to her feet.

If you are not too tired. Aren't you hungry?

I shook my head, and she had smiled; that quiet, sweet, familiar smile. As I helped her with the digging, neither of us wearing gloves and both of us enjoying the feel of the soil on our fingers, she spoke in bursts, relating short anecdotes of her mother, Ammachi, who, in the tradition of mothers of her generation, had never once wondered whether her children were happy, well adjusted, well cared for. It was enough to provide food and a place to sleep. Ammachi, who had completed six years of schooling but no more, and who had met my mother's wish to study for a degree in Trivandrum with utter incomprehension – apparently it was my grandfather's employer who had paid my mother's college fees.

I was surprised to find my mother so loquacious, but did nothing to stop her. I knew this was a singular opportunity; she would never repeat these stories. I simply listened and lost myself in her voice. Neither did I trouble her with a request to talk of my father. I had long relinquished those incursions and why would I choose this occasion to burden her? She was speaking of her past and the past and at that moment in time, working in the garden with my mother in the soft evening light, that was enough for me.

7

THE next day, the first Sunday without my father, Rahul drove us to church in the morning. He had a small car of his own which he would be selling in a few weeks when he went off to university in Bombay. I watched from the back seat as he talked to my mother. She had a teasing tone to her voice, and he often smiled at her. It was only when we arrived at the small church at the bottom of the hill and I noticed the other Malayalee families, among the rest of the congregation, that I wondered why it was Jonah who had come to help us with the water, Miss Munroe who had taken my father to the airport.

As my mother was climbing out of the car, balancing Danny on her hip, her bag fell onto the ground, upside down, and its contents spilled out. Rahul quickly walked around to her side to pick up the objects: her hairbrush, her small mirror, an address book, a purse with a brass clasp, her kohl pencil, Danny's teething ring. An unexceptional collection of items, nothing one would not expect from a woman's hand-bag. But as Rahul handed it back to her – here you are, Aunty – and as she smiled up at him – thanks, mon – the crowd of Malayalees stood still and watchful, like a dense clump of trees, menacing, shutting out the light; behind them a warmer, sunnier glow. As if we had all witnessed an act of great intimacy. As if Rahul touching my mother's possessions was tantamount to Rahul touching my mother. I saw his mother watching us, her expression cool, impassive. But when we were in the church, all seemed as normal.

We sat in the same pew that we usually did, with the same collection of aunties, some of the men separating from their wives, observing the custom from India, even though we were thousands of miles away in this unadorned church in a tiny hamlet. From the pew in front, a small child with patches of hair not obscuring a dry scalp stared at me, his nose running, until his mother pulled him to her and wiped it on the end of her chitenge. Across the aisle I saw Bobby and Aravind, but I felt nothing. I was not sure I would try to play with them again.

It was then that I felt a sensation of being both crushed and empty; my father's absence was impossible to ignore. It was so peculiar not to have him at my side. It was he who would hold Danny, my brother hanging off him like a koala bear, and it was he who patted my knee at intervals as if trying to prod me awake. And it was he who made a show of attending Mass under sufferance of my mother's wishes, ending the responses with a slightly ironic edge – and peace be with *you* – until he received a reprimand from my mother. Spending the homily with his eyes closed as if in reverent contemplation before emitting a soft snore, getting an elbow in the ribs from my bemused mother, and then making a show of blinking rapidly, staring at his environs with wonder, while I shook with silent laughter beside him. Quite the comedian, my father.

The sycophancy irritated him; the rituals and how they were followed amused him. Somewhere along the way my father had discarded the piety that dripped off the fronds of the coconut trees in Kerala, coursed through the veins of the people below. I would not say that my mother had a particularly strong faith, but she was more willing to abide by conventions and less inclined to question, to settle for an easy compliance in order to enjoy attendant benefits. My First Communion, which had taken place in Kothamangalam – we had returned to India in between contracts and had a protracted stay, my mother only just beginning to recover her strength – had been, I could see, rather than a celebration of my induction into the Church, an opportunity for my mother to showcase her good fortune. To order a tailor-made dress for me, to arrange a celebratory meal for after, to parade me in front of her family. A Kothamangalam girl done good, with husband and child in stock, a career in a foreign land. Yes, only one child and a girl at that – will she have more? Yes, it was Africa, but at least the remittances were generous. My father had spent that day, throughout the Mass, and all through the family gathering that followed, under strict instructions from my mother. He had behaved impeccably, crossing himself and kneeling and rising solemnly, never once catching my eye, and only disobeying right at the end, when he had come to say good night, with a pious expression, his hands pressed together, and my flowery veil perched like a doily on top of his head.

The memories rushed through me as we stood in the church, only three of us now, and when we returned to the campus, my mother was quiet. But, as if to compensate for corralling herself in her room the previous day, she strived to be cheerful: let's weed all around the vegetables, we can make another banana-leaf tent for Danny, let's plant the seeds Papa left us.

We spent the rest of the day outdoors, digging and clearing, the sun warm, but not summer-hot yet, and the fresh air and exercise meant that we were tired enough that night to fall into our beds and close our eyes and block our ears from the constant hum that my father's absence brought.

Rahul took me to school, as arranged, for the first week. It was a detour, but he could drop me off before he delivered Aravind, Bobby and his older brother Benjy to Kabulonga High School. I was dwarfed by the boys in the car, in their uniforms of long trousers and blazers, their bursting school-bags and kitbags. I sat unencumbered, with my cardigan, small satchel and juice bottle. Rahul and Benjy sat up front, communicating in monosyllabic grunts. I was sandwiched between Bobby and Aravind in the back seat, but they did not speak to me, or one another, each choosing to gaze out of their separate windows.

When we arrived at my school, I clambered over their legs, turning back to say thank you to Rahul and meeting his eyes. His smile managing to convey that he understood, he understood everything: the indignity of being the only girl, the precarious standing I had with my playmates. Who was *that*? the girls waiting outside the school asked as I tumbled from the car and waved goodbye; and all through the day, and the days that followed, they continued to ask, would gawp and giggle at the long-haired, handsome young man who drove me to the gates, and I would feel a glow, answering their queries with an indifference designed to make them even more curious. But by the second week, Rahul only drove me to the Coopers'; they had returned.

In the afternoons, where I would spend an hour or so before I was dropped back at Roma, I trod a well-worn route in the house from the kitchen to the bedrooms. And as I passed Mr Cooper's study, I could spy him along with groups of men of varying builds, arranged in chairs and leaning against the wall, in serious discussion – about the plane, and the inevitable retribution. It's only a matter of time, was the refrain. God knows what they'll do, was another. I was a veteran eavesdropper, having acquired the skill of squirrelling away snatches of conversation to be collated later at leisure, for more coherent analysis. While I may not have understood exactly what was being referred to *then*, now I remember the conversations as if I had. Perhaps I have conflated what I read many years later, in the library in Washington Square, with what I heard. And in the same way, I cannot claim to know exactly what words were spoken to my mother a few days later; I have only pieced together what might have been said from what happened.

Another weekend without my father, another journey to church and back in Rahul's car, after which he said quietly, without looking up: 'Aunty, Amma wants to talk to you.'

I watched my mother as she walked down the road to the Devasias's house. She held a bag of guavas from the tree in our garden as a present. Rahul's mother was a biology teacher; his father taught mathematics. They were proud of their sons, hard-working people. But, not unlike many of their milieu, they were small-minded and petty, imbued with a strong conviction in their narrow ideals, and thus prey to a resentment towards anything which or anyone who strayed from convention. I can only imagine the scene when my mother arrived. Uncle lurking shamefacedly in the background, Aunty squaring up to my mother: why should my son have to pick up after your husband? It's inappropriate for him, a young man, to be spending so much time with you.

Not long after going to the Devasias's house I saw my mother returning. She was walking briskly, her back straight, but holding the palloo of her sari around her waist as if bandaging a wound. She looked as if she had been struck but was determined to carry herself erect. Only her face was composed, but that was what unnerved me most. She had no expression, no frown line between her eyebrows, her lips were closed and set, as if she were asleep. Even her eyes had a vacant aspect, as if she were sleepwalking. She did not look at me as she passed me on the veranda, as she moved to the bedroom. I heard drawers opening and closing, and then she re-emerged to ignore me again, to walk towards my father's car: the green Toyota Datsun, an old model but one my father was extremely proud of, one which he lovingly washed and tended to. She opened the car and sat behind the wheel, closed the door so that I could not see her hands fiddling with the controls, or see her turn the key in the ignition. I only heard the rev of the engine.

On the road in front of the house, suddenly appearing at the top of the steps that led to the netball courts, I saw Jonah. When he spied me on the veranda he raised his hand in greeting. But I did not return it, only stood frozen as I turned my head and saw the car jerk forwards, stall, shudder, lurch again and then, at a terrifying speed, jump forwards. There was a flash of green as it shot down the drive like a predator suddenly spotting its prey, and then it crashed into the acacia tree, the bonnet of the car folding elegantly like an accordion.

Jonah was running now, and behind me I could hear doors opening, and people appearing, but the car did not stop. Instead it backed away from the tree, the metal groaning as it was separated from the bark, the wheels turning grudgingly, and the engine making a staccato sound as if overwhelmed by its efforts. It started slowly and then accelerated so that in an instant it had reversed the length of the drive into a mulberry bush, the fruit smearing the back windscreen with purple-red juice. And there was a matching red streak on my mother's face, I could see. A delicate, spidery trail of red that sketched a line from just above her eyebrow to the start of her cheekbone. Otherwise, my mother looked ethereal, untouched.

At that moment, perhaps that car encapsulated all that my mother regretted. That we were captives on the campus with no means to leave, that she had all those years ago not made more of an effort to learn to drive despite my father's attempts to teach her. He had then indulgently given up. What if she had persevered? If she had acquired her own way out, a freedom? I wonder now if that utter dependence she had allowed herself to impose on my father, even if unintentional, had weighed down on him, become a burden, a lodestone, so that if the need should arise for him to leave it could be no small decision, but a stark choice – her or them. Once he had shaken off that burden, perhaps it had then acquired an impossible allure – to be unattached, weightless like my mother had been that time, laughing over her shoulder, swimming away from him in the lake. By driving my father's beloved car up and down without care, wounding it, I can see that my mother was unleashing her anger against my father. What we were witnessing was an act of violence; the metal body of the car had become my father's dark cheek to slap and claw at.

There were steps behind me and as the car jerked forward again I knew I had to run and save her. I did not want the people who were gathering to hurt her, or judge her. But a hand caught me by the elbow, and held me back, Jonah's voice – no, Sissy – as I saw Miss Munroe draw up to me, her face pale and her eyes glistening, and behind her Mr Lawrence, who skirted around us to approach my mother. He strode towards the car just as it lunged forward again, but he did not jump back in fright. It stalled halfway down the drive with an ungraceful jolt and he jogged to its side, reached forward and opened the door. I had a glimpse of my mother's sari again, a vivid orange.

'Mrs Olikara, perhaps I can help you.'

My mother did not look at him, but stared straight ahead, so that for a moment we were all positioned as if for a still shot: a motley collection of actors and props, the arid ground showing between the blades of grass.

Only then did I see her face crumple, and she raised a hand to brush the spider's line of red, so that it became a smudge. I saw Mr Lawrence shut the door, so she was again half-shielded from our eyes, to walk around the car to the other side and get into the passenger seat. For a moment I thought he would give her a driving lesson, teach her how to manipulate the pedals, change the gears, in our battered car, the bumper hanging off now and scraping the ground. But he simply sat with her until I saw my mother lean sideways to rest her head against the window. She looked broken, as if a faulty mannequin in a shop window.

'Go inside, Sissy.' Jonah's voice behind me.

But I shook myself out of his grasp and ran to the car, laid my hand against the window so that I was holding my mother's head up, holding her pieces together, against the glass.

'Mama! Mama!'

She did not turn her head to look at me or acknowledge that she had heard my cries. And all I remember is the different shades of the tiny orange triangles on her sari, as again I felt Jonah's hand on my arm as he pulled me away.

8

I WAS the fly in the ointment. If I had been old enough to attend Roma, then I would not have had to attend a primary school in the city and my mother would not have had to make these increasingly complicated arrangements to ferry me to and from the campus. Years later, I tried to calculate the distance between Roma and my school: eight miles. I worked out that if we took about half an hour for the journey, as my father had often recounted, but only ten or fifteen minutes to drive to the Coopers', they must have lived only four miles or so from our bungalow.

Their house was located in a pleasant neighbourhood of large trees shading large houses, fenced lawns and post boxes nailed to the gates; the residents of this area enjoyed having their post delivered to them directly. One of Ally's chores was to check their box every day, insert a little iron key into the keyhole, and reach inside to lift out a pile of envelopes. If opening an aerogramme had pleased me, then this task enthralled me even more.

The sound of sprinklers and lawnmowers and the splash from a swimming pool accompanied the birdsong, not unlike the American suburbs of my later life. The Coopers' road was neat and clean, recently tarmacadamed, with a white painted kerb, leading to a small green roundabout at the end, the centre of which was decorated with topiary. We turned right onto a longer road which ran past a bottle store, now becoming dustier and patchier, pavements and kerbs falling away, past a small supermarket which had rows of empty shelves, to arrive at a steep hill. Here we turned, the spot marked by a tree that had been burned down but never been removed, its blackened branches pointing the way. Then, after skirting the cluster of small tin-roofed houses in the low valley to the right, where Grace lived, we were on the road that led directly into the campus. Up the hill, and curving round, we arrived at our bungalow.

It was decided that I would stay with the Coopers during the week, from Monday after school, to be dropped back at the campus on Friday afternoons. Mr Lawrence was instrumental in this arrangement; he will have recounted to them the incident with my father's car, and everyone will have agreed that my journey to school had become another stress on my mother's energies. Taking care of Danny and the house, especially with the water supply becoming increasingly erratic, all the while trying to keep up with her marking and lesson preparation, would not be as onerous for my mother if I were removed. The Coopers had a spare bedroom and the girls would enjoy my company. But I feared that in actuality they didn't; the household was less bright, less convivial than it had been before their visit to Virginia. It was not that the practicalities had altered in any way. The constant stream of visitors continued unabated, and in the mornings, I would meet a series of men in various states of dishevelment, in the living room, rolling up a sleeping bag. I was now the occupant of the guest room. The room I slept in was as comfortable and cosy as I could have wished; the meals as regular. But with an acute sensibility that I was destined to develop, I realised something had changed. Mrs Cooper was brittle, the girls were sullen; perhaps they had not wished to return after the reminder of their homeland. Certainly, my aptitude as raconteur, which the Cooper girls had once enjoyed, was now obsolete. Ally seemed more inclined to retreat to her bedroom, door closed after school; Mary-Anne and I kept company but half-heartedly. Mrs Cooper no longer volunteered at the adult education centre in town; the number of students had dwindled to a handful. Too difficult to travel when the public transport was unreliable and the street lighting scant, with rumours spreading of thugs and vandals prowling the streets when darkness fell. When Mr Cooper arrived from work, he appeared inordinately cheerful, as if to bolster Mrs Cooper's spirits, and once she had snapped at his breezy 'hello, ladies' with 'I wish you wouldn't do that, Sam. It makes us sound like a harem.' There was a plague of flies and mosquitoes which made playing in the garden unpleasant. We stayed indoors, and even the Coopers' spacious house began to feel confined. Grace made a point of complimenting me on something nearly every day – ah, beautiful plaits, Sissy, look at how you are growing – as if she knew how discomfited I felt. Perhaps I, too, had changed.

My first weekend back in the small pink bungalow, I scoured my mother's face for signs that she had missed me, but she only appeared tired, even a little thinner. Her only question was: did you eat well, mol? But on the Saturday afternoon she offered to wash my hair whereas previously she had castigated me for whining about having to do it on my own, an indication that she was aware I might be feeling displaced. While Danny was having his nap, we set up in the bathroom. I sat on a stool and leant back over the tub as my mother poured the hot water over my head. My hair was long, as was common for Indian girls of my age – as my mother's had been, she often told me. It reached my waist nearly, and while it was manageable when in two plaits, I often begged to have it cut shorter, at least to shoulder-length. But my mother prevaricated; perhaps that was a rite of passage she wished to delay until she could no longer enforce her wishes on me. But that afternoon, I was grateful for her attention, and while I am sure my mother did not notice, I had a lump in my throat as she wet my head and massaged in the shampoo. I missed her dreadfully, I missed my father, even

Danny in his uselessness. She might have thought that the creature comforts the Coopers' house offered would have compensated for much, even enchanted me, but she little knew that I felt strange and alien in their household.

'Papa phoned earlier this week,' she said suddenly.

I knew this meant my father would have called the convent. None of the houses had telephones, a fact that I had heard Miss Munroe complain about to Mr Lawrence: I mean, do we have to be quite so godforsaken? Why can't we have a phone to ourselves?

I said nothing, only waited for my mother to continue.

She chucked me under the chin. 'Not asking?' She was smiling. 'Did you hear? Papa called.'

'How is he?' I asked, feeling a reluctance as I spoke which made the words sound slow and heavy. I realised, suddenly, that I was angry with him.

'Fine. And he sends his love. Next time, he'll call on a Friday when you are back. I told him you are staying with the Coopers.'

I studied my fingernails as my mother combed the coconut oil through my hair. Then she handed me the comb, plaited my hair. She had always said, count to two hundred, Sissy, at least, before you wash it out. I had never had the patience to last beyond twenty. Now she put a towel around my shoulders so I would not get cold, and we waited together.

'Has Jonah been coming?' I asked.

She glanced at me, carried on pulling the stray hairs out of my brush, then nodded.

'Are you still helping him?'

'Yes.' She smiled at me. 'He does the shopping also. He always asks how you are.'

I stared at my toes.

'Are you enjoying at the Coopers', Sissy?' Now her voice was soft. 'Isn't it nice to have some company?'

I shrugged my shoulders. Where could I begin? That I was anxious about putting the clothes that needed washing in the wrong basket, they had so many. One for white clothes and one for colours, another for woollens, one for hand wash. That I found the food dispiriting, my least favourite being something they called 'meatloaf' but which tasted like sawdust. That I was awkward with a knife and fork, that I was terrified my table manners fell short of theirs. That I missed hearing Malayalam.

She didn't press me, as if worried I would voice these exact concerns, but bade me lean back again so that she could wash out the oil and then wrapped my head in the light cotton towel, the thorth, we had brought back with us from Kotha-mangalam. In the evening we played cards, and when I had yawned five times in succession, my mother smiled and asked me whether I didn't think it was time to go to sleep, and if I did, would I like to join her. I slept on my father's side, and once during the night I saw her get up and adjust the blanket in Danny's cot, then move to the window, holding the curtain slightly open. She stood there for many minutes before she turned away and climbed back into the bed, lying on her side, facing away from me.

Back to the Coopers' house for Monday evening, back to a stilted evening and a bedtime much earlier than my own, which left me lying in bed, wide awake, wondering at the Cooper girls who seemed capable of oblivion when sleeping, unlike me. Eventually, I got out of bed, admitting defeat, switched on my light, and after reading for some time, decided to visit the bathroom for a final visit before trying to fall asleep again. Returning to my bedroom, shuffling down the hall, I could hear Mr Cooper on the phone in his study and as I passed his door, I could hear his intonation drop, low and sombre. His door was ajar, but I could not see him, only his feet crossed at the ankles, in red socks with blue toes. I remembered how he had leant against my father's green car, that day when I had seen them both talking about Ezekiel, and I remembered how he had always seemed to enjoy my father's company, even though he was not short of people to talk to. Perhaps they had found a commonality, both visitors to this land, both family men. Now I saw Mr Cooper's foot curl around the door, and he started opening it a little more, before he seemed to change his mind and kicked it shut. Perhaps he knew I was standing outside; my heart thudded guiltily. I moved on, grateful that he had not seen me, but I found that my feet still shuffled reluctantly, as if they knew sleep did not await me on my return to the bedroom.

The house had a surreal air, like I was walking through a dream landscape. It was quiet and dim, with its warren of corridors and closed doors. But as I approached my bedroom, which was at the front of the house near the entrance, I saw a light coming from the living room. I had not noticed it earlier. Perhaps the door had been closed; perhaps Mr Cooper had forgotten about the lamp when he had gone to answer the phone. I had been taught the economics of saving electricity and so I pushed the door open, thinking to turn off the lights. The room was bathed in a warm golden hue; there were three lamps positioned around the room. The curtains, thick and long, were closed, and added to the snug, intimate air. There was no one inside and I moved to the desk, which held a messy stack of paper, one of which remained in the typewriter. I drew closer and read the heading: *Spiritual Healers: Accusations, Target Groups and Development*. I was leaning closer to read more when Mr Lawrence walked in.

'Sissy,' he said, swapping the drink in his hand, a golden liquid filling the bottom half of his square tumbler, from one hand to the other. 'Hey there. How are you doing?'

I stared, unsure what to do, and he drew closer. 'Can't get to sleep?'

I shook my head, and then glanced involuntarily back at the typewriter.

His eyes followed mine. 'What do you think?' He smiled. 'An eye-catching title?'

But before I could respond, he continued: 'It's my research. This project I'm working on. Why I am here.' He raised his hands, gesturing to the world around us and spilling a few drops of his drink in the process.

'Oh shit . . . Oh sorry.' He was bending down, rubbing the whisky on the rug with the end of his sleeve. Then he straightened up and laughed. 'Excuse my language.' And as I made to leave, he said, 'Don't go. Come and sit here for a bit.'

He moved a pile of books off the sofa and he settled down next to me. He gestured first to his drink – 'I can't offer you this, I'm afraid' – and then to the coffee table in front of him. 'I was looking at these. It's something I like doing.'

I saw the table was covered in a pile of maps, and underneath them was a large hardback atlas. I recognised the topmost map immediately, a single political map of Africa, and I identified Zambia easily, coloured in pink.

'So we're here,' he said, following my eyes and placing his finger on Lusaka, 'and my hometown is all the way over here,' and he dragged his finger across to the left, off the table and further on, his arm stretched out wide. And then he paused, and I saw a look of uncertainty flit over his face as if he was thinking: now she will place her finger and drag it to the right, saying, and my father is somewhere over there. He cleared his throat, and his apprehension made me relax.

'Where is your hometown?' I asked.

'Tannersville, New York State. Up in the Catskills,' he replied, smiling. 'Have you heard of it?'

I shook my head.

'Not many have,' he said. 'Let's look at what we have here . . .' He sifted through his papers and drew out another large map. 'Now what are we looking at, Sissy?'

I perused the large rectangle; this was a more complex diagram of the physical features. I saw shaded areas and thousands of delicate blue lines, triangles and squares; hundreds of names written in tiny italics, and a series of red dots spotting the area. It was a magnified area of the nexus of the three countries – Zambia, Rhodesia and Mozambique – tied together by the river which fed them all. I let my finger trace the Zambezi and he looked impressed.

'That's right,' he said. 'And just a few days ago I was here.' He pointed to a dot, and I squinted at it – Tete. 'And Ally and Mary-Anne's dad was here.' He pointed to another: Lourenço Marques. 'Although,' he grabbed a pen from the table, 'I've been meaning to do this for ages.' He crossed out the two words with a line and wrote above it: *Maputo*. 'The name's changed.'

His words had an unforeseeable resonance: names change. Just as mine would a year later, just as another country's name would change, another city's. A man picks up a pen and draws a line and writes another name. A child watches as her mother signs a paper on her behalf so that a name disappears. Now I watched as Mr Lawrence regarded his handiwork, no doubt wondering what the next suitable conversational move would be.

'What are the red dots?' I asked, pointing at one adjacent to Tete.

'These are the wells that Sam Cooper's agency have dug. You know, some people, mostly women, have to walk miles to get water from the nearest river. But if you dig down deep enough, you'll hit the water table. And now they can get the water from the well, right in their village.'

He spoke as if he thought I knew nothing of wells, and I wanted then to tell him of the back yard of my mother's family home in Kothamangalam. How I could conjure up easily a picture of the well with its mossy surround, and of how once, when I was drawing water, my foot had slipped, and I had for a second feared I would plunge into the dark hole. But I felt shy, sitting next to him, barefoot, in my powder-pink pyjamas – my mother's sartorial tastes for my wardrobe did not always coincide with my own – so I said nothing.

'Do you like drawing?' he asked suddenly. 'I have these with me.' And reaching down to the side of the sofa, he retrieved a pile of coloured papers, the type to be found in a stationery shop, and a half-filled flat tin of pencils. My eyes must have lit up at the sight of the rainbow of colours in the sheaf – green, purple, yellow – because he smiled with some relief.

'Here, you have them.'

'Thank you.' I put them on my lap, willing myself not to act too enraptured. I was, I knew, too old to be so taken by the gift.

'No problem.'

Then, as we both must have been scratching inside our heads for the next topic, he asked, 'What do you like drawing?'

'Well,' I hesitated. I did not consider myself talented in any way. 'Boats.'

'Boats?'

'Papa takes me to see the boat races when we go back.'

'Does he?'

I was warming up. 'And birds.'

'Birds?'

'Mama's family live in a nature reserve. A bird sanctuary.'

'Really?' Then, perhaps because I had introduced my parents into our conversation myself, so he felt he could pursue the topic without upsetting me, he sifted through his piles, retrieved the atlas. 'Can you find it for me? Where in India?'

I scanned the map and placed my finger easily on Kerala, and the dot – Cochin – and then I trailed my finger a little way to the right, to the Western Ghats. 'Somewhere here.'

He leant forward so that he was inspecting the image, showing an unselfconscious interest I did not associate with grown-ups. His hair fell over his ears, and covered the back of his neck, and I could smell the faint tang of the whisky, either from his glass or his breath.

'What else do you do when you go there?'

'There's a river and a lake, so we swim.' I added, 'Mama's a very good swimmer.'

'Is she now?' He was smiling as he picked up his glass.

We sat for a few moments in a silence that was now comfortable. I glanced at him and back at his typewriter on the desk across from us.

'Do you know about Ezekiel?' I blurted out.

He looked at me blankly. 'Who's Ezekiel?'

'Grace's son. Ezekiel.'

'Oh, I see. Yeah, right.'

'I heard Mr Cooper and my father talking about him one day.'

'Did you?'

I flushed, hoping I would not have to furnish the details of my lingering behind the car in shameless, unedifying eavesdropping. 'They said he was always getting ill.'

'He doesn't look in great shape, that's true.'

'And Mr Cooper mentioned something about a witchdoctor.'

'Oh right.' He nodded, kept nodding, said, 'Well, yes,' as if I would understand what he meant. Then he began: 'We all need something to believe in, right? You know how you and your family go to church?' He waited for me to nod before continuing. 'Well, some people believe that there are people who live among them, you know in the same village maybe, with special . . . powers. You know, people who can heal you if you're sick . . .'

'Witchdoctors?'

He made a face. 'I'm not very fond of the term myself. You know, tag on the word "witch" to make it sound really crazy . . .'

'So you think they *do* have powers?'

'No.' He shook his head, smiling. 'I didn't say that, Sissy. Listen . . .' He faced me more fully. 'When bad things happen, people need to find an explanation, you know, or even a scapegoat. So, take the Greeks. There would be a storm, and they believed there was a god who controlled the wind and rain, and that god was angry with someone, angry with what they'd done. And over here, in some places, something bad happens, like . . .'

Then he stopped. I could see him struggling to find an example he believed would be an appropriate illustration for the young girl sitting at his side. I opened my mouth – like a man falls to the floor because his girlfriend is troubling him and loses his job, like my father leaves us, like a plane is shot down and people die – just as the door was pushed open.

Mr Cooper stood there, and did not query what I was doing, sitting in my pink pyjamas near midnight, in front of a pile of maps with Mr Lawrence, only said, 'That fax has come through, Charlie. Do you want to take a look?'

Mr Lawrence stood up and Mr Cooper continued: 'I think you should go to bed now, Sissy.' He opened the door wider for me to pass by him. I feared he was angry with me but as I scuttled past him I felt his hand briefly touch my head. 'Good night, honey.'

I had forgotten that I had already tried to get to sleep, so I was surprised to see the bed already open and the sheets pulled back, as if someone in my absence had readied the room, turned off the lights and shut the curtains. I clambered into the bed, my heart racing, playing over the conversation I had just had. I had enjoyed talking with him, but I had not told Mr Lawrence everything. Just as I had not revealed that I had my own knowledge and experience of wells, I did not tell him about those years back when my mother was ill, those days when she lifted herself out of bed to greet me from school, then retired again until my father persuaded her to join us at the dinner table, to pick at my father's best efforts of an evening meal. I had not told him that Grace had once arrived at our house, late at night, when she must have believed that I was fast asleep.

I heard her talking with my father in the same place as years later I saw my father and mother face each other: behind the house, near the vegetable patch. There was my father in a mundu and a shirt open over his chest, for he must have been ready to go to bed; there was Grace in her knitted hat, cardigan and dress, white canvas shoes on her feet; and there was someone else. A small wiry man, who wore spectacles fixed with tape, a fur-trimmed hat, a leather waistcoat over his bare torso showing off his muscled arms, and khaki knee-length shorts. I remember staring at him because, despite his shambolic, inelegant attire, he emanated a charisma; his posture was arresting, his expression haughty and this made him fearsome. Looking at him, protected by the distance of some metres and a glass window, I felt scared. And as if he could feel my fear, he turned at that moment and his eyes found mine. For a long time – seconds, minutes, even an hour – his gaze froze me, and I could not breathe. Then he turned his head, releasing me from his spell, to face Grace and my father once again, and I ducked down beneath the windowsill where I remained, hand clamped to my mouth, heart pounding.

My father re-entered the house some time later, on his own, and I opened my bedroom door a crack. He was sitting motionless on the sofa, the television set turned on but turned to silent. In those days, before the power lines were cut and the water pipes severed because of spiteful wars in neighbouring countries, we had little worry of power or water cuts. As I stepped into the room, he turned to look at me, and said, much as Mr Lawrence did all those years later, 'Can't sleep, mol? Come and sit with me for a little bit.'

I curled onto his lap, leant against his chest and watched the pictures on the television with him – a boxing match.

'Who did Grace bring?' I asked eventually.

'You saw?'

I nodded.

'Someone she thinks can help Mama feel better,' he said, and his voice was so tired I felt my stomach contract.

When he did not continue I whispered, 'And do you think he can help Mama?'

He smiled and stroked my hair, shook his head.

We stayed like this for some time and I must have fallen asleep because when I woke again, it was dark and I was back in my bed.

9

THERE was a subdued feel to the following days and nights, as if we were all waiting for the next instalment, knowing that we could not fall back into the unchallenging routine of old. On the Friday, after Mrs Cooper dropped me off back at our house – Laila, she's such a delight – my mother took my hand, Danny in her arms.

'Come, Sissy. Papa is phoning.'

As we reached the steps leading to the netball courts, I saw the figures of Bobby and Aravind. I had hardly seen them in the last few weeks, and the days I had spent with them, all those afternoons, felt as if they belonged to a previous life. There was someone walking across to them, one of Bobby's brothers; perhaps the boys had grown up enough to appeal to the older brothers' company. We walked down the steps, across the netball courts and along the road that led to the convent building. The convent was surrounded by a low wall enclosing a verdant garden, at that minute being tended to by a novice, complete with white headscarf, who greeted us with a shy smile. At the door, we rang the bell and then waited as we heard footsteps tapping across the floor. The entrance hall was large and wide and airy, with tall stained-glass windows along each side, and smelled of wax polish and candles.

Other than the nun who opened the door, there was no one else in sight. In their rooms above us, I imagined the nuns, gathered together around a table, playing cards, their veils discarded, a crate of beer at their feet and cigarettes between their lips, aping all the Malayalee men at our gatherings. I must have been daydreaming for my mother poked my side and we were led into an office, lined with filing cabinets and in the centre of which stood a desk. On the middle of this was placed a telephone, reverentially, on its very own crocheted mat, so precious was this rare instrument on the campus.

The nun left us and my mother said: 'Sit, we'll wait.' It was clear that my parents had arranged a time and, sure enough, only five minutes elapsed before the phone rang, a shrill tone which startled all of us in the silence. My mother picked up the receiver just as Danny bumped his head on the side of the desk and began to wail. She spoke into the phone, her voice curt, while simultaneously leaning forward to grab the back of Danny's T-shirt, dragging him along the floor to where she was. A few more words and then she passed the receiver to me.

I took it and held it to my ear. I said nothing, only listened to the background noises: voices, a rhythmic swoosh, most probably a ceiling fan.

'Sissy? Mol?'

My father's voice reached across the oceans, and the familiar tones ran through me like a current. I swallowed and found I couldn't respond; tears were pooling in my eyes, my throat was constricted.

'How are you, mol? How is school?'

My voice was a squeak. 'It's all right.'

'And the Coopers? Are you enjoying staying with them?'

'Yes, Papa.'

'Tell me what you did today.'

'We had maths first thing. We measured angles and stuff . . .'

He started to say something, which meant I paused, then he stopped, and I heard my own voice echo back to me: angles and stuff. After a moment, he spoke again. 'Carry on.'

'We played rounders because Mrs Green was ill . . .'

He made a kind of noise in response, but which broke the flow once again. I felt tired and pressed the receiver to my ear, and then we fell silent. Even my father was finding this difficult, I could tell, but I could feel something prickling at my skin: petulance. He was the adult, he should shoulder the burden.

'I miss you, mol,' he said, his voice light. Then, without waiting for me to respond in kind, he asked, 'What do you want me to bring back for you?'

Now I glanced at my mother, who was studiously attending to Danny. I took a deep breath and spoke: 'When are you coming back?'

My voice sounded determined, as if I was convinced my words would have an irresistible pull, ensure his return. Soon, he said. Soon, soon. When, he paused, when Raju's case is in hand.

But now I ask myself: did my father even say those words? In truth, my memory of that conversation must be inflected with my memory of the letter I received six years later from Professor Tharoor, in which I learned of Raju Kumaresan. Only then did that name enter my dream lexicon, embedding itself so deeply that now I cannot remember a time when it was an unknown.

I looked across at my mother, who must have heard my question but seemed to be avoiding my eyes, seemed uninterested in the reply. She was sitting on the floor, her legs tucked to one side, her sari palloo falling off her shoulder, rolling a ball to Danny, who grabbed it and rolled it back, bumping up and down on the ground with excitement.

'What are you having for supper?' my father was asking, and as I watched my mother roll the ball again, insouciantly, as if the three of us over here and him over there was the most normal set of circumstances, I allowed any determination I had harboured to ebb away. I muttered, 'I don't know. I've only just got back from school. Mama didn't say.'

At the mention of my mother, he did not repeat those last words he had said to me – take care of Mama, okay? – perhaps because he knew now that this would be a burden I was ill-equipped to shoulder.

I forced myself to ask: 'What are you having?'

He laughed. 'Not sure . . .' And then there was a sudden eruption of music behind him, shouts of laughter, and he said, 'I won't talk any more, mol, okay? Love you, okay? Pass the phone to Mama now.'

By now I could not speak anyway. I wordlessly held out the phone and my mother smoothed down her sari as she twisted onto her feet. Then, taking the receiver, she whispered, 'Go outside with Danny.'

They did not talk for long. I had only led Danny to the entrance, he had only then suddenly dropped down onto his bottom and refused to walk, so I had only just lifted him up and carried him to deposit him on the border-wall around one of the flowerbeds when my mother appeared, dry-eyed, her face set in an expression I could not discern. But before she reached us, the novice announced that the Mother Superior had asked that my mother see her in the school office upstairs. As my mother went back inside the convent, Danny sat unmoving on the low wall, and I put my arms around him to ensure he did not fall. He was tired, I could see from the glazed expression in his eyes. I sniffed his head. 'Did you miss me?' He would not have understood, but he gave me a sudden, wide, gummy smile, which warmed my heart. But soon after, I felt an ache, remembering my father's voice in my ear. My mother appeared behind us. 'Come, let's go.'

'What did Papa say to you?' I asked.

But she only shook her head, half-frowning. 'I have to hand in a report to Mother Superior. I'd forgotten about it. So we'll go to the lab quickly, okay?'

'But I'm hungry.' I could not stop a whine entering my voice.

'Only a few minutes, Sissy . . .'

She walked quickly, Danny bumping against her hip, and then I sat with Danny on the grassy verge outside, watching as my mother leant over her lab bench. It seemed like a long time since my escapade – I think Ezekiel's having a heart attack. My mother looked tired, as did Danny. Perhaps neither of them was enjoying each other's company, I thought with some malice, but knew that was not the reason. Some hairs had escaped her plait, and fell around her face as she copied the marks from a pile of tests to a grid. I could have offered to read them out to her, to help her, but even as I had the thought I refused it. I did not want to do any more. Was I not doing enough? Removing myself from her care? Looking after my little brother at every opportunity? Who was looking after me?

'Finished.' She tried to smile but there was a strained look in her eyes. She locked the door and we retraced our steps to the convent, then climbed uphill towards the row of bungalows. My mother's head remained fixed ahead as if she was unwilling to turn and look at the windows we passed, in case she saw a curtain twitch, a neighbour watching us. I trudged behind my mother's swishing sari, and I saw the boys again, a trio under a tree. In contrast to their demeanour of old – when they had always appeared occupied, intent – they looked more sullen and lethargic, as if they had suddenly realised the limits of their environs and a malaise had befallen them. I lifted my hand in a wave, but they did not return it. They stared at us, their eyes barely resting on me; they seemed more interested in watching my mother. By now my stomach felt as if its juices were eating me up from inside, but I found I was reluctant to return to the house even though I had longed for it all week. Now I found myself thinking of the brightness and the neatness, the polished furniture and floors, the patterned curtains, packed bookshelves and bedside reading lamp that awaited me on Monday in the Coopers' guest room. On the steps to the back door stood a basket full of fruits and vegetables and packets of milk, a small loaf of bread: Jonah's delivery.

'Oh good.' My mother sounded pleased.

She bent and lifted the envelope, which gave off a small clinking sound, the change. I felt a rush of disappointment. I had wanted to see him. I had not seen him for a week, even more. Only my mother and Danny were lucky enough to see him. And then I thought, resentfully, I had missed seeing Jonah because of my father's phone call.

My mother put her arm around my shoulder, kissed me on the cheek. 'Welcome back, mol.'

Her eyes were dark, but she was trying to make them shine, I could tell, and she was trying to keep her voice upbeat. I could smell her hair, which always held the scent of lemons and coconuts and fresh air, and her skin, which smelled like cocoa butter.

'What do you want for your snack?' She was whispering. 'Do you want some cinnamon toast?'

My favourite. She was being compliant; perhaps she had missed me. I nodded, and as she turned away I saw a wave of relief move over her features, as if she believed she had, by making this offering, righted every wrong. And I felt suddenly, viciously, misunderstood and unappreciated. I seethed inside, the anger a bitter ball in my stomach as I watched her butter the hot toast, sprinkle it with cinnamon and then more liberally than usual with brown sugar – another bribe. So that when she came to sit with me, and even before I had taken a bite, I asked again: 'What did you talk about with Papa?'

She did not seem to notice the edge to my voice. 'We didn't talk much.' She glanced at me. 'You saw how difficult it is to talk with the delay and everything—'

'But did you ask him to come back?'

She looked at me then, raised her eyebrows. 'There's no need to ask him that—'

'But does he *know*,' I spluttered. 'Does he *know* that you *want* him to come back?'

She stared at me. 'Sissy. Mol. Of course he does.'

'But what is he doing over there?'

'He said there is some work he has to do.'

'You mean he's teaching somewhere?'

'No, not teaching . . .'

'Then what?'

'I'm not sure.'

'So how long does he have to work there?'

'I don't know.' Then, 'I'm not sure he knows either.'

'But—'

'That's it, Sissy. That's all I know myself.'

'But why can't you ask him to come back?'

She fell silent; the only sound around us was Danny, sitting on her lap, growling now as he tore up his own piece of toast.

'Even if I asked, he will only come back when he's ready,' she said finally.

'Ready for what?'

'Sissy, thinnu, mol. Eat, you said you were hungry.'

I lifted the piece of toast, my stomach in knots, and threw it at Danny, who looked befuddled before picking it up and tearing it in half, with a smile.

'Don't do that.' She was wiping the crumbs and crystals of sugar out of his hair. 'Why did you do that?'

I grabbed the piece of toast out of Danny's grasp and he started to cry.

'Sissy, what is this behaviour?'

I laughed at Danny, then stuffed the toast in my mouth while his face puckered and turned bright red, his fingers splayed in protest. My mother suddenly got to her feet, put Danny down on the rug in the living room, then went into the bedroom and closed the door. I swallowed the wad of dough, nearly choking on it, my throat was so dry. Danny stopped crying and we both stared at each other. 'I hate you,' I whispered, and he rewarded me with a tentative, toothless smile. From my mother's room we could both hear the notes of a song; she was playing her records, just as she had done those weeks earlier. And just as that day when my father had left, we were left alone.

I ate all the scraps of toast left, even Danny's mangled efforts. Then I changed out of my school uniform and into my favourite comfy top and corduroy dungarees. I paused in front of my mother's bedroom door but heard only the sickly-sweet tones of yet another maudlin love song. Danny was quiet. I saw he had positioned himself on his stomach on the rug, bottom in the air, with his head turned, his cheek against the ground, thumb in his mouth, readying himself for a nap. The rug would aggravate the soft skin on his cheek. I looked around and found a colouring book, tore out a sheet of paper, and slipped it under his face to provide a buffer, feeling proud of my ingenuity, and hoping that this act of kindness and maturity was one step on the road to my redemption. But then, immediately, the resentment returned: why should my mother have the luxury to barricade herself in her bedroom, to leave me alone with my baby brother yet again?

'Don't sleep.' I rolled him onto his back with my toe and he unplugged his thumb with a squelch of surprise.

'Come with me.' I lifted him up.

His bottom felt heavy and damp but I would make him wait; I found the keys in the sideboard next to the dining table. We went out onto the veranda, and then I walked across the grass to where my father's car remained, under the mulberry bush. I opened the door and bundled Danny inside. It was stuffy; it had sat in the sun for days with the windows shut. I rolled the window down and slipped behind the wheel. Beside me, Danny pulled himself up on the back of the passenger seat and began babbling. He was singing, I realised, a song he must have sung with my father in the car. I felt a stab of sorrow for my baby brother – clueless, unconsulted, passed around – and then he fell back, bumping his head on the dashboard. He didn't cry, only whimpered as I rubbed his head, set him back on his feet. 'Idiot,' I whispered, feeling a sense of power surge through me. How easy it was to talk to him this way out of anyone's earshot, without fear of punishment. How easy it would be to leave with him. We could go where we wanted. He started jumping up and down, holding on to the back of the seat, babbling again. I glanced at the window of my mother's bedroom; there was no sign of her. She would be lying down on the bed, uninterested in what was carrying on outside. Had she abdicated all responsibility?

I put the key into the ignition and placed my hands on the steering wheel. The sun was setting and the tops of the trees in front of us were lit up in a golden glow.

'Where shall we go, Danny?' I asked. 'Paris? London? New York?'

I imitated the mellifluous tones of the voiceover of an advertisement we had seen in the cinema on our last visit to India. The actor had listed a selection of glamorous destinations in answer to his own question – *Where did she buy her beautiful necklace from? Paris? London? New York? No, she went to Lakshmi's Boutique in Chalakuddy.* Chalakuddy, a dusty strip of earth if ever there was one, with one fiercely air-conditioned, tightly sealed jeweller's. There had been some guffaws from the audience that night at the sheer effrontery of the ad, and in my father's car I laughed at my own joke while Danny joined in good-naturedly.

I looked at the key and contemplated turning it, but at the same moment I saw Jonah appearing at the top of the steps leading to the netball courts, just as he had done that day when it was my mother in this same driving seat. He had materials of some sort tucked under one arm and was carrying a tool bag in his other hand. For a moment I felt that I was her, Danny not my brother but my child next to me; I was in my mother's body, the orange sari soft around me. I watched as Jonah's eyes searched the windows of our bungalow, then he turned and glanced at the car, and I waved at him. He stopped short for a moment and then started jogging, laid his bag and the materials he had been carrying on the veranda, before he changed direction and strode towards us. He leant into the window, just as Mr Lawrence had leant into the window.

'Hello, Sissy.' He smiled at me and I smiled back, and inside my chest, inside me, I could feel a lifting, fluttering sensation, my heart soaring at the sight of him. 'How are you?'

'Fine, thanks.'

'I have not seen you these days.'

I shook my head, supremely pleased that he had noticed my absence.

'Danny.' He reached forward and patted my brother's head, then his eyes dropped down and without saying a word he pulled the key out of the ignition and put it in his pocket. There was a short silence.

'So you are well?' He was still smiling, but there was a darkness in his expression as he looked at me.

I nodded.

'And your mother?' He looked back at the house.

'She's lying down.'

He nodded, still smiling. Then he opened the door and held it open. 'Come, Sissy. I need to speak to your mother.'

He waited for me to climb out, before reaching back inside and extricating my brother. I found myself reddening with shame. He would feel Danny's damp bottom, and he would know that I should have changed him, that I was a neglectful sister. But he said nothing, only followed me to the front door, my brother on his arm. When I opened it, he deposited Danny inside, but remained outside.

'Call your mother, Sissy.'

There was something in his voice which made me run to my mother's door and, without any hesitation, knock on it. 'Mama, Jonah is here.' I held my breath and waited. I heard the music stop, heard steps and then the door opened and my mother appeared.

Her hair was loose around her and hung to below her shoulder blades in long, black waves. She was wearing her sari blouse and underskirt and nothing else; she had not tucked a lungi or a shawl around her. The blue of the blouse and skirt contrasted with her skin, the goldness punctuated only by the redness of her lips, the dark arches of her eyebrows, the fan of her eyelashes and then her hair framing her like a cloak. She glanced at me, then at Danny, who started scooting excitedly towards her making small, satisfied grunts. But she ignored us both, and I watched as she walked barefoot past me to the front door, her legs scissoring under the flimsy skirt, to Jonah, who was standing on the veranda. His eyes swept over my mother: over her face and hair, her slender, golden midriff and her navel dotting her belly neatly just above the drawstring of her skirt, down the shape of her legs under the skirt. I wanted to laugh; at his obvious amazement, his eyes moving up and down, up and down, absorbing the vision in front of him. Yes, I wanted to say with a proprietary pride, she's beautiful, isn't she, my mother. And I felt a joy at seeing the two of them before me: Jonah back at our house, my mother re-emerged from the bedroom. Then he lowered his eyes and gave a little cough.

'Jonah?' She opened the door wider. 'Come in.'

He opened his mouth again as if to protest, but then closed it and stepped inside. She bent to pick up Danny, who was now tugging at her skirt, and he immediately shoved his little fist into her blouse. She shook her hair off her shoulder, then settled Danny on her hip, and arranged his limbs around her like a lungi, one leg poised in front of the other.

'Madam,' Jonah said, cleared his throat, and started again. 'I came to tell you. There is to be a curfew every night.' He paused. 'Because of the plane.'

His words hung in the air and I stared at him. So he knew about the plane. Until then I had only heard the other men speak of it.

'A curfew,' my mother repeated.

'Yes, madam. There will be a . . .' he searched for the word, 'there will be a revenge.'

My mother glanced at me briefly, then nodded. 'I understand,' she whispered.

'I've brought some things, madam,' and he gestured to his bag and the supplies on the veranda. Within minutes, he had set to work. He had brought pegs for the curtains and cardboard sheets which he intended to use to cover the two bare windows – in the kitchen and next to the back door – and those in the living room, which only held thin cotton curtains. He cut the cardboard to size, measuring the frames exactly, fashioning a slit which we could use as a handle of sorts. We all watched him; even Danny did not squirm. All of us, I believe, taking some comfort from having this male presence in the house. He did not speak, declined the offer of a cup of tea from my mother, preferring to concentrate on his task.

He was beautiful to watch. His movements were deft, and his calculations and execution were skilled and precise as if he was an engineer or an architect, not the odd-job man of a convent school. We could see he took pride in performing the task in hand well. He was, as always, clean-shaven and his hair was neatly cut. And while his clothes were plain – a collared blue shirt and dark workman's trousers tucked into work boots – they were fresh and pressed and fitted his strong frame well. He took pride, we could also see, in his appearance. When he had finished the cardboard cut-outs, he walked around the house, entering every room, closing the curtains, pegging each tightly. When he was finished, he walked over to where we had stood, the three of us, motionless, watching him.

'This is very kind of you, Jonah.' My mother's voice was soft. 'Thank you.'

I think he said, don't worry, I'll come every day if you want me to, but I'm not sure. All I can remember is how they stayed like that for some time, facing each other, and how I watched them both.

'Sissy,' he suddenly spoke to me without turning his gaze from my mother, 'don't open the curtains. Not until the morning.'

'I won't,' I piped up.

'Not even to wave goodbye,' he said, looking at me now, and then grinned. So he knew I always watched him ride away. I blushed, but returned his smile.

'Jonah, I'll give you some money for your time and the materials . . .'

He shook his head, but my mother turned and walked to the sideboard, and as she walked away I saw his eyes move over her again, before he seemed to wrench them away as he turned to me. 'How is school?'

'Fine.'

'Study hard, Sissy.'

Then he reached into his pocket again and held out the key of my father's car. When I had grasped it, he did not let go immediately, but tick-tocked the index finger of his other hand from right to left. I gripped the key tightly.

'I will,' I said. 'And how are you, Jonah?'

'Well, Sissy, well.'

Then, to my delight, he reached forward and tugged at one of my plaits, in the exact same way that my mother did; perhaps he had seen her do so. He gave me another small smile, and then my mother was standing in front of him offering a collection of notes.

'No,' he shook his head. 'I did not come for this.' He opened the door, caught my eye again before the door closed and he was gone.

There was a silence; it was just the three of us again. I put my hands behind my back so my mother would not see the car key in my fist, but when she turned to look at me she fixed her eyes on mine, and did not waver.

'I didn't want Papa to go, Sissy.' Her voice was icy but her eyes were hot. 'He decided to, not me. And, yes, I'm angry with him and I know you are too.' Her eyes flashed at me, challenging me to deny what she had said and I gulped. 'But don't take it out on me, just because I'm the one who is here.' Then she gestured around her. 'This is hard for me. But I'm not going to disappear.'

The sole light glowed dully. We would be alone with the dark for hours ahead. I said nothing. All I felt was a gnawing fear in my heart, at the word she had used – disappear – at the anger I could see brimming beneath her skin, but also the cold resolve in her voice. She might have wanted to continue, but she didn't, choosing silence over explanations as she would do for the rest of her life. We spent the evening getting ready for bed, as if the rituals of mindlessly eating, washing up, washing ourselves, were enough to alleviate a life without any cultural pursuit to cultivate or any beauty to behold, any sound to soothe or image to enjoy. The little house was a boat suspended in a lake of darkness, its occupants floating on its waves, the gentle wind outside stirring its sails.

Part Three

IO

I FINALLY returned to India, to Delhi, to attend a conference, 'Translation in a Technological World: New Developments and Challenges'. The opportunity was the first of three to present themselves to me – all within twenty-two months of each other – to reconnect with my past. This first emerged without any warning. I was teaching a class at NYU on translation theory, supplementing my meagre stipend with translations for commercial catalogues and interviews for fashion magazines, finding that after a relative flurry of requests to translate literary texts – three novels in quick succession – the work had dried up. A colleague rang to say that a professor in the department who had been due to attend the conference had dropped out on account of illness, and the organisers had asked if someone could step in. Could I knock up a quick paper? The department knew of my India connection, deemed me therefore suitable for such a last-minute venture, and were happy to fund my flight and conference fee if I would pay for my own accommodation. I found a cheap hotel in the area of the city near the train station, Paharganj, described as 'perfectly decent' in my guidebook and a snip at 500 rupees a night; at that time, approximately seven dollars. My mother, when I had called her to let her know I was going to India the following week to a conference, only said: I've never been to Delhi. Neither of us mentioned that the trip would be a homecoming; we only discussed how our plans for my visit back to Philadelphia would have to be rejigged for the following month.

It didn't feel like a homecoming, although I had a sudden, surprising lump in my throat as we descended into Delhi. The airport looked nothing like the tiny shack where we had always landed in Cochin, to be met by Monuchayan. And outside, waiting for a taxi, the air was not thick and moist like a warm, wet towel, but hot and dry. I heard no Malayalam, or at least I did not pick out any from the cacophony of voices surrounding me. The taxi-driver into the city kept meeting my eyes in the rear-view mirror, until he asked, speak Hindi? I shook my head, although, as a true linguist would, I had crammed up the previous week and now had a passable knowledge of basic phrases and numbers. My response provided the death knell to any further conversation and we proceeded in silence. As we drove past the grand hotels and boulevards, and skirted around Connaught Place, I was thinking how dissimilar the capital was to the chaos of Ernakulam, which to my memory had looked half-made and badly made by turns, until we swerved into the road leading to Old Delhi, into a familiar vista of shabby stalls and unremitting traffic, human and animal jostling against each other.

The hotel was neat enough, and comfortable enough, staffed, it appeared, entirely by men, and the stares I attracted were disconcerting. While I filled in the police registration form I felt the eyes of the young receptionist on me in a piercing gaze. After suffering his scrutiny for many minutes, I raised my head and gave him a weak smile, which he then returned with an astonishing, sudden brilliance, his Adam's apple bobbing up and down in his throat. Perhaps, I thought, he had not been appraising the scar that veiled half my face, but was simply curious about a woman in rumpled clothes, travelling on her own.

In the evening I wandered through the stalls of Paharganj, fingering the blouses and trousers and kameezes – madam, this way, madam, good price – and bought myself a shawl, for the night had grown chilly. I slung it around me and continued meandering, braving the blatant curiosity; at least, I thought, I was not invisible. I marvelled at the familiar – the dust on my toes, the colours and the clothes, the smells of cooking, the stalls where hot, sweet milky tea was served in steel cups, the tailor with his sewing machine in full view of the street – and the unfamiliar – I understood hardly any of the language, the children on the street seemed plentiful, pitiful and unsupervised. There were several groups of well-dressed, well-heeled young people with modern swinging haircuts, trendier and cooler than any I had seen in Kerala, who must have been visiting from more affluent areas of the city, and who were regarding their environs with as much ethnographic interest as I was. All these sights and sounds swilled around in my no-doubt jetlag-addled brain, so that when I found my way back to the hotel and lay on the bed, I wept for many minutes, perhaps even an hour, surprising myself at the quantity of tears I could produce, soaking the pillow. Wept at the sheer strangeness of being back in India, but not where I knew, and not as I had been; not a smooth-faced young girl but a young woman who felt rudderless and adrift.

I hadn't seen my father for eighteen years. My mother had been married to my stepfather for longer than she had been to my father. I was thirty years old and, until a few months previous had been in a relationship I thought would last for ever, but which had since gone awry. I seemed always to be working, yet I paid my bills with difficulty. I had moved back to Bed-Stuy, having given up the lease of an apartment near Central Park, one I could not afford now that I was living alone again. I was back on Nostrand Avenue, which I still felt great affection for. But the neighbourhood had become more expensive and the return was a reminder of how little my circumstances had changed materially since my early twenties. I had no idea what the rest of my life would be like, but I knew I wanted it to be different. My scar had faded a fraction over the last few years but I had long stopped hoping that, just like the colour of a flower's petals can alter with a variance in the acidity of the soil, one day, by some trick of hormonal changes or by some strange concoction in the air, I would wake up and the veil across my face would have been drawn back, my skin would have resumed its original hue to match the rest of my face, my eye fully healed.

After wallowing all night in my thoughts, I was glad the next morning to find my way to the conference venue on the outskirts of the city. To be reminded that I was not purposeless, that I was educated, had a profession and a reason to have taken myself across the ocean. That my trip had been paid for because someone had thought of me as a deserving recipient. In the first coffee break I got talking to another woman of my age, Prithi, who was originally from Delhi but was now living in Bombay, and who worked as a translator in the film industry. We gelled immediately and kept each other company over the next three days. I appreciated her confidence and enjoyed her irreverent humour.

And then, on the fourth day, I absconded; woke up that morning and decided that I would not go to the conference. I had already given my paper to a group of fifteen unenthusiastic delegates. The experience had been rather deflating, but I knew that was not the reason for my sudden disinterest. I felt that I was being untrue to myself, by being in India and not conceding to this significance. I ordered room service for breakfast. I was reluctant to descend to the soulless, airless dining room, to drink a cup of 'English' tea under the eyes of a swarm of over-attentive waiters. I ate my toast and slurped my tea while lying in bed, the television I had ignored until now tuned in to a soap opera.

It was after I had lazed in this way for a couple of hours that I began to feel restless. The hotel room did not assuage my disappointment of myself, and so I dressed, threw my shawl around me. I would wander around the shops on Connaught Place.

The sun was out, and there was a bustle. Surrounded by young couples, families and tourists, I walked past shops selling Levi's, saris and jewellery, a McDonald's, takeaway kiosks offering masala dosa, cheese sandwiches and pakora. I could pretend I was on vacation. I loitered on the pavements, enjoying the snatches of conversations in English that I could understand. And then, on advice from my guidebook, I approached an autorickshaw driver who was parked in a rank, cleaning his wing mirror, and asked him to take me to Humayun's tomb. He was a Sikh, with an impressive maroon-coloured turban and extravagant moustache. He accepted the fare I suggested without any haggling and my appearance with a refreshing equanimity – perhaps he had seen much worse – just a slight inclination of the head and gentle smile. And then, as if he offered entertainment as part of the service, as we buzzed through the streets he started singing – a Hindi love song. Neither the noise from the autorickshaw's engine nor the traffic that sped around us failed to drown him out. He sang with great feeling, beating time on the steering wheel, pausing at significant moments, in a voice that was deep and melodious. And I was transported; I was the heroine of a story being driven to meet her lover. We arrived at the tomb, and the driver slowed down so that when he stopped and turned off the engine it coincided with the end of the song. Perfect timing. He turned around, grinning, and I smiled back, my spirits revived.

Large manicured gardens, surrounded by trees. Beyond, the elegant red stone building and white dome. I turned off the path leading to the tomb, found a quiet spot on the grass. Others had come for the same respite; when the emperor's Begum built a mausoleum for her husband, she would not have known what a haven it would offer from the sprawling city that Delhi was to become. Among those tranquil surroundings – the beautiful Persian symbol of the love between a husband and wife before me – I mulled over what I had been thinking when I had agreed, so easily, to come to India, after so many years. There was no reason that I should not have made this journey five, ten years ago; instead someone else had presented me with the opportunity. And what had I learned so far? That it was a vast, diverse country; that this city, and the people in it, bore little resemblance to the river and the lakes in which my mother had swum, in which I myself had swum with her, all those years ago, the coconut trees swaying around us, with my father watching us from the bank. If I indeed wanted a homecoming, I would have to make another journey, further south.

I got to my feet, walked up to the tomb, and climbed the steps to the terrace. There was hardly any noise here. The city could have vanished, and apart from myself there was only one other person: a woman in a green sari, bent over at the waist, sweeping the inner room with a bamboo brush. I stood still, absorbing the serenity, appreciating the elegance of the ornate window cut out of the stone. The vista was scrubland; the smog above the city hung not far away. When I turned around, I saw the woman was watching me, her eyes softening when she saw my face.

Then she pointed and said, Mecca. Humayun head, Mecca.

I smiled and nodded, and she smiled in return – a smile of very large teeth with a prominent overbite. We held this position for a few moments and then she returned to her brush. I left the tomb, walked back through the gardens where three young men were sprawled on the grass. When they saw me, one sat up and waved, and then, as if galvanised by his friend's actions, another blew a kiss while his friends hooted with laughter.

I returned to the hotel – in pensive mood, but feeling I had made the correct decision to have missed the day at the conference – where the young receptionist said: the lady left a message, madam.

It read: *Where the hell have you been? I'm coming back at six. Dress nicely, I'm taking you to see some friends. Prithi.*

And when she arrived, punctually, and found me waiting for her downstairs, she said: what happened? I thought you were eaten by wolves or something. Then: what on earth are you wearing? You look terrible.

I had chosen to dress in a salwar kameez that I had bought an hour earlier from a stall, filled with nerves over the prospect of meeting Prithi's friends. Not wanting to attract attention to myself, not wanting to be the outsider. But I agreed that the outfit swamped me, the colours clashed with my already two-toned face, the salwar was heavy and I had no idea how to arrange it over myself. Around my neck? Draped over one shoulder? In the end I had twisted it around my chest like a straitjacket.

Those jeans you were wearing the other day and that black sleeveless top? Prithi said. Go and change, I'll wait here for you.

I laughed to myself as I climbed obediently back up the stairs to my room. I was not offended; I only felt an affection for my new friend. I changed, brushed my hair out from its bun and swapped my earrings.

When I descended, she said: that's better. Followed by: what were you thinking?

Trying to fit in I guess, I muttered. And I'm a bit nervous, truth be told, about meeting your friends.

This, she flapped her hand in my face. Don't think about it, Sissy. Don't think about this.

But it was a glamorous gathering, as I had suspected, and she had made me wear the exactly right clothes. The whole party – two young married couples, two other single women and a single man – the whole party wore studiedly casual jeans with shirts or blouses or kurtas which could not have been anything but designer-made, were all glossy-haired and had dazzling smiles, spoke mostly in rapid English with only the very occasional dip into Hindi. They were welcoming and interesting, and I enjoyed watching and listening to them, surprised at the quantity of beer and whisky everyone drank as we munched on plates and plates of pakora and samosas that one of the women kept bringing in from her kitchen. The apartment was modern and modishly East-meets-West. The colony, it appeared, was much sought after, with a shopping mall close by, and for most of the gathering, aside from Prithi and the single man, only a short drive away from their work.

You're an American, aren't you? the man said. Aren't you supposed to be loud and brash or whatever?

He was at my feet, literally, sprawled out on the rug while I sat in a low chair above him.

I sipped my beer. I don't think of myself as an American, I said, maybe a New Yorker. But I suppose I am. I've lived there most of my life.

Don't be rude to Sissy, Ashu, Prithi called out from across the room, quite drunk by now. She's adorable. She's an Italian translator *and* she's a Keralite, you know.

Kerala? I've never been, he said. Do you go back often?

I could have lied, but perhaps because of my earlier disdain for shirking from the truth, I answered: not for many, many years. My parents divorced, and my mother's family really disapproved. They're Catholic, you can guess how badly that went down. She hasn't seen them since.

He raised his eyebrows. And your father?

My long-lost father, George Olikara, I said, raising my beer bottle in salute, and I furnished him with the few details I had relayed to many people, on many occasions.

Don't underestimate Sissy, Prithi called over again, and I realised she was as worried about how I would fare in this gathering as I was. She's a dark horse, she said.

But, the man continued, ignoring her, have you not tried to get in touch with your father yourself?

You're right, I said, I should. But when I was younger, this was what took up all my energies – I gestured to my face – and then life moved on. My mother remarried and I love my stepfather.

He peeled himself off the rug, sat up and brushed down his jeans, put his glass on the floor next to him, held out his hand and, surprised, I took it.

I'm Ashok, by the way. Drink makes me unpleasant, he said lightly, but smiling apologetically. In my real life I run a business and on occasion we have call to investigate potential clients et cetera. You know, run background checks to make sure they aren't child traffickers or terrorist motherfuckers. I can ask my team to look into your father for you.

I shrugged. Why not?

But by now I wanted to leave, because my heart was thumping at the possibility that this man and his pool of investigators would uncover my father deftly. And that with a quick flick through a phone book, the opportunity would present itself to me: do you want to meet him? The likelihood that this man would find my father, the chance of success when a search was done in the country itself, by professionals, was very high, and this appalled me.

The following day, back at the conference, I felt ill with the several scenarios that were jostling in my head. My father, bedridden and unconscious, the nurses and doctors berating me: you must pay for his care, his bill is so high! My father, as tall and dark as I remembered, emerging with a woman on his arm: I remarried too, Sissy. This is your stepmother, and our five children are inside waiting to meet you. My father, in prison. He was, in fact, Raju Kumaresan, the pseudonym he had assumed when he left my mother.

Are you all right? Prithi dug her elbow into my ribs.

Just hungover, I managed to whisper back.

The next day, the last of the conference, and the day before I was booked on a flight to leave for New York, back to my life of almost-penury, my solitary class and freelance work, Prithi passed on a message that Ashok wanted to take me out to dinner that evening, during which he would report on his findings.

He arrived at my hotel in a huge 4×4 better suited for a safari than the narrow streets of Paharganj. As we drove back into New Delhi – he was taking me to a new Japanese restaurant that had opened not far from India Gate – he said, I won't keep you in suspense, Sissy. We haven't found him. But we can talk more over some food. Then he patted my arm.

I stared out of the window. I did not feel relief that none of the scenarios I had envisaged would come true, I felt bereft. Here, in this city in which I had no investment, I had nevertheless felt that he was close, nearby, within touching distance. Was it because of the break-up a few months ago with my boyfriend, whom I had loved but who could not have loved me equally in return, choosing to leave me rather than stay? Was it because I had seen so many men in the streets, even at the conference venue, who looked like my father? Was it because I had imagined that the reverse might happen, that my father would look for *me*, learn that I was visiting New Delhi, sweep into the conference venue and step into my path: mol, it's good to see you again after all those years. You've grown into a woman, but what happened, Sissy – touching my cheek – what happened?

Ashok did not try to engage me in small talk, with a measure of tact that I would not have attributed to him when we had first met. Perhaps, as he had said, drink did make him unpleasant. Only when we reached the restaurant, and after he had parked the car, did he take my hand and lead me upstairs where a smartly suited maître-d' showed us to the table. The restaurant was filled with an impossibly stunning clientele: every woman seemed to have the face and figure of a starlet, and every man seemed to be blessed with chiselled cheekbones and an enviably strong jawline. But compared to my gentle collisions earlier in the week – with the hotel receptionist, the autorickshaw driver, the woman in the tomb – here, the preening and posturing, the shrill voices, the wine bottles and music, the raucous laughter, were vile, ugly to me.

As soon as we sat down, a man from the table across from us approached ours, threw his arm around Ashok: Sala! I heard you were engaged to that Rohini! What are you doing here with a beautiful stranger?

But as he spoke he turned to look at me more directly, his face falling; either because of the scar that eclipsed half my face or because of the tears that had gathered in my eyes. Ashok shook his friend off, and as the man moved away, he took my hand.

Is this a bad idea? Shall we go somewhere else? Somewhere quieter?

But I was loth to stand up and leave, make even more of a spectacle of ourselves, so I shook my head. Just give me a minute, I whispered.

And he did, giving me more than a minute, ordering the specials, and arranging for water and wine, fussing with the table setting, as I felt the gale inside me settle until it was just a flutter in my belly, like the first tiny kicks of a newborn baby.

I did the whole American thing, he started, and prepared you a dossier. He pointed to a slim folder he had placed on the table. You can read it in detail later but basically, there has been no official registration of a death, no marriages, bank accounts, no businesses listed. That doesn't mean that none of the above have *not* actually happened. What it means is that there is nothing we can find through official channels about him, after the court case you mentioned. Before, in the sixties, there's plenty, but I'll let you read all of that yourself. Your father was involved as a party member when the Communist Party split, and he joined the Marxist branch, so he features in records and minutes and things, and there's evidence of his friendship with the Kumaresan fellow.

Our food arrived and we each made a good fist at pretending to enjoy our meals. It was when we were halfway through that he spoke again, choosing his words carefully: Sissy, sometimes men abandon their wives. Sometimes wives abandon their husbands. They leave their children. Something happens inside them and they just can't face going back.

His voice was gentle and he was looking at me intently, even though I found it difficult to meet his eyes.

I'm not saying that you need to accept or even understand that, he continued. I just don't want you to think that a positive outcome is solely in your hands. You mustn't feel that you are the only one who can solve this and then blame yourself for not succeeding. I mean, your father could try and find you, couldn't he?

He added, after a few moments of silence: it might be sometimes that you have to be on the ground, asking around, talking to people.

I knew what he meant. I could take myself to Ernakulam, find the house of my great-uncle Monuchayan, who would surely have seen my father, at least when he had first returned to India; who could point me in the direction of the mountain, the cave, the seminary, the lonely hut at the top of a hill in which my father had spent the last eighteen years.

Did you find anything about Raju Kumaresan? I asked finally. Did he have a wife and children that my father might have wanted to take care of?

He frowned. Then, still munching, he slid a finger into the file, glanced through some pages. His mother and sisters are mentioned, as you already know, no one else.

But there was no need for further clarification. I had found a plausible fairytale that cast my father in the role of protector and chivalrous knight. The storyboard was already designed in my head: my father taking charge of a poor illiterate woman, husband imprisoned and children hungry, a scenario not uncommon in India. This would be the narrative I nurtured, not by any means outlandish, and this would be the narrative that would enable me to return to my former life, pick up from where I had left and carry on. For the other – that my father had simply left, turned his back to face forwards to a future without us – was a story that deserved to be as buried as that story of the plane I had uncovered those years ago in a library on Washington Square.

Ashok drove me back to the hotel but parked at the top of the street where it was quieter. He took my hand and drew me close. I felt his breath against my forehead as he pressed my face into his chest. I did not resist but neither did I melt against him. He might have been feeling pity or desire. I had no idea, and felt no inclination to understand. When he released me, I got down from his ridiculous vehicle, the file clutched in my hand, and as I was fumbling with the door he said, goodbye, Sissy Olikara.

I entered my hotel bedroom alone, lay down on the bed alone, and wondered whether I should have invited him to stay the night. Anything to displace the memory of this trip as being a failed attempt to connect with my father. I read through the dossier that night, met Prithi the next day and exchanged contact details with promises to keep in touch, took myself to the airport, and in a blink of an eye was back in the studio apartment I was renting – back in Bed-Stuy, phone messages to listen to, a class to teach the next day.

That night I called my mother: I'm back.

How was it? How was your paper?

Fine, it's an interesting place.

She laughed. I've never been, but it's something, isn't it, to visit the capital?

I said: I had someone look for Papa.

My mother fell stone silent, even though, *surely*, she must have expected, at least in passing, mention of my father.

I added after some moments: he found nothing.

She said: I'm very sorry, mol.

Have you not heard from him, Mama? I asked the question that I had long stopped asking, and received the very same answer as before.

Not since the divorce, mol. I'm sorry.

I put my hand over my eyes, the light in my apartment seemed suddenly too bright.

Are you there, Sissy? Her voice was soft.

My head hurts, I said. And I have a class first thing in the morning. My voice trembled suddenly with self-pity.

Drink lots of water, my mother said. Don't work too hard, Sissy. Get some sleep and you'll feel better tomorrow.

THE curfew enveloped our lives. The darkness it brought was like a pall. Being trapped indoors from just before sunset, with curtains pinned and cardboard cut-outs in place, was stifling, especially when on the other side of our walls was open land under a wide night sky. Even though before, because of the crickets and the insect life and the ever-present fear of snakes slithering into our yard from the bush behind us, we did not have a habit of sitting out in the warm nights, now we felt compelled to enjoy the veranda and hence felt thwarted by the edicts issued daily on the radio, repeated by the school authorities. We lowered our voices, heard every glug from the fridge as it battled through the night, every gurgle from the pipes if we were lucky enough not to have a water cut. Windows were closed; at least the nights were always cool and we did not suffer from the heat.

I did not sleep in my mother's bed that night, our first under the curfew; I stayed in my bedroom. On Saturday afternoon, she dug out the old, rickety pushchair that we had been given by a neighbour and which Danny hated. But we held him down, his body arching in resistance, his face bright red with fury, slipped on the straps, and belted him in. Then we wheeled him off the veranda, down our short drive and onto the road, turning left, to walk past only two bungalows before reaching the steep descent to the entrance gates of the campus. We passed through the gates and carried on walking. Past the settlement of tin-roofed houses, carrying on and on, with no destination in mind, only to find a pleasing space: an outcrop of rocks or a patch of grass under the shade of a tree.

My mother was wearing one of my father's shirts – light blue, made of a faded, thin cotton – oversized on her but she had rolled up the sleeves. And the navy-blue stirrup pants, bought at a department store in Bombay on our way back to Cochin, this purchase made under duress from my father. It was my mother's very first pair of trousers, and he had coerced her into trying them on, and then swept away her coyness and taken them to the till. This was a couple of years ago, and the stirrup pants were worn rarely. But they suited her, and combined with my father's shirt, she looked carefree, unbounded by the respectability of a sari. You look nice, Mama, I had said on seeing her, and she had grinned. Not so sure, mol. But she did. She looked young and bright; she had tied back her hair, unplaited, in a ponytail. She was small and small-boned, I was beginning to realise. I reached her forehead now; she was not much taller than me. Danny was gabbling contentedly, and we exchanged a glance and smiled. She took one hand away from the handle of the buggy, and tucked some of the hair that had escaped my own ponytail behind my ear, then laid her palm against my cheek briefly. It was my birthday. I was twelve. We were taking a picnic of cake and cordial to enjoy in the fresh air.

That morning my mother had crept into my bedroom, gently pushing me across and, climbing into my bed, pulled the covers over us both.

'Before Danny wakes up,' she whispered, then kissed me. 'Happy birthday, mol.' Her eyes were sad. We both remembered our words from the previous evening. I searched my mother's eyes for any lingering anger or resentment, and only met her gaze: bright, loving, a hint of regret somewhere behind her lashes.

'Sorry no party, mol,' she whispered.

In fact we had agreed, weeks ago, that we would wait until my father returned before booking a trip to the cinema with my school friends. In years past, we would invite all the Malayalees for an afternoon of songs and cake, but I knew without asking that this would not happen today. She produced a small parcel: a new anklet and bangles, bought, I knew, on our last visit to India, in preparation for this day. And I thought of how she had to think ahead but had probably no inkling when she bought the trinkets that my father would not be with us. I slipped them on to please her and she exclaimed at how well they suited me, how elegant my limbs appeared decorated with the jewellery, not mentioning how incongruous they were against my pyjamas. This pair were in lurid stripes of orange and green, another of my mother's bizarre choices.

She also produced a neatly ironed trio of cotton training bras. So she had noticed how I was growing. She had made a cake during the week, with the chocolate she had asked Miss Munroe to bring back, months ago, from Ireland, and which she had saved for the picnic. We spread out a blanket and released Danny, who grabbed the side of the buggy and raised himself on his feet, then after looking around with surprise, dropped back down onto his bottom.

I poured out the squash, my mother arranged some candles on the cake; after I blew them out, she handed me the paper plate. We both sank our teeth into our slices and munched in silence. I was in heaven, the cake melted in my mouth. She had brought our pack of cards. We could play rummy, she said, but I shook my head and stretched out onto the blanket, on my stomach. Maybe later, I said, after more cake. She laughed, then lay down on her side beside me. Danny was rolling the squash bottle between his legs.

'You know,' she spoke suddenly, and reached across to smooth my hair down, 'I wanted more than this for you. When

I was your age,' she said smiling slightly now, but with that same sad look in her eyes, 'I had my brothers, my cousins, so many friends. We ran around, there was always something to do, someone to play with. We had the lake, the river. There was always a party at the church to get dressed for, to wear nice clothes. My dancing lessons. It's so quiet here. I know you have friends but we live so far away from them. And now with Papa not here and me not driving . . .' She stopped. 'I wanted more for you.'

We were silent for a long time, and then I said, 'But I like it here, Mama.'

'Do you?' She smiled widely. 'Tell me what you like, mol.'

'I *like* the quiet,' I said. 'I like our house . . .'

She burst out laughing, but covered her mouth quickly, 'Sorry, carry on, mol.'

'I like Ally and Mary-Anne and Grace and Jonah . . .'

She had stopped laughing, and while a smile still played on her lips, her eyes were now grave.

'. . . I like it when the holidays come and me and Bobby and Aravind can play all over the campus.'

She said, 'You haven't played with those boys for some time now.'

Those boys. She was not looking at me now, her eyes were on Danny.

I replied, 'I think they've grown out of me.'

She glanced at me, with a brief rueful smile. 'I think *you've* grown out of *them*, mol.' Then she sat up, pressed her knees together, laid her chin on them, facing forward. 'I wanted you to have piano lessons or singing lessons or even dancing lessons,' she said. 'I could find someone in town, I knew. But then we would have to drive somewhere. Papa didn't like that. Then there was the petrol shortage.' She shook her head. 'Always something happening. Always an excuse.'

I sensed it was the right moment to ask, 'Why don't we go back as well, Mama? To be with Papa?'

She did not stir, did not look at me, and stayed quiet for so long I wondered whether she had not heard or whether the question had so affronted her she would pretend I had not asked. Then she hugged her knees tighter and looked at her toes. 'I wish it were that simple, Sissy.' She turned to me. 'But where would we stay? With Monuchayan?' My father's uncle in Mattancherry. 'Or go back to Pappan?' My grandfather in the Ghats. 'Back to Kothamangalam?' Her childhood home. 'When a woman marries she leaves her family. They will not be happy if I come back. They don't even know Papa is there . . .'

'But—'

'And what would we live on? Do you think Papa will find a job easily? Or me? Why do you think we're here?' She shook her head and bit her lip, and stared fixedly at her feet. 'All our savings,' she spoke quietly, 'all the money we made, all these years, Papa has given it away. To help his friends from college. To help friends of his friends. To pay for the weddings of his friends' sisters.' She shook her head again. 'There is always someone asking.' She turned then, to look at me. 'But he never thought to ask me first. To see if *I* was happy for the money *I* earned to be given away, to people who . . .' Her voice broke off, and there was a silence, but then she resumed. 'When I lost the baby . . .' Her eyes flickered over me. 'Do you remember?'

And I nodded, a chill settling into my heart that she would mention this, that which we never spoke about: the little sister I should have had, some years before Danny. I should have told her then that I remembered everything, even how my father had flung her carelessly into the lake in Thattekkad, and how I knew that was the reason for the terrible occurrence and her illness those months after. How I knew that my father had done something wrong then, that there had been something in the water, some black sadness that she must have swallowed which had made the baby die inside her and my mother's spirit wither. That I remembered how a witchdoctor stood in our back garden even if she had not known, and how, secretly, even though I knew it was not rational, I believed he had helped us; because it was not long after his appearance that my mother roused herself and began to regain her previous self.

'When I needed to stay in hospital,' she was saying, 'do you know we had to borrow money from Rahul's father because we had nothing in the bank? How do you think that made me feel?' She shook her head and mumbled something under her breath. What did she say? I seem to remember something like 'He's not what you think,' or maybe it was 'It's not what you think,' but maybe I am projecting to, weeks ahead, when I would watch my mother take a path she determined for us.

I did not speak. I felt that we had entered deeper waters than I could navigate. She shook herself, tried to smile, offered to shuffle the cards, and I agreed. Danny was by now mewling, and so we let him join in, but he refused to let us hold any cards, angrily snatching them from our grip, and so we admitted defeat, allowed him to monopolise the pack, which he did with an unencumbered selfishness, the thought flashing through my mind: like father, like son. I was allowed another piece of cake, and Danny, too, my mother wrapping the remainder in some tin foil she had brought. She would ask Miss Munroe round for a cup of tea later if she were available.

And when we returned and we found her, Miss Munroe produced a gift. A book, *Little Women*, bought for me by a friend on a visit from Dublin, at her request. I was touched by her thoughtfulness, and raced through the rest of the evening, so that I could lie down in bed, with the candle for a night-light, and lose myself in the words. Miss Munroe stayed for an early dinner, taking her leave before the curfew began, so she could ready her own house for the darkness. And when, the next morning, Rahul appeared at our door, his face flushed – his mother had said he should drive us to church – I could detect some satisfaction when mine informed him that, in fact, we did not need the lift, Miss Munroe had offered already to take us. Then my mother softened her pose and she touched his arm, while he blushed further before catching my eye: 'Hi, Sissy.'

He turned to my mother, asked quietly: 'Anything I can help with, Aunty?'

'No, we're fine,' my mother replied. 'Thanks anyway, mon.'

He said: 'Just ask, Aunty.' And then mumbled, 'Amma doesn't need to know.'

'She'll find out!' My mother laughed, throwing her head back as she said the words, and Rahul smiled back, his eyes glancing down to her throat before he squared his shoulders and stood up straighter.

'Can I go with Rahul, Mama?' I asked, suddenly aching to win some of his attention, and my mother shook her head, still smiling at Rahul while absently patting my shoulder.

But when she turned away to retrieve Danny from the kitchen where he seemed to be finding the dustiest, stickiest space under the sink, Rahul bent forward and whispered, 'I'll take you for a drive one day, Sissy. Your mother doesn't need to know. And she won't find out.' And he winked.

The exchange kept my spirits lifted all through the monotonous church service with the saintly Miss Munroe, who I had heard say to Mr Lawrence not long ago: now why would I want to be going to Mass when there's no one here to tell on me? And as we were leaving the church, I felt a hand on my arm. It was Bobby, who had grown it seemed like half a foot since I had last stood next to him. He looked down at me as I blinked up at him, the sun in my eyes. Ahead of us, I saw my mother exchanging bright smiles with the other Malayalee ladies, all of the adults luminous in their falseness. Miss Munroe was talking with the older boys; I saw Rahul among them.

'Uh . . .' Bobby's voice sounded deeper as well. I waited and then he pulled something from his pocket. 'I made this at school. You can have it.' He cleared his throat. 'For your birth-day, you know.'

It was a small wooden box with two brass hinges, an inlay of patterned leaves carved into its top. I took it from him, ran my fingers over the surface. It felt smooth and luxurious and the box rested in my palm with a pleasant weight.

'For your earrings I thought,' he muttered.

He had never before treated me like a girl; I had never thought Bobby and Aravind regarded me as such. That was why his crass imitation and insinuation those weeks back had felt so unfair and hurtful. But much had shifted over the last weeks. He had not only grown taller, and my father had not only left: I had also changed. I could feel the cotton brassiere brushing against the fabric of my dress, which was shorter now as my legs had grown longer. I breathed my thanks and he shrugged, his face reddening. And then, as if he were in collu-sion with Rahul, he added, 'Just let me know if I can help in any way.' He did not, however, add that I could play with him and Aravind, or join them later that afternoon, as if he too could feel that we had outgrown each other.

Alongside my bracelets, anklets, the book from Miss Munroe, the box from Bobby and the promise from Rahul – I did not think to count the underwear – my birthday haul was looking highly respectable. I realised that the phone call from my father had been his present, even if we had both forgotten to refer to the occasion. The well wishes and the warm thoughts I could feel emanating from all around me sustained me well into the next week and my return to the Coopers'. The return to the routine of school, the days bright and full, then the stilted atmosphere at the house, Ally's reticence and Mary-Anne's company.

It was after one particularly stiff dinner of the dreaded meatloaf, with Mr Cooper commenting, 'Delicious, Cindy,' to which she laid her cutlery down, 'Good God, Sam,' – an exchange which perplexed me, but which seemed to drive the Cooper girls to an even earlier bedtime – that I was left lying in the bedroom surrounded by the beautiful things, but sleepless and restless. I tossed and turned helplessly and then crept out to use the bathroom, and only then did I hear the voices coming from the main bedroom: rising and falling, like moans. My cheeks grew hot. It was embarrassing hearing my friends' parents making love. But I quickly realised the noises were not amorous; the cadences were different. They were having an argument.

I flushed the toilet, washed my hands, all in the light of the candle each of us had been given for night-time prowls, then padded back down the corridor. I could feel my feet tingle with curiosity and as much as I knew I shouldn't, I couldn't stop myself from slowing down until I was positioned outside their door and could hear Mr and Mrs Cooper.

'. . . who you fetishise . . .'

'That's an unpleasant word to use, Cindy.'

'But you do. You fetishise them. Because you can't accept that there might be dishonesty and sloth and slovenliness just as *anywhere* else. Because you *love* being this white *explorer* guy . . .'

'Jesus Christ. Where is this coming from?'

'Just admit it, Sam. Just admit that this is not going how you expected—'

'I'll do no such thing.'

'Don't hang your head like that, Sam. Don't play the browbeaten husband.'

He must have raised his head, because his voice was suddenly clear. 'Listen, I thought we were talking about Ezekiel.'

My heart jumped into my mouth and the candle tumbled from my grasp, extinguishing itself as it thudded onto the rug, and then I was in darkness, on my knees, my hands scrabbling around until they met the stick of wax and I stood up again. The darkness seemed to magnify the words.

Then, there was a silence, so deep and so long that I was sure they had heard me, or if they hadn't, could hear me now, my heart thundering in my chest, my hand covering my mouth so that my breathing would not betray my presence. But then I heard a creak and Mr Cooper spoke, his voice coming from lower down; he had sat on the bed.

'Treat me like an idiot,' he said, low and measured, 'and take me step by step through what's in your head.'

But when she spoke Mrs Cooper's voice was strangled with tears. 'I just don't recognise you any more, Sam. And I hate myself as well for hating it so much here.'

'Cin, baby, you don't have to feel that way.' His voice was suddenly gentle. 'It *is* difficult to live here . . .' he tailed off. Then, 'You've given up a lot for me.'

She made a barking sound, a rasp more than a laugh. 'God, listen to yourself, Sam! Where do you *get* these lines from? It's like living in some third-rate movie set or—'

'For *fuck's sake*, Cindy.' Now his voice was like a whip. 'Try to be nice, will you? You seem to mock *every fucking word* I say these days—'

'I didn't *give up anything* for you, Sam,' scathing and trembling at the same time. 'I did this for *me*. And for the girls. Not for you. I thought it would be enriching.' Then, her voice breaking, 'But it's just not . . .'

They fell silent again, and when Mr Cooper finally spoke his tone was calm but persuasive, and because of this, I imagined him standing like Jonah had stood, his arm pinning the cook into place. 'Tell me about Ezekiel.'

'I know you want to give him a break,' she said. 'And God knows Grace needs a break. But I don't like it, I don't like him.'

'Has he not been doing any work?'

'No, that's not it. He fixed the gate. He cleaned up the backyard . . .'

My heart was thumping. So Ezekiel had been working for

them? *Here?* And then I understood: the Coopers had arranged it so that he would only come on the days I did not, to avoid our meeting.

'You've seen him. He's sick, there's something wrong with him . . .'

'It's his epilepsy, Cindy. He's on medication now.' His voice was almost stern, and Mrs Cooper must have heard the same inflection for she snarled, 'Don't patronise me, Sam.'

Mr Cooper did not respond, and I heard Mrs Cooper continue: 'And he's strange. I don't like having him around. I don't like having him near the girls—'

'I think you're being a little—'

'I can't *believe* that the Olikaras left Sissy alone in the house with him. I can't believe they just left her with him like that. I mean he could have done *anything* to her. How do we know that he didn't . . .'

I turned away. Just as I had run that afternoon, when Ezekiel had fallen to the floor, clutching his chest – get your mother! – I knew with a scorching certainty that I had to run again. I had to reach my mother, all alone in the bungalow. That was where I belonged, not here. Danny would be fast asleep, too vulnerable himself to offer her anything: support, aid, protection. He could offer her nothing.

I returned to my room, packed my bag, changed out of my pyjamas. As I went back into the dark hallway I saw Mary-Anne's door open, and there she stood, in her spotted nightshirt, her eyes as wide as saucers, and her mouth forming a perfect circle of surprise. We stared at each other.

'Mommy and Daddy are fighting,' she whispered.

I said nothing.

'Is that why you're leaving? They'll stop soon.'

I shook my head. 'I need to go back to Mama,' and as I spoke I thought how babyish was the sentiment.

She nodded, her mouth still open.

'Will you tell your parents where I've gone, please? In the morning?'

She nodded again, her eyes huge.

I slid back the latch of the front door and stepped out into the night. I walked quickly down their path and onto the road, past the roundabout. It was surprisingly easy to see my way; the curfew had meant that the interiors were dark but outside the moon shone brightly, albeit intermittently between the scudding clouds. The temperature was cool and I was glad I had pulled on a jumper. My bag flopped against my back as I passed the blackened tree, then walked along the long straight road. No one was in sight.

Often, I think of how I must have appeared that night: a slight figure, with long plaits framing a small face, my dungarees flapping loose against my legs, my tennis shoes clumping against the path. I was lost in my thoughts. Each step I took, each beat of my heart, underscored the urgency I felt: the conviction that I had to be there, with her, rather than in that house behind me. I could never have imagined Mr and Mrs Cooper speaking in that way to each other, just as I can never forget, all these years later, what I heard; it remains a stark reminder of the child I was, how I only ever saw a fraction of the adults' true selves. And I deserved to have heard those words, a fitting punishment for listening at the door. But they had not only wounded me, they had startled me out of a slumber, shone a light as if exposing a darkness that had until then been beyond my view. My feet slapped against the compacted earth, the tarmac of the road, unhemmed now, with no kerb or edge, no pavement, only a messy margin, melting into pebbles and sand. To my side, the silent trees. Not the majestic oaks and beeches of my later life, nor the sinewy giant coconut trees of my past, but low and flat-topped, respectful, some with bursts of flowers in the branches.

When the hand grasped my elbow I yelped, then screamed, but the voice calmed me, even if it was not calm, overladen as it was with incredulity. Child, it said. Child. Her face was dark in the night, but I saw the whites of her eyes and teeth, her lips stretched wide as Mary-Anne's had been. I realised I had reached the cluster of tin-roofed houses. I was more than half-way home. The woman had a bucket in her hand, and had braved the curfew for some errand. Now she put it down and grabbed my shoulders, peering at my face, the smell of her evening meal on her breath. Her hands were strong, but I realised she was old, older than Grace. She stared at me for many minutes, and then, beckoning but without releasing her grip, led me away from the road, down the track that she had walked along earlier, towards the houses. I could not resist. Her grip was vice-like, but neither did I feel in danger. Her voice had been full of concern and it had prompted a realisation of the foolishness I had shown; it could easily have been someone else to have jumped out at me in the dark, a man. It could have been Ezekiel, with his crooked smile, the monster. He could have reached out and pawed at my small breasts. My stomach turned over at my thoughts and the erosion of my loyalty.

We stepped through the silent dark shapes. It was harder to see here, but each home gave off its own heat, its particular aroma of earth and wet leaves and stewed meat, as we passed. I saw her lips moving soundlessly, as if she were chanting or praying. We stopped in front of a small dwelling, no different from the others, with a doormat, a clean porch and a red tin door. She rapped on the door, calling something, and I heard voices inside, murmurs, a man's voice and then a woman's, and the old woman called again, sharply. Footsteps, and then the door opened. It was Jonah, in trousers not fully buttoned and an open shirt, as if he had hastily thrown on his clothes, and behind him I glimpsed a low bed, and the arm and shoulder of the woman he had been lying with.

I was then pushed forward, and as his eyes fell on me I saw his astonishment.

'Sissy.'

I tried to smile but my eyes filled suddenly with tears. Those deep notes, and this coupled with the mixture of surprise, admonishment and concern in his tone, only made the tears spill out onto my cheeks. I wiped them away. The old woman now released a stream of talk, to which Jonah listened, respectfully at first, but as her litany continued and continued, his expression began to wane, and eventually he blew out a sigh of exasperation. Finally, she gestured to him and to me, even to the bed behind him, chastising, as he closed his lips and nodded, and then with a quick backward glance, pushed the door half-shut, to reach behind it. I heard a woman's soft voice in query, his own brief response, and then the door reopened and he was lifting his bicycle out, clicking the door shut behind him.

The old woman turned and left without a word, and Jonah said softly, 'Come, Sissy.' He wheeled his bicycle to the path, I followed in his wake, and when we reached the top where the road began again, he threw his leg over his bicycle and sat on the seat. When I stood staring at him stupidly, he reached forward, took my bag and slung it over his shoulder, leant forward again to put his hands under my arms and lifted me like a bag of sugar onto the bar spanning the frame of the bicycle. Then, keeping one hand on my back to steady me, he used the other to button his shirt, but not before I glimpsed the taut muscles on his chest and stomach, the thin gold chain around his neck with its delicate, tiny pendant shaped like a hand. He leant forward to grip the handlebars, we glided off together. I knew to lean back into his chest so my head was tucked under his chin, to stop myself from falling off. I felt safe and enclosed, and he felt warm and strong behind me. He smelled of wood smoke and soap. The sky was clear now and the stars shone. The night air was fresh and we zipped past many dark shapes.

144

'Are you married, Jonah?' I asked. 'Was that your wife?'

'Be quiet, Sissy.' His voice was curt but I could hear a smile.

Somehow, he stayed on the road. Perhaps it was a journey he knew so well he had no need for a light, for now the moon was less bright and the night seemed blacker. When we reached the hill leading up to the staff bungalows, he stood up on the pedals, his body arching over my head, but we climbed the incline without any apparent effort.

Of all the men in my life at that time, and it seems that there were many, it was Jonah who made my heart sing, my twelve-year-old heart, thudding in my chest as I leant against him, my protector. In short, the man who filled the hole that my father had left. He even had a thin gold chain around his neck like my father. Did my mother feel the same way? Certainly, when Jonah told me, on arriving in front of our bungalow, that we should try not to alarm her, that we should knock firmly but not bang on the door, when my mother came to the window, pushed aside the covering, her expression when she saw Jonah first did not hold any fear, disgust or disdain, only an assumption that if he had arrived in this way at night there would be a good reason. But then her eyes dropped down to me, her mouth shaped my name, and her face blanched. I can only imagine what went through her head when she saw me standing outside in the dark with Jonah, when she had assumed I was tucked up in bed at the Coopers'. The door rattled; she could not turn the key. I heard her sobbing, and I realised with a chill how much anguish I was causing her. The noise was not loud but it was terrible to hear, and awful to witness, the key for some reason sticking, the door shaking with her efforts.

Then Jonah spoke, his voice deep and low. 'Take calm, madam,' he said. 'Sissy is well. Take calm.'

His error only added to the comfort the sound of his voice gave, an alternative to my mother's whimpering. When my mother finally opened the door, she came out like a banshee, and grasped my shoulders like the old woman had, her eyes piercing mine, then running all over my face and body – for symptoms of pain, scratches, tears and tears – although at that age I had enviably untarnished skin, two utterly symmetrical eyes. On seeing her I could not cry, fearing now that I had made an inexcusable mistake, to cause her such distress.

'I just wanted to see you, Mama,' I whispered and then my throat tightened.

Her eyes wide, she turned to Jonah.

'She was walking on the road,' he said. 'And my neighbour she found her and brought her to me. And I brought her to you.' He gestured into the dark at the bicycle, propped against the side of the veranda, in a pool of moonlight.

She said nothing, only continued to stare at him.

'She is well, madam.' And then he added: 'She is brave to walk in the night alone.'

Now she cleared her throat. 'Thank you so much, Jonah,' she whispered.

He shrugged and then laid his hand briefly on my shoulder, before turning to leave.

'Shouldn't you stay here, Jonah?' She gestured inside the house. 'Until it's light?'

And to our surprise, on this, he grinned suddenly, widely, his teeth shining in the dark. His reaction was like a shaft of sunlight falling through dense storm clouds, a reminder that we could still smile and laugh, that the darkness was only that, nothing indelible or ineffaceable. That morning would come, and we would still be ourselves.

'I don't think so.' He was shaking his head, and then he lifted his eyes to hold hers. 'It will make trouble for you.' And because he did not end his pronouncement with his customary 'madam', and because I saw his eyes move over my mother's face and her slender frame, moth-like in her nightgown, with a tenderness and not a little appreciation, as she must have done as well, we both watched soundlessly as he retrieved his bicycle and kicked off, disappearing instantly into the night.

My mother put her arm around my shoulder, led me into the house, and without discussion we both knew that I would sleep in the bed with her, on the side left empty by my father. Although I am not sure how much sleep she got. At one point I opened my eyes and saw her staring at the ceiling, her arms folded over her chest, her gaze unseeing.

12

I WOKE to my mother, already dressed in one of her cotton work saris, shaking me gently, Danny staring at me from her hip, unperturbed, sucking on his thumb. She was leaving for her classes, but it being a Friday, would be back with Danny for a late lunch. I would not go to school today; she would phone both my teacher and the Coopers from the convent to explain. Would I be all right on my own? Could I get some things ready for lunch? Then she leant forward and kissed me on the forehead, and I heard them leaving the house.

I turned over and must have fallen back to sleep because when I opened my eyes the sun was bright and my throat was dry. I got up and made the bed, made myself some toast, and unpacked my small bag. Then I lay on the cool parquet floor of my bedroom and imagined that I was walking on the ceiling, that everything was in fact upside down. Five steps from the bed to the window, another four to trace the outline of my wardrobe, six back to the other side of the room. It was a favourite game, one I realised I had neglected since Ezekiel's departure, as if his leaving had triggered the end of childhood and the start of more serious growing up.

I found the bag of clothes that the Coopers had brought some weeks back and chose a pair of smart, dark blue shorts, and a T-shirt with red and white horizontal stripes. Both fitted me nicely, more nicely than my own clothes did, and had a foreign, stylish cut. Then I stood in front of the mirror propped up on my desk, pulled my hair from my plaits and brushed it out so it lay spread over my shoulders, framing my face. Pulled up my T-shirt and examined the small crescent-shaped swellings on my chest, not really breasts yet. But I quite liked the way they looked, and I liked the way my midriff seemed to narrow now at the waist before curving out slightly at the hip.

When I ended my examination the clock in the kitchen showed it was nearly ten o'clock, still three and a half hours before my mother would return. I went back into my parents' bedroom – my mother's bedroom –and opened the bedside cabinet on her side of the bed. I knew that was where she stored the blue aerogrammes, and sure enough, in that neat stack, sandwiched between one from my cousin-aunty and one from my grandfather, the latter a few lines and no more, I saw my father's handwriting on a blue rectangle. He had printed her name in capital letters – Mrs Laila Olikara – above the post box of the school; he knew that it would be difficult for her to leave the campus to check our personal post box in town.

I opened it. It was not dated, but when I turned it over and scrutinised the postmark, I saw that the letter had been posted three weeks back. It began with *My dearest Laila*, but continued in the familiar curls and ticks of Malayalam. Only the words 'Sissy', 'Danny', and 'school' were written in English. He had not filled the whole sheet like my cousin-aunty, nor had he written barely a paragraph like my grandfather; two-thirds of the allotted section were covered with his writing. Then, signed at the end, *Yours, George*. He had sent this aerogramme three weeks earlier, but when had my mother received it? Perhaps this week, while I had been at the Coopers' so she had not had time yet to mention it. And he had written to my mother, but not included anything directed to me. I stared at the Malayalam. I only knew how to write my name, Priscilla, and Danny's and could recognise those phonetic building blocks, but nothing more. I rifled through the other letters; no more from my father.

The discovery left me in a bad mood, and although I knew I was forbidden during school hours, I opened the door and walked out of the bungalow, down to the bottom of our front yard where there was a makeshift seat I often sat on, made from a low-hanging tree branch. I heard from across the road the strident voice of a teacher above the clatter of typewriters, a secretarial class. I was hoping that I would see Jonah, and I did not have to wait long before he appeared at the top of the steps leading to the netball courts. He immediately looked over towards our house and spotted me sitting just across the road. He walked over, and without waiting for an invitation lowered himself onto the tree branch, which dipped down and then up again like a see-saw with the addition of his weight. In his hand was a basket of bread, eggs and milk – his weekly delivery – which he laid on the ground. My legs dangled from my shorts from the branch but his stretched out on the ground in front of him.

He smiled. 'No school today?'

I shook my head.

'And did you sleep well?'

I nodded before asking, 'And did you?' and then I blushed as I remembered the slender arm and bare shoulder among his bedclothes.

'I fell' – he laughed – 'I fell into a . . .' He motioned with his hands.

'A ditch?'

'A ditch.'

I risked a tentative smile, because he was grinning. 'You didn't get hurt?'

'A little.' He pulled up his shirt and pointed to his ribs, and I caught a glimpse of the gold chain again with the tiny hand against his chest. Then his shirt dropped. 'But more important is that my bike did not get hurt,' he added.

'I'm sorry, Jonah,' I said quietly. 'It's my fault.' When he did not respond I said in a small voice, 'Are you angry with me?'

'Of course, no,' he said. 'I like to help you. And your mother.'

'Why do you want to help my mother?'

'It is not only me.' He gestured around him, with a little chuckle. 'You can see every man here wants to help her.' He was smiling. 'She's very beautiful.' And then he inclined his head at me. 'And you will be a beautiful woman, Sissy, like your mother. And you will have beautiful children.'

His words warmed me; they were unexpected, but said so naturally and with such sincerity. As he spoke I could feel something pushing against my chest, as if it was the older me, my future self, bursting to come out of its chrysalis.

'If someone wants to marry me . . .'

He burst out laughing. 'So many will. You will see.'

'Why do you like helping my mother?' I repeated, wanting to show him that I knew he had not answered the question.

'Well, your mother is helping me.'

'With your school work?'

He nodded.

'Why are you still at school, Jonah?' And then I bit my lip because I could hear how rude the question sounded. 'I mean . . .'

He shook his head. 'No, I understand you, Sissy.' Then he smiled. 'You see me, and I am a man, but I still need to take exams and my English is not so good—'

'Your English is very good, Jonah . . .'

'It isn't.' He laughed. 'I started my school in Mozambique but then I came here before I could finish.'

'Mozambique?'

'My mother was Mozambican. She didn't speak English. She learned Portuguese.'

'And do you speak Portuguese?'

'A little.'

'And where did you live in Mozambique?'

'In Tete. Do you know it?'

I thought for a while. 'I think Mr Cooper and Mr Lawrence have been there.'

He raised his eyebrows, and was quiet for longer than I had imagined my announcement warranted. Then he nodded. 'It's possible.'

'Why did you leave?'

'Because she died and then my father brought me with him, and my brother.'

'You have a brother?'

'Older than me.'

'Does he work in Lusaka?'

He shook his head. 'In the Copperbelt.'

I said: 'How do you say hello in Portuguese?'

'Olá,' he said, smiling.

'And thank you?'

'I say obrigado. You must say obrigada, because you are a girl.'

'Why was your mother Mozambican? Where did your parents meet?'

He stretched his legs out, and I watched his profile. 'You see, Sissy,' he said, 'we are tribes, not countries, in Africa. My father and mother are both from the same tribe. But my father was born on this side of the river, and my mother on that side. My mother's father was a very good fisherman, and he had his own boat as well, which was a big thing at that time. He caught the fish, and every day before she went to school my mother had to sell the fish, in Luangwa. There was an Arab man who bought for his business and there were Portuguese and South African families. So my mother had to walk to their houses, deliver the fish, and then walk to school. My father, he worked on the river, and when he saw her one day he wanted her to be his wife. But first he helped her to carry the basket of fish to the houses, before she went to school. And when she was older and finished her school, she became his wife, his only wife. Even after she died, my father didn't take another wife.'

It was a beautiful story, simply recounted in those sonorous notes.

'What was your mother's name?'

'Zakira.'

'That's a lovely name.'

'Yes.'

'When did she die?'

'Ten years now.'

'How did she die?'

'It was her heart.'

We were quiet, and I began to worry that I had reminded him of something sad that he preferred to forget but when I glanced at him I saw he was watching me, a small smile on his lips. I reached towards him tentatively and drew out the gold chain from under his shirt, my fingers brushing against his skin, to expose the small amulet that it held, so that it now nestled in my palm. It was a gesture of some familiarity, I knew, and my heart was thumping, but he did not seem to mind. There was still that smile playing on his lips as I asked him: 'Did she give you this?'

He nodded. 'A hamsa. The Hand of Fatima.' Then, when I said nothing, he added, 'My mother was a Muslim, and she worked for an Arab family who gave this to her when she helped with their baby. They believe it protects us. Then she gave it to me because she believed it would protect me.'

'Protect you from what?'

He gave me a wide, toothy smile. 'I don't know.' But the way he said it, it was clear that he did.

'Are you Muslim?'

He shook his head. 'No, only my mother.'

Then he plucked the amulet from my palm and dropped it back into his shirt. Still smiling he continued: 'Now I ask *you* a question, Sissy. Did you talk with your mother?'

'About what?'

'About why you were walking in the night like that?'

I shook my head. 'We went to bed and then she woke up early.'

He said gently, 'Will you tell me?'

'What?'

'Why you left like that?'

I took some time, turning over the events in my head. 'I heard something,' I began and then started again. 'I overheard Mr and Mrs Cooper talking about Ezekiel.'

He was watching me.

'Grace's son, Ezekiel.'

He nodded, his face attentive.

'Do you know him?'

'Yes.'

'Did you hear what happened, Jonah? Why Ezekiel stopped working here?'

He nodded again.

'It was my fault.'

'No, no.' He shook his head. 'He should not have tricked you. He has this illness. And some people believe it is because of spirits. They believe the nganga must cure him. Until then, they think he will bring them bad luck also. That is why it's difficult now for him to find a job.'

'And do you believe that?'

'No, no, Sissy.' He smiled. 'I believe in science.'

'What do you want to be, Jonah, when you finish your exams?'

'Maybe a doctor. Or maybe a science teacher like your mother.' He grinned. 'Maybe I could wear a sari.'

I burst out laughing and he watched me. Then he looked away, stared at his feet, and kicked at the ground with the toe of his boots, before speaking again. 'But they were talking about Ezekiel, Sissy. Why did you want to see your mother?'

I waited, and didn't answer, unwilling to repeat what I had heard: he could have done *anything* to her. And he did not press me, so we remained sitting side by side surrounded by unspoken words.

Then I whispered, 'Jonah, has my mother spoken to you? About my father?' He raised his head, held my eyes as I continued. 'About why he went away?' And as I said the words the tears came to my eyes. Jonah looked away, was quiet for a long time, his eyes on the ground in front of us. He remained still, his hands clasped, and I watched his face, stroked his jawline with my eyes, the high cheekbones and full lips.

'Jonah?'

He turned to look at me as if he were suddenly reminded of my presence.

'Has she, Jonah?'

His eyes ran over my face as mine had run over his, and then he reached over and pinched my chin, a gentle playful gesture completely at odds with the solemnity in his eyes.

'No,' he said finally, quietly.

'So you don't know why he went away and when he is coming back?'

He shook his head, his eyes soft with gentleness. 'He will come back soon. Don't worry.'

'How do you say don't worry in Portuguese?'

'Não te preocupes.' He smiled.

'Obrigado, Jonah,' I whispered.

'You need to say obrigada, Sissy. Because you are a girl.' He pinched my chin again. 'A beautiful girl.' Then he stood up and handed me the basket of groceries. 'Can you take this inside? It's not too heavy?'

I stood up and took it from him. Now the difference in our heights was evident, as he towered over me as usual, and he seemed to notice that as well as he smiled down at me. He turned to leave but then stopped, turned back.

'Why do you think your mother would talk to me?' he asked.

I shrugged. 'She likes you.'

He smiled again, but said nothing, and turned away. I watched as he walked back down the steps to the netball courts, as first his feet, then calves, legs, shoulders and head disappeared, and I went back into the house.

13

I MADE lunch, and my mother arrived, slightly harried, to say that the Coopers had asked if they could pay us a visit: to see me, and to assure themselves that we were all in good spirits. Perhaps, I thought, but did not say, they were worried that I had told my mother of the noise they had made, arguing. And it was not long after we had cleared away the lunch things and tidied the house – my mother plumping our few cushions and straightening rugs like I had never seen her do before – that we saw Mr Cooper's blue car pull up and park in front of the wreck of my father's car. Both adults got out, bearing bags of biscuits and tins of fish and meat, avoiding looking at the carnage – while Mary-Anne gawped with frank interest – before walking briskly up to greet my mother effusively.

Mrs Cooper bent down and hugged me, 'Are you all right, sweetheart?'

I mumbled, 'Sorry to have worried you, Mrs Cooper.'

She hugged me tighter, 'Don't be silly, we know it's been difficult for you. But we'll talk with your mom. You're so welcome in our home, Sissy.' I was conscious that I was wearing hand-me-downs and, sure enough, Mrs Cooper cooed over me further: 'They suit you a treat!' while Ally rolled her eyes, muttering, 'I don't know why my mom's so *enthusiastic* all the time.'

Mr Cooper ruffled my hair as he joined us, leaving Mrs Cooper to accompany my mother to the kitchen, and then stood with his hands in his pockets as the girls and I took turns to push Danny on the swing. At one point, Ally, nearly as tall as her mother now, leant back against her father, and he took his hands out of his pockets, smoothed her hair down with both palms, in a gesture that was at once loving, paternal and familiar, making my stomach contract. 'Who made the swing?' he asked, and on hearing about Jonah, he turned to Ally saying, 'Your granddad made you one when you were little, remember?' Another innocent comment that stabbed through my fragile sensibilities. I was relieved that my brother remained loyal, chuntering discontentedly when one of the Cooper girls pushed him, but chortling when I took over, and my heart turned over in gratitude to him. Mary-Anne clamoured to be lifted up to reach the highest guavas from our tree, and with Mr Cooper's consent, she scaled up her father with practised steps, putting a foot first on his knee, then his hip, then his elbow which was extended in readiness, before swinging onto his shoulders.

Mr Lawrence appeared in his car; he was visiting Miss Munroe. Mr Cooper walked over to talk to him, Mary Anne sitting at a great height on her father's shoulders, her legs dangling on either side of his neck, her hands in her father's hair, and his gently clasping her ankles as the men faced each other, both tall, both speaking in that easy, relaxed way they had. I turned away, my throat felt scratchy and while it all felt convivial, while we all gathered for tea and the leftover chocolate cake from my birthday which garnered many compliments – as if we were having an ad hoc celebration for the event of my running away in the dark – I noticed the extra effort everyone was making, adults and children alike, to ensure that our gathering did not feel contrived.

They left afterwards, the Coopers, in their blue car, to get back home before the curfew began, and as they left, Mr Lawrence appeared again with an invitation: he wanted to take us on an outing the following day, Saturday, to cheer us up. As soon as he said the words he tried to backtrack, pointing out that my mother rarely left the campus and needed a break, an announcement which in turn caused him to back-pedal, just as my mother laughed and accepted.

And then later that night, in the quiet after our unusually sociable afternoon, my mother asked gently if there was anything I would like to talk about, regarding the previous night. No, Mama. She did not persist; surely the afternoon's visit and the Coopers' obvious affection for me had allayed any fears she might have had that I was in some way maltreated in their home. She assumed that I was homesick. I did not mention Ezekiel.

The outing the following day with Mr Lawrence was to Munda Wanga, the animal sanctuary and botanical gardens on the other side of Lusaka, an outing for which my mother wore her stirrup pants and my father's shirt, and I reprised the Cooper girls' shorts and T-shirt combo, both of us gaining a compliment from Mr Lawrence, who then added for my mother's benefit, 'But you always look very elegant, Laila.' I watched as my mother laughed, flattered, her cheeks flushed. Every man here wants to help her. Miss Munroe, it appeared, was spending the weekend at her friend's house and would not be joining us. My mother offered to pack a picnic, but Mr Lawrence revealed he intended to buy us lunch at the café near the recreation area which promised a swimming pool and water slide. It was a generous offer from Mr Lawrence, who was soon apprised of the enormity of taking out a mother and two young children minutes after leaving the campus when Danny upchucked the contents of his stomach over my mother's chest and the front seat of his car. Back we returned to the house where I cleaned up Danny in the bathtub, Mr Lawrence cleaned up his car with liberal amounts of soapy water, and my mother changed out of my father's shirt into one of the thin cotton sleeveless kurtas, light green in colour, she sometimes slept in. It cannot have been in any way deliberate, but my mother succeeded in emerging from the house looking even more appealing than before, her arms bare and the kurta accentuating rather than hiding her slender frame. She had brushed her hair and changed her earrings to match her new top: dangly green beads. I saw Mr Lawrence open his mouth and then shut it; perhaps he felt a third compliment would be excessive. A blanket was thrown over the still-damp front seat, the doors were shut and we were on the road again.

Usually I was an avid adult-watcher and proficient eavesdropper; now I felt more inclined to sift through my own thoughts. The conversation with Jonah, Mrs Cooper's words. I turned over and over all the interactions I had had with Ezekiel. Each was wholly innocent, but as if a story was being retold, I searched now for evidence of monstrous, inhuman behaviour: this game chilled me. When we arrived at the botanical gardens, I hung back as we walked past the bushes and trees and over the lawns. Mr Lawrence had Danny on his arm and my mother appeared relaxed and comfortable with him, even though she had rarely met him. As I dragged my feet behind them, I saw that they made an attractive tableau: Mr Lawrence's fair hair contrasting with my mother's black ponytail; Danny content, his thumb in his mouth. I had packed my swimming costume, and my mother changed Danny into his trunks. I heard Mr Lawrence say, 'Sissy tells me you're a good swimmer, Laila. Are you sure you won't join us?' But I hoped she would not and felt a disproportionate relief when she declined. I could not have borne it if she had revealed her golden body, only for Mr Lawrence to put his hands on her waist, lift her onto his shoulder in a fireman's lift and throw her into the pool, to wild applause from onlookers.

I swam up and down, and Mr Lawrence gamely took Danny in with his armbands, and it was pleasant and enjoyable. But even as I appreciated the different environs, and the sight of so many people we never usually saw, even as I could see my mother genuinely looking relaxed, reclining on the blanket with a magazine, her head supported by her bag, even as I could see that this outing was exactly what we had all needed, I resented Mr Lawrence for presuming correctly.

My brother became querulous, and the pool became crowded and splashy. We showered by the poolside, dressed, devoured chips and fried chicken at the café, walked away from the crowds into a quiet spot in the gardens, and found a shady area where Danny could have his nap. He found his sleeping position and plugged in his thumb, gaining an admiring 'why, look at that' from Mr Lawrence. I left the adults, with some paper and my pencils. I found a tree with a convenient low branch which I climbed onto, grazing my bare legs, but along which I spread, like a tiger I thought, my sketchpad and pencils carefully laid out beside me.

But I found I was now reluctant to pick them up. From my vantage point I could see them: Mr Lawrence lying on his side, propped up on his elbow; my mother hugging her knees as she had done on my birthday picnic. Their lips moved in constant conversation. He often threw his head back to laugh; was my mother indeed so witty? A smile never left her lips, the teasing smile that she used with Rahul. She seemed to play with her hair a lot. At one point, he brushed something from her shoulder and I noticed she did not shrink from his touch. She looked content; she did not look like she missed my father. And this thought made me remember the assurance from Jonah: don't worry, he will come back soon. I felt disgruntled even as I thought, why not let her be happy? I was no longer sure *I* missed my father any more. But from my position on the branch, I seethed. I felt I was witnessing a courtship. I turned myself around, so I was not facing them, and watched a pair of birds in the tree opposite me, then a family with three small sons. The mother and the father made a slow journey across my view, exhibiting an incredible curiosity, examining each plant with care and reading each information card, each son listening to his father, rapt with attention. They eventually left my vision, and I dropped to the ground. As I made my way back to the picnic mat the breeze brought the conversation over to me.

'. . . old enough to be your mother.'

Mr Lawrence's response: 'Now, I believe that would be biologically impossible . . .'

'Well, older sister then.'

'I can honestly say,' and he exaggerated his sincerity, 'hand on heart, that I have never thought of you as a sister, Laila.'

She laughed and he grinned at her. I deposited myself on the edge of the picnic mat but not before I saw them exchange a glance, co-conspirators, and Mr Lawrence sat up and cleared his throat. I opened a bag of crisps without asking permission and met my mother's eyes defiantly. She looked away. Danny turned himself over and lay on his back, his legs falling back like a frog's, his arms bent at the elbows and his fists by his ears. My crisps crunched in the silence.

'I thought,' Mr Lawrence said, 'when Danny wakes up we could visit the pavilion on the other side. I think there's some exhibition or something arty going on . . .'

'We shouldn't take up your whole day.'

'Nonsense.' He glanced at his watch. 'We only have to keep in mind the curfew . . .'

Thank God for the curfew, I thought, the invisible chaperone. They were both looking at me. I realised Mr Lawrence had asked me a question, and my mother appeared irked at my distraction.

'Pardon?'

'I wondered if I could see what you were sketching over there.'

'I didn't sketch anything.'

'Really? I thought you'd taken your stuff with you.' He was smiling into my eyes, with affection or amusement. Whatever, it grated.

'I was watching a husband and a wife and their sons,' I said, and my voice sounded unpleasant even to my ears. 'On a family outing. As a family.'

My mother's cheeks had coloured and she opened her mouth to say something, but Mr Lawrence spoke first: 'Well, that's nice, Sissy,' then glancing at my mother. 'Perhaps, Laila, we should just head back . . .'

'Of course.'

'I've got some work to catch up on.'

'You've been so kind to take us out.'

There was much to pack away and much with which to busy ourselves, so I could hide my face and pretend I did not feel wilful and unlovable. I glanced often at Mr Lawrence, hoping I could meet his eyes and smile, try to make amends, but he seemed intent on avoiding my gaze, and then I felt sullen and misunderstood. I stared out of the window on the drive back.

Thank you, Mr Lawrence, I said as I climbed out of his car, and now he smiled at me, no problem, Sissy, and so I could smile back gratefully, my heart lightening, until my mother said, with easy familiarity, thanks again, Charlie, and I felt it tighten again with annoyance. He drove away, and it was just the three of us again, and we went about our business as usual. Danny was tired from the outing, sucking his thumb with eyes half-closed already, and my mother declared she would give him an early bath and put him to bed. I heard my mother singing to him as she bathed him, a short Malayalam ditty that ended in a tickle, and I heard him crowing with delight. But I refused to be charmed by their performance. She had not sung that song in my hearing for many weeks, and I was sure she had chosen this evening for a revival expressly to demonstrate the maternal adeptness she possessed.

Later, as my brother lay in his cot, making a crescendo of gurgling noises, a sure sign that he would fall asleep, and deeply, until the morning, my mother and I skirted around each other, making polite exchanges. Would you like to have your bath first, Mama? No, thank you for asking, mol. You go first, I'll finish clearing up.

And then we found ourselves behind the cardboard cut-outs and pinned curtains, only one dim lamp on, in the gloom of the evening curfew. I was curled up on the sofa with my book; my mother was sitting in a chair, her sewing basket on her lap, with one of my school skirts that needed letting out and Danny's pyjamas which needed a new button. I read about the daughters, their father gone to war and unreachable, how they maintained their industriousness, their faith, their sewing and their prayers, and the book should have rung true and real and should have consoled me. But I felt peeved and was irritated by my mother, sitting there placidly, in an aura of silence, and not asking me anything: what made you run away that night, did Ezekiel ever touch you, why can't you let me enjoy myself? Not weaving any tales either: Papa wrote the other day and said he will write specially to you next. He will be home soon, don't worry, just as Jonah says. I laid my book down and went into the kitchen, opened one of the cupboards to retrieve a glass and closed it with a bang. I heard her enter the room behind me as I slopped some milk into my glass, carelessly, and then gulped it down, messily, wiping my mouth with the back of my hand in the way I knew she hated.

She spoke: 'Are you all right, mol?'

I shrugged. 'Of course I am. Why shouldn't I be?' And then I glared at her.

She held my eyes for a short time before looking away. 'I think you were a little rude to Mr Lawrence, Sissy.'

'I thought you called him *Charlie*.'

She looked bewildered by my tone. 'I might call him that but you know him as Mr Lawrence so—'

'Well, why don't *I* call him Charlie as well?' I retorted. 'Or Mr Charlie? Or Uncle Charlie? Or Charliechayan?'

My taunt was unexpectedly alliterative and suddenly tremendously funny, and I felt a bubble of laughter in my throat, which I dampened down until I saw my mother's lips quiver. And then we both collapsed into giggles. It felt good to laugh, and to laugh with my mother, and I found I enjoyed it so much the ripples of mirth came rolling and rolling until my ribs were aching and I was hanging off the kitchen counter, gasping. My mother wiped her eyes, and we regained some composure.

'Mol—'

'He likes you, Mama,' I said, and my words quietened and sobered us both.

'Sissy—'

'And Jonah says you're beautiful.'

Now my mother blushed, and she opened her mouth and her eyes grew wide. Did he say that? *Really? Jonah?* I could see she wanted to ask, but she waited a few moments before saying, her voice soft, 'You will find, Sissy, that men often say these things, but they don't always mean them.'

'I think he meant it,' I said quietly. I didn't tell her what he had added: and you will be a beautiful woman too, Sissy.

'And if he did?' Now she looked impassioned. 'What does it matter? What does it change?' She shook her head. 'And Mr Lawrence,' her eyes flashed at me, daring me to interrupt, 'who is he to us? Just a friend. None of this matters at all, none of this means anything at all.' She held my eyes for a long while and then said, 'Because it's me who has to look after you and Danny.'

'I can look after myself.'

'Yes, that's true,' she nodded. 'True in some ways, Sissy, but not in others. You are still my responsibility and that's what I am here for.'

I felt suddenly tired, and suddenly no longer angry with her. She slipped next to me, put her arm around me, squeezed my shoulders.

'It's been strange, I know. But I'm proud of how you are being so helpful.'

'I don't want to be helpful all the time, Mama.'

'I know, mol.'

'Sometimes I just want to understand what's happening to us.'

'Nothing is happening to us, mol!' My words seemed to alarm her, and she became animated. 'You'll see. When Papa comes back, we'll feel better. We just miss him, that's all.'

But she did not convince me, and when I glanced at her, I suspected she had not convinced herself. I should have said then: he wrote a few days ago, why didn't you tell me? But for some reason, possibly because by now I was aching with fatigue and perhaps because I wanted to spare my mother the need for further platitudes or even untruths, I said nothing and allowed her to indulge me – she would let me use her special face cream, she would boil some more milk and add some chocolate for a bedtime drink, I didn't need to brush my hair, it looked fine as it was – and allowed her to imagine that I had recovered: all forgiven, forgotten.

I woke in the night with a terrible dread, one which I now realised I had felt when I had left the Coopers' house that night to walk back to Roma on my own. I had not simply been concerned for my mother. The comments about Ezekiel had served to highlight how vulnerable and unprotected Danny and I would be with not only my father gone, but my mother too. I stared at the ceiling, unable to tell if I was indeed awake or if I was in some protracted dream state; all I could feel, with the soundtrack of my pounding heart in my chest, was a terrible fear that my mother had left. She had got up quietly in the night, dressed, given Danny a last look, not opened my door for fear of wakening me, and left. Out the door, down the road, into the night.

I forced myself to sit up, rubbed my hands against my thighs, pinched my forearms and did not wake up. I tiptoed out of my bedroom and pushed open her bedroom door. For a moment my heart stopped, because I could not see her in the bed and I realised that I had known all along that she was biding her time. But in that same instant I noticed a mound on the wrong side of the bed, my father's side, which was more in the shadows and hence difficult to see. She was lying on her side and her face was just visible in a streak of moonlight. It was a warm night and she was sleeping in her cream-coloured sleeveless nightdress, her elbows bent, and her palms clasped together under her chin, sleeping on his pillow. She looked like a girl; not a woman, a mother, and in her sleep all her anxieties and responsibilities were suspended. She was dreaming of the river, the lake, I was sure, dreaming of ducking in and out of the water, with her brothers, maybe with me, her hair streaming behind her like a black wave, the water cool against her naked skin.

I shut the door, crept back to my bed with my heart full of something: relief, gratitude, sadness. I closed my eyes, and replicated her sleeping position so that I could feel even closer to her. I fell asleep again quickly, I must have felt reassured, but I woke with the wind – it seemed only a short time later – to the unfamiliar sweeping sounds. Like a storm that came and went, came and went, but faster, much too fast to be a storm. Juddery thuds, a noise that was too loud, intrusive, it did not belong in the dawn. Early morning light filtered into my room and I closed and opened my eyes again to make sure that I had indeed woken up. I realised my mother was calling me, and then she appeared at my door in her nightdress, and pulled me out of the bed, back into her bedroom, where Danny lay, still asleep, but out of his cot, in the middle of the bed. Her grip was strong and her expression terrified.

'What is it, Mama? What's happening?'

Her eyes were wide, and she did not speak, only made a little sound, held me tighter. 'Sissy!'

But I pushed her arm away, ran to the window and pushed aside the curtain.

The helicopters hovered – five, six of them, angled in the sky – but not so high, not so far: in the space between the land and the heavens. Their bodies not moving, but their giant blades cutting through the silence, churning time and churning up dust from the ground, with that groan that I would remember decades on. And one helicopter, its gleaming metallic body cold and hard in the light of dawn, hovered in front of us, so close I was sure that if I opened the window I could stroke it, feel its hot metal heart. At its opening, a man, a boy really, with blond hair showing beneath his helmet, his body encased in a khaki uniform, a diagonal strap across his chest, tools of some kind in his hands. He was watching the scene below him unfold, but then he turned to see me as I looked up.

'Sissy, no!'

But I stood transfixed, framed in the window, the gusts of wind swirling around outside, exchanging a gaze with this stranger above me. And he, too, seemed disturbed by the sight of me, pushing the machine gun that extended from his hands to his calves to between his ankles, as if to reassure me that he would not raise it, take aim. His eyes were open and troubled, as were mine, while all around us, growing clearer, like the swell of the sea – but not, it couldn't be, we were as far from the coast as we could be – a gathering chorus: the screams.

I had by now pushed the curtains wide open and we watched the girls run, their hair in curlers or hairnets or in disarray, some not fully clothed. They were pouring out of their dormitories, their voices being carried in all directions by the wildness of the wind. One girl tripped, was flung headlong, and shouted out as her friends thundered past her, until another slowed, with one hand caught her friend's, lifted her, so she could join the others, their legs a blur. They screamed and ran – past the houses, through the backyards, and into the bush beyond.

Part Four

14

T HE past jumped out again at me, coming on the back of the publication of my book, *The Wild Wind: Translating the Poetry of James Joyce in Post-war Italy,* six years after I had finished my doctorate, and not quite two years after my sojourn in Delhi. It was published by a small press in Maryland, was stocked in several university libraries including, to my great pride, the university in Rome where I had spent my halcyon year as an undergraduate. A pleasing side-effect of my publication was the modest collateral publicity that the novels I had previously translated received. And it was possibly for this reason that, hearing I was in town, my supervisor from my doctoral studies insisted I come to a drinks and nibbles party at her apartment. The writer from Brooklyn, my first writer, was also invited and had expressed a wish to see me.

He was separated from his partner and a weekend dad to his four-year-old son, who accompanied him to the party. Parenthood had made him even more attractive. He was less groomed, but this new scruffiness only added to his appeal, as did the obvious love and tenderness he had for his son. A touching addition to his armoury and I could see why some people toted children as accessories. They made a fetching duo; when he proffered a sandwich to his son, the child munched on it obediently before silently giving the half-eaten triangle back to his father, who gobbled it whole.

I've heard about your book, he said. I must order a copy.

My supervisor joined us. I never told you, but Sissy here was so intimidated by you she wanted to talk herself out of the job.

I blushed – never a good look on a facial burns survivor – but the writer laughed: I might have been intimidated by *you*, in fact.

I don't believe that, I managed to say, as, her work done, my supervisor drifted away.

Well, I always wanted to study, he said. I dropped out of college. I'm not saying that I've suffered for it, but I confess I'm envious of anyone who managed to stick it out. And you were on your way to getting a PhD, for Christ's sake.

I shook my head, laughing: well, you could have been nicer about it.

I stand corrected. He grinned back. His son tugged at his trouser leg and he picked him up: meet Doctor Sissy, buddy.

I spent most of the time with him at the gathering, and his son eventually warmed to me when I revealed my secret superpower – a skill at making paper aeroplanes, something that had kept Danny occupied for hours on end at the same age. I left the apartment having talked and talked, having soaked up a warmth from the writer that was a very welcome contrast to our first encounter, feeling prouder of my achievements than ever before.

Although the irony of it all was that I had long left academia, long stopped translating literary texts and long left New York. I had not managed to sustain a livelihood through my endeavours. I had clung on for years, and to no avail, to the hope of getting tenure or even more than just one, unpredictable class at NYU or Brooklyn College, or any of the institutions I had diligently turned up to, cap almost in hand, to teach the subject that no one else wanted to, at the most inhospitable hour, with the lowest remuneration, with the heaviest marking load. Not long after my strange week in Delhi, I had shelved my romantic ideals, and had moved completely into commercial translation.

For nearly two years I had been working for a firm of engineers, based in Boston, and subcontracted by an Italian oil company. Their funds seemed endless, the financial ambience in which they operated contrasted with my frugal existence of the previous years. I could charge for subsistence and overheads if I worked from home. I was paid overtime if I needed to meet a deadline. They flew me out to Houston and New Orleans and Montreal, paying for flights, expenses and hotel rooms for a one-hour meeting. And then, a few weeks after that party in my supervisor's apartment, to Douala, Cameroon, for a four-day workshop, a trip onto which I tagged an extra three days of unpaid leave. For I intended to use this visit to the continent to make a pilgrimage to Zambia.

As always with these work jaunts of late, the logistics were taken care of with seamless precision by the well-oiled cogs of the firm, and before I could fully process the fact that I had had a yellow-fever jab and a tetanus vaccination – just in case – I was on the plane, and soon after in a hotel room in the Akwa area of the city, preparing for my first meeting the following day at the offices nearby. Unlike my memories of Lusaka – of its quietness and staidness – Douala was brutish, its pleasures more visceral. It was a large sprawl, its streets crowded with vendors, who annexed the pavements outside air-conditioned, guarded shops and cafés. It had a busy port that obscured the beauty of the sea, and large sections of the city were replicas of themselves: a long busy road with tower blocks on either side, the repetitiveness only broken by the occasional green space or market. What it lacked in aesthetics, it made up for with energy. The city pulsated as if it were a living organism, fuelled by the needs of the oil industry, and these visitors, such as the clients I was visiting, viewed the city with a mixture of awe and contempt. I was taken for dinner to a restaurant on the estuary of the River Wouri, during which my Cameroonian colleague switched from French to English to Italian with panache.

But I had once again misjudged – as on my return to India – and I soon discovered that it was not so easy to just book a flight and go to Zambia. They were on the same continent but travelling between the two countries proved as complex, and as expensive, as flying across the Atlantic. There were only four flights per week, the timings of which ate into the three days I had at my disposal. In order to return to Douala in time for my return flight to Boston, which could not be altered, I would have to arrive in Lusaka in the morning and catch the same aeroplane back later, leaving me with only the day to spend there.

On the phone to my fiancé I bemoaned my lack of planning, the cost.

The fare is astronomical, I said, and it feels so extravagant to spend it for a few hours' sake.

I think you should go ahead and do it, he replied. You don't know when you'll next be that way. He was being tactful; he could have said, you'll never go that way again.

I hummed with hesitation.

Sissy, charge it to my card, he said impatiently. What's the point of having a sugar daddy if you don't spend his money?

I had, of course, fallen in love with an older man. Not old enough to be my father, not quite – fourteen and a half years older – he would be forty-six next month. Not even what one could call rich, not the best of sugar daddies. He was an engineer, and we had met at the firm that employed me. He was recently divorced, and I would have two teenage stepchildren, a girl of fifteen and a boy of thirteen, whom my fiancé adored with a guilty terrified love, and who regarded me with caution. I was still being tested. We had met after his separation from his wife, but even so, he had fallen back into a relationship within a few months of the divorce being finalised. And he had chosen a younger woman, such a cliché. The only point in his favour was that, although his ex-wife was gorgeous, always immaculately presented, his wife-to-be was disfigured.

I murmured my agreement and thanks on the phone. I'll make it up to you, I said.

He had replied: you can begin by telling me what you're wearing, down to the very last detail.

And I had laughed out loud, gripping the handset. Wishing he were with me, but knowing that I was too immersed in thoughts of my return to miss him after I had hung up. Knowing that I needed to make this personal journey alone.

From Douala I contacted a travel agency and arranged for one of their guides to meet me at the airport and ferry me around Lusaka. No, I was not interested in a tour to Victoria Falls or the game reserves, I would only be in Lusaka for a few hours. Roma? Yes, of course they could take me there, although it was certainly one of their more unusual tour requests. I had, before leaving Boston, contacted a professor at the university in Lusaka. Some years earlier, I had read his analysis of the last stages of the Rhodesian bush war, which included his first-hand account of what became known as the Green Leader Raid, one of a series of incursions made to avenge the shooting down of the plane. The professor, in his youth, had been part of the same Rhodesian SAS regiment who had made the daring sortie across the border, to attack the camp on the outskirts of Lusaka, and on learning this I imagined that he must be the young fair-haired man who had tried to reassure me from his lofty heights: not you, we're not looking for you. He had since interviewed several members of the Patriotic Front who admitted to their involvement in the catalyst of the events: the downing of the plane and subsequent civilian fatalities.

In the late seventies, the event had thrown the talks-in-progress regarding a future new government in Rhodesia, to be renamed Zimbabwe, into disarray. The missile that had brought the aircraft down had been indisputably launched from the Zambian side, by Nkomo's men, but from there on, details became vague. The men interviewed declared that they had had intelligence that the aircraft would be carrying ammunition; it was therefore considered a legitimate wartime target. Who would have provided such faulty information? The list of potential sources was long – the Soviets, the Renamo rebels in Mozambique, the South Africans, the Americans? There had been many actors on Africa's stage during that time. The men's assertion was either false, and the assault was simply a spiteful, vindictive act on holidaymakers returning from Victoria Falls, or there was a more Machiavellian strategy at play, one that orchestrated Nkomo's removal from his favoured position. For why would Nkomo sanction such an act when he appeared on the brink of winning favour over his rival Mugabe? Why would he jeopardise his future ambitions? But most chilling were unsubstantiated rumours that some of the survivors, having crawled out of the wreckage, were then shot and killed. The men refused to talk of this.

In his book, the professor had explored his own ambivalence: of the injustices that were atoned with more injustices; of how, on gaining its hard-fought independence, the country's liberators had turned on each other. Soon after a new flag was raised, thousands of Ndebele, followers of Nkomo, disappeared, presumed killed – a secret genocide orchestrated by his nemesis Robert Mugabe. *The Gukhurundi operation*, he wrote, *documents the violence with which Mugabe has been willing to conduct his politics. While the Rhodesians, and I include myself as a young man, cannot be condoned for engaging in warfare to uphold a political system that was committed to a disproportionate role for the white minority and racist policies over the black majority, a war which would cost the lives of an estimated 25,000 civilians, including civilians in Mozambique and Zambia, history now looks less favourably on the actions of the Zimbabwean liberators. Mugabe has shown his ruthlessness, not just against hated colonialists, but his very own people.*

His very own people. While I was fascinated by his book, these words jarred. He was, here, building a dramatic tension that was unfair, I felt. Pitting brother against brother, Cain against Abel. But were they not, ultimately, just men, written into the same country by a map drawn at some point in history? While the professor's frank admission of his own involvement in historical events and his detailing of how he had latterly agonised over his youthful convictions moved me, I longed also to correct him on this point. I needed to impart to him the words that I had not forgotten: you see, Sissy, we are tribes, not countries in Africa. I was grateful for the professor's willingness to meet, and although it was I who had initiated our acquaintance, he was now the more interested party. He wished to interview me and record my memories of the events. I could see that I would, with my child's perspective, provide a different texture to the story that read like the pages of an international espionage thriller but which was a real event and which had touched real people's lives, some now scattered all over the world.

But by the time I attended the last meeting and workshop in Douala, my mind was already elsewhere; my interest in his project faded, my desire to explain the politics of the past evaporated. I could only think of my own return, to where I had spent so much of my childhood, to where I had had my rebirth. I avoided looking at myself in the mirror. With this pilgrimage imminent, I did not see my scars as friends. It seemed the decision to go back to the space where I had been whole and unblemished was reigniting a bitterness that I had suppressed. I was alive, I reminded myself; I hadn't died. And yes, I was now marred, but it could have been so much worse. My fiancé often told me I was beautiful – not an adjective I would ever have chosen for myself. Already, in Douala, I had had my share of attention, equal parts pity and revulsion. I imagined this would be magnified when the land recognised the child who had lived there before, and it was only my innate conscientiousness – a need to see a project through – that made me board the plane early in the morning. And in fact, when I landed, despite my fears, nobody paid me any attention. Save for a brief spark in the immigration officer's eye, I could discern no reaction to my appearance.

When I approached the travel agent, who was holding up a card with my name, I saw her eyes falter only for a second and then she was extending her hand: I'm Veronica. Veronica Sibanda.

She was slim and elegant, her hair straightened into a sleek, chin-length bob, and she wore a silk shirt tucked into smart trousers. What did she make of my request? I felt embarrassed about the lengths I had taken to revisit my past. Her cousins had attended Roma, she informed me, straight off the bat, but she had gone to the American International School.

Yes, I knew some kids who went there as well, I said, and she nodded without saying anything as she unlocked the doors of her car, as if she expected nothing less from a foreigner such as myself.

But then she turned around and smiled at me. Well, welcome back.

As we drove through the city and then on the long straight road leading outwards, memories started slotting back as if finding their favoured position. The trees looked familiar, and it was likely they were the same, for twenty years was a whisper in a tree's life. But the settlement, the cluster of tin-roofed homes a mile or so outside the campus, was gone and in its place I saw white and pink villas, arranged around a swimming pool, so that the tension I had bottled inside me over re-viewing that particular location seeped out. Before I knew it – the distance covered with little effort in a modern car – the entrance to the campus loomed in front of us, now boasting a wider road, a glass-fronted cabin in which sat an attendant, who waved us through after a few words from Veronica.

I phoned ahead, she said. The Mother Superior has been here now ten years, but she did not know your family.

We drove up the steep hill, and I remembered, my heart in my throat, as if it were yesterday, how Jonah had stood up on the pedals of his bicycle, and then we were on the narrow road, freshly tarmacadamed, the netball courts still visible down the steps on our left, and the row of bungalows to our right.

It's school holidays, Veronica continued, so no classes, no girls, which is why we could come just like this. She stopped the car and we got out. There's no staff housing on site any more, it's no longer a boarding school. Day pupils only. She pointed to the bungalows: they're offices and suchlike now. Then she said gently: I'll wait for you here. Take as long as you like.

The small brick bungalow was still pink, the door was still blue. But the windows looked freshly painted, and I could see through into what had been the living room – now housing two desks, computers and printers, and beyond – through the door, into my parents' bedroom – a larger desk and chair. Two ladies lifted their heads. I smiled and raised my hand in greeting, and that was enough; they returned to their work. I could also see, to the left, through the door into what had been my bedroom, shelves lining the walls, packed with files. It was a tiny space. Had we really all lived there? All four of us at one stage? My horizons had grown wider; it looked like a doll's house.

The tree with the perfect branch that had held Danny's swing remained, as did the one with the low branch on which I had sat with Jonah, but the garden was otherwise unrecognisable. Landscaped now, with a fountain, flower beds and pebbled pathways, and to one side a green lawn on which benches were arranged in a semi-circle, perfect for the office workers' lunch hour.

Miss Munroe's house was now the infirmary; the Devasias's a home economics unit, complete with counters and hobs fitted around the perimeter. I walked the length of the row of bungalows in what felt like minutes, even though as a child the time I took had felt endless when I was pelting down the road in agitation, fearing that Bobby and Aravind had abandoned me. I rounded the curve at the end that led to the convent, which was still surrounded by a low wall and still looked over a verdant garden, and took the turning which was the alternative route to the netball courts. Then I went down the steps to the science laboratories. I found my mother's lab without much difficulty, and peeped through the window, much as I had done when I was twelve years old. You left Danny alone? It looked largely unchanged; the benches were polished, but they had always shone. There was a new glass-fronted cabinet at one end, but the large roll-up blackboard still stood at the head, extending to the width of the room, and in front of it, as before, the teacher's desk. I tried the door, but it was locked. I could not satisfy my urge to go inside and stand where she had stood, rows of navy girls in green dresses before her, and so I went to sit down on the patch of grass opposite the lab. I remembered how she had bent over the marks that afternoon, after my father's phone call at the convent, as she filled in a report sheet.

I had not told my mother of this visit; she knew only of an exciting expedition to Cameroon. Perhaps I had wished to reserve the right to change my mind, and I was glad I had kept her in the dark. For this belonged as much to her memory as mine; I was trespassing on her past just as I was visiting mine. She had spent most of her twenties, into her early thirties, teaching in this laboratory, chalk on her fingers, preparing chemicals for practical exams, manipulating pipettes and burettes and Bunsen burners. She had climbed back up the steps nearly every weekday afternoon, basket in hand with lab coat folded inside, to return to the bungalow and her children and domestic responsibilities.

Returning to a place where my mother had spent so much of her life as a young woman, as a young woman myself, made me feel an extraordinary oneness with her, despite the fact that she was thousands of miles away. My own early adulthood had been a rush of experiences. I had slept with three men before meeting my fiancé, not an extensive list by many standards, and I had had what could be called a relationship only with two of those. But I had fallen in love, had my heart broken, all those things, and after each episode I was left unencumbered. For my mother, by the time she had had her first experience of heartbreak, presumably when my father left us, she had two children to consider. At my age now, nearly thirty-two, she had been married for nearly all her adult life, had lived in that tiny house, lived on this campus nearly all that time, surrounded by nuns who did not understand and Malayalee women who begrudged her. Miss Munroe, with whom my mother still kept in touch, had been a unique female companion. But even then, the chasm between their personal circumstances had limited their friendship. Would I tell her of this return?

By now my appetite felt sated and clawing at once. I had not expected to fall into floods of tears but neither had I expected to feel so discomposed at seeing, brilliantly alive and present, in mint condition and vividly coloured, not sepia-past, the familiar places. I had hoped, I realised, for something more, as if returning to that point would ensure that time and space converged, so that I would be that young, smooth-skinned girl again. But I knew it was not only so that I could shed my yin-yang appearance, like a snake would shed its skin, that I had wished to return; I was searching for someone. I got to my feet and walked up and down the walkway in front of the laboratories, and for some reason, my mind went back to the day of the school anniversary celebration. A day which I recalled as a series of vignettes playing before me in the clear, bright light of an African spring. My playmates conspiratorially leaning over something unseen, their backs to me; the figures of Miss Munroe and Mr Lawrence sitting cross-legged on the grass as if at a music festival, not in the grounds of a Catholic school. And Jonah leaning into the young cook while, her eyes shining, she looked up into his; this image leaving a familiar ache in my chest. But as I paced up and down, what I could not conjure was an image of my parents. I had left them on my travels around the campus, and they remained outside my vision, sitting next to each other, their shoulders touching, in their best clothes.

I left the science laboratories, walked up the steps, past the storeroom which, remarkably, looked untouched, only mossier. But I did not linger. I walked on, up again, up the second set of steps, and in front of me, as always, was the small pink bungalow. I found Veronica on one of the benches in the green space, stubbing out a cigarette. She had reapplied her lipstick – a deep vermilion. She smiled as I sat down next to her. It must have changed, she said.

It has, I replied, and so have I.

She smiled again, then glanced at her watch. You are due to meet with the professor in forty-five minutes.

I was floored. I had spent more than an hour and a half in a reverie, but it had felt like minutes, as if I had returned to a childish ignorance of time.

She was saying: before that, we can pay a visit to the new Mother Superior or go back into town. You mentioned your old convent school?

But then, without having thought about it, but I *must* have done, because it was not a request to suddenly emerge from nowhere, I asked if we could renege on the visit with the professor. Drive back into the city and visit the hospital. Veronica did not query my capriciousness, only offered to phone and cancel my meeting with the professor herself, pass on my apologies. She perhaps assumed a masochistic desire of mine to revisit a place in which I had spent weeks, months, bandaged and broken, inside and outside. But then I mentioned

I had no wish to visit the burns unit, and explained what I wanted to find. She told me as we got back in the car that she would try her hardest to find someone who would be able to help us in the hospital, but that we could not just pitch up as we had done on the campus. This was a teaching hospital, once the best in independent southern Africa, and there were regulations over visitors.

We drove back into the city and returned to the travel agency. While I looked in the shops on the street, Veronica made some phone calls. It was a quiet time of day, and I marvelled at how Lusaka was not dissimilar in temperament to my memory of it, so very unlike its more extrovert cousin, Douala. I could not recognise much of it; nothing looked familiar from my faded collection of memories. I had no memory of the city as a panorama, a fact that disturbed me more than I had expected. Was a child's memory really so selective, so unformed? What else then had I forgotten or not noticed in the first place? I was standing outside a large department store, the ground floor of which was given over to selling stationery, when I saw Veronica's reflection in the window, crossing the road to approach me.

I've found someone, Sissy, she said, and I murmured my thanks, adding: this is more than you expected to do for me.

But she interrupted me: no, not at all. Only let's go right away, because I must make sure you get back to the airport on time.

The hospital was east of the city centre, and, handily, on the way back to the airport. I remembered nothing of it or its environs. We could have been driving into somewhere I had never ever been. And the corridors we walked along, to enter a pleasant courtyard, then re-enter another corridor, then yet another courtyard, only served to make me feel I was indeed on a road to discovery, passing through layers of time to arrive back at the past.

We met our guide for the next hour, an obstetrician on her break, who introduced herself with her first name, Cleopatra, and who spoke in low tones, as if advising on an academic interest of hers, of the perils of childbirth. There was a high percentage of stillbirths in the seventies, she informed me, which led in 1979 to a seminal study of two hundred women in the unit, alongside two hundred women with healthy deliveries, for parity. A huge undertaking, and one which found that prenatal visits were rare in the unfortunate cases, leading to a drive for more midwives in the early eighties. These women were dispatched all over Zambia.

But all this happened a few years after what you recount, she said with a sad smile. Then, on reaching the medical registry, Cleopatra spoke to the registrar, who listened, then nodded. I had not understood the words, but the music of the language was comfortingly familiar.

Cleopatra turned to me – Veronica now waiting at a discreet distance – you think it's 1972 or 1973?

It's awful, isn't it, I replied, but I'm not sure. I didn't ask my mother before I came here. I didn't plan this.

Don't worry, she replied. We'll start with those years.

I feel sure, I continued, that I would have been six or seven.

In those days, Cleopatra continued, there was not much acknowledgement of the need for a grieving process. She added gently: what I mean is, nowadays there might have been a funeral arranged or at least counselling offered to the parents. This would have been rare at the time you are looking into. She sounded apologetic, and so I reassured her: yes, yes, of course. Then her eyes moved to the side as the registrar returned.

I caught a glimpse of the white label taped to the spine of the folder. *Neonatal Deaths 1968–1974.* We looked together. She was more adept at reading the notes in the columns, handwritten in faded ink, and I let her turn the pages, one after the other, until, suddenly, there it was: *Baby Olikara, female, stillborn, 12*

May, 1973. There followed some more details, of weight and length, and then the parents' names. *Mother: Laila Olikara. Father: George Olikara.*

I stared at this insignificant confirmation of an event that had held so much significance for my family, and I felt a loss so deep inside me that for a moment I believed I was my mother, looking at the handful of words that told me that the baby inside me, the baby I had carried, had died. My body became my mother's, so that I felt I needed to hold the page, read those words, wet the paper with my tears, to reassure her that she was not forgotten, never forgotten, and that we – me, my mother, my brother – each carried a fragment of her soul within us. The mention of my father's name here seemed unnecessarily cruel, and relentless. Part of me wanted to take a pen and scratch it out, so that my mother, who had raised us – me and Danny, the survivors – could claim this baby, my baby, my sister, as my mother's alone, to give breath to or to send from the living world.

Now, the women fell silent and watched me: this alien, descended on Lusaka for a few hours, with clothes bought abroad, a voice from across the oceans, with a half-painted face. I stared and stared, at one name in a list of many, until Veronica appeared next to me and gently touched my elbow, reminded me that we needed to leave, my plane was leaving Lusaka that evening.

15

E IGHT girls had not returned by sunset. Those who had emerged from the bush at various points on the campus perimeter were escorted back to their dormitories by the staff members who had been positioned to welcome them. Their hair was matted with leaves and thorns, their skin dusty. I watched as some passed by our window, in reverse of their flight early that morning, holding hands with each other; some with arms linked, some being supported by their teachers, docile and silent. Most were wearing nightgowns, now torn into shreds by the bushes they had run through. Others were barely clothed, having either shed or lost their clothes in their desperate flight. But all of us – the teachers and staff and families on the campus who had watched the raid through our windows, the girls who had either stayed or fled and returned, and by the following daybreak all had returned – all of us were alive. Whereas hundreds had lost their lives not far away, in the camp just a few miles to the east.

Jonah came to the house first thing in the morning, but I was in the bathroom and only heard him speak briefly to my mother, his voice concerned and reassuring at the same time. When I rushed out, he was already gone. My mother, her face still pale and her voice tinny, told me that Jonah would be join-ing the search for the missing girls and then would be charged with repairing the damage done to the school – from the wind the helicopters had unleashed and the ensuing stampede of the girls. He would not be able to come to our house for some time, but before joining the other men, he had wanted to make sure of our wellbeing.

Miss Munroe spent the morning with us. She had heard from Mr Lawrence, who was helping Mr Cooper's agency set up an emergency relief tent in the camp and assess what rehabilitation was needed. All the teachers remained at home, relieved of their duties, as a queue of cars arrived on the campus bearing distraught parents who, after emotional reunions with their daughters, spirited them away for the planned fortnight's closure. I was also exempt from my own school for a few days while Lusaka recovered from the trauma. Both Rahul's father and Bobby's father came to our house, full of bluster, enquiring after us and assuring my mother that if she needed any help, she was not to hesitate. If she was scared at night, if there was an intruder at the window, she only had to call out into the dark. They would hear her and rush to our aid – a proposal that I'm not sure comforted my mother in any way. And then, having lavished these promises on us, the two families decamped in convoy. They were taking advantage of the school's closure to visit some family friends in the Copperbelt, leaving Rahul to stay with another friend on the university campus in the city. Miss Munroe arranged to stay with her friend in the fancy house, coming to see us before she left, my mother interrupting her explanations with: but of course, you should go, Fee. Don't worry about us.

Everyone, it seemed, could tap into a network of friends and associates. In contrast, we could not muster up anyone.

In short, the aftermath of the raid – when all the girls were accounted for, and when people had made their arrangements for the fortnight's closure, when the hubbub had removed itself from the campus – brought an unremitting boredom to our life, the three of us keeping sole company and my mother rationing our supplies. The only silver lining was that the curfew that had been so ineffective was lifted temporarily. There needed to be traffic between the hospital and the camp, and there were reports of dignitaries and diplomats scurrying around Lusaka at all hours, in an attempt to bring calm to a fevered situation. There was no mention, either, after a few days, of the need for me to attend school; the logistics were too much for my mother to consider and I did not complain about the unexpected holiday.

The first evening that followed the raid, my mother excused herself, asking if I would look after Danny for a short while. I could see from the direction she was walking that she was going to the convent, no doubt to phone my father and inform him of the events. Perhaps entreat his return, or arrange for us to join him. I was not party to what she said, and when she returned she had some other news to convey. She had also spoken to Mrs Cooper, who had informed her that, with much regret, she would be returning to Virginia, taking Ally and Mary-Anne with her. The news was apt in a cycle of events that seemed bent on unpicking our life and leaving it unstitched. I was less heartbroken by the loss of my friends than anxious about the questions their departure provoked. Who would I go to school with, which presumably I would need to do at some point? Would I now stay on the campus with my mother every day? And what of the few items I had left in the Coopers' guest room? Three school books, two hair grips, a pair of socks and fresh underwear. I did not interrogate my mother because she looked pale and exhausted, chewing her lip, smudges under her eyes. I strived to be as supportive and as helpful as possible over the following days. We whiled away the time playing cards and hangman and checkers, testing the television intermittently and cheering if we had one hour of electricity and thus one hour to watch a re-run of the previous year's independence celebration, or a snippet of an American detective show, before the power cut returned.

When night fell, my mother tried to act as if all was as it should be, but I saw that she continually got to her feet, to check that the doors were locked, the windows closed. For, alone on the campus, our house felt insubstantial, a flimsy barrier against any big bad wolf skulking in the bush behind us. I helped her during the day with washing the clothes in the tin bucket outside, and with tidying the house. We tended to the vegetable patch and picked the fruit from the trees. But not with abandon as before; now counting and allocating the bananas and guavas so that they would last, freezing the mulberries. As the days passed, we forgot to think of any end to this existence, but accepted our fate, became submissive to whatever would happen next. Our lives then entered a passably pleasant routine. My mother sewed and cooked; I read to Danny, bathed him, and pushed him on the swing ad nauseum.

I was doing just that one afternoon when I saw Rahul drive up the road and pass by. I could make out a wave – he would be returning to check up on his parents' house – and I had a mind to go and ask my mother if I could pay him a visit when a blue car swung into the road in front of our house and then up our short driveway to stop abruptly in front of the cadaver of my father's green car. I could not help but stare as I watched Mr Cooper struggling to extract himself from behind the wheel. He had in his hand a plastic bag which seemed to have lodged itself by the gearstick, and which he seemed to have difficulty in retrieving. Eventually he disentangled himself and appeared, blinking at me from across the roof of the car.

'Sissy. Hello, honey. How are you doing?' He walked over, stumbling on an uneven patch, before righting himself with a soft 'whoa'. He gave me a wide smile. 'Haven't seen you for a while.'

I shook my head.

'Is your mom in?'

I nodded. 'Shall I call her?'

'Well, yeah. Why don't you do that? Thanks.'

He looked odd: strangely informal, with sandals on his feet, in blue jeans and an open-necked shirt showing his chest. His beard was flecked with grey, but the hair on his head was thick and clean and shiny, his arms and face were tanned. He looked wholly otherworldly, incongruous in our surroundings, and, I could see, handsome. He squinted at me as I turned and went into the house.

My mother was in the bedroom, ironing.

'Mama, Mr Cooper is here.'

'Mr Cooper?'

'He's outside.'

She returned my gaze wordlessly, then followed me to the front door and then onto the veranda, from where we could see Mr Cooper pushing Danny on the swing with one hand, the plastic bag in his other. My brother looked put out.

'Laila!' he called out on seeing my mother. Then approached. 'I've brought provisions. I got a load of stuff sent over by the American consul and I wondered if I could invite myself for dinner.' He pulled out a bottle from the bag. 'I even have some sparkling wine to toast the occasion with.' He raised it in mock salute. 'Here's to two abandoned spouses,' and then, catching my mother's worried glance in my direction, he added quickly, 'I mean, one spouse. *I* have been abandoned, not you, of course,' making a courtly bow.

We both looked on, goggle-eyed, our mouths now dropped open, my mother and me, at Mr Cooper, who had clearly had at least some of the wine or something else already. And then Danny bellowed. His body was stiffening in protest, and he was thrusting himself out of the swing. My mother darted forwards and caught him, settled him on her hip, then turned to face Mr Cooper, who was now looking less assured.

'May I?' He cleared his throat. 'May I invite myself for dinner?'

My mother glanced at me, and then at Mr Cooper. 'Of course,' she said.

'That's wonderful, thank you.' He grinned, a hand now on his chest. 'I've got a chicken here, some eggplant, some ice-cream, various items I thought you could work your magic on . . .' On seeing my mother purse her lips, he added hurriedly, 'I'll help of course. I'll do whatever you say.'

Now my mother laughed, shaking her head, and, gesturing to me, she said, 'Sissy can help me.'

'No, I insist!' He looked genuinely pained that she would deny him the opportunity. 'Sissy, it's your day off, honey,' and returning to my mother, 'I'd enjoy your charming company, Laila.'

At least my mother had the grace to blush before she glanced at me again, a query in her eyes.

'I'll take Danny, Mama,' I said. 'We'll go and see Rahul. I saw him go into his house.'

She hesitated as I held her eyes, but then nodded, handing me my brother. 'Don't stay for too long.'

I did not bother to reply, but allowed Danny to lead the way, holding his hands while he soldiered onwards. But before we reached Rahul's house, I lifted him up and turned off the road, down the steps towards the netball courts. I had a notion that I would find him where I had seen him that day, leaning into the cook, so I was disappointed when I arrived at the storeroom and saw no one. I deposited Danny on the ground and he pulled himself up against the wall. And then he took his first tentative steps, all on his own, as if he had chosen this moment to remind me that one day, if I was patient, he would become a worthwhile companion. I caught sight of my reflection in the dusty window of the storeroom – there was a smile plastered on my face. And my brother lifted his chin and smiled back.

'Well done, Danny,' I whispered, and then he toppled, bumping his head against the wall, but he did not cry, only pulled himself back up with the determination he would show all his life. I walked around the storeroom, snooping through the windows, but could see nothing; it looked dank and dark and uninhabited. Then I sat on the steps and watched my baby brother, not reprising his earlier success, but sitting down now and investigating his environs, tugging at blades of grass, and then placing his palm, empty-handed, against his mouth. I was just thinking to retrieve him and indeed knock on Rahul's door when a figure passed us, at the bottom of the hill, carrying two bags, one in each hand. But even though he was evenly balanced, I saw the uneven gait, the distinctive sloping shoulder: Ezekiel.

He put the bags down. Whatever he was carrying did not appear to be heavy, but he put them down anyway, and I thought, now he will turn to look this way and he will see me, and the feeling did not fill me with anticipation or pleasure at seeing my erstwhile friend. A dread consumed me: don't look this way, Ezekiel. For I could not look at him without feeling a profound unease. He was almost skeletal, his hair uncombed and knotty, and there were dark marks on the back of his neck as if he had been scratching himself. How could I have thought him a friend when he was so unkempt, his demeanour so ungraceful? I could imagine him coming up the hill to stand over me, take note of how my legs had grown longer in the months since we had last seen each other, take note of the swellings on my chest, of how my face had matured, and I resisted that eventuality, disturbed by the change in my sentiments. Could I have grown so much in so short a period of time, grown so far away from the child I was, just months earlier? I glanced at Danny. Maybe I could use him as an excuse, walk over and pretend to have been so engrossed in his play that I had not noticed Ezekiel at the foot of the hill. But I remained frozen, my eyes focused on a spot on the ground, just as I had always been told to behave in the presence of a snake. Remain as still as you can; they fear you more than you fear them. I did exactly that, I stayed statue-still, and when I finally raised my head a fraction, I saw he had gone.

I stood up, my heart thudding. At my disloyalty, with disbelief at myself and my previous feelings, and with incredulity at my parents – how could they leave her alone with him? I gathered Danny up into my arms, and he bumped against my chest as I jogged back up the steps, our house just ahead, back onto the road, just as Rahul's car pulled in beside us. He rolled down the window, smiling, but when he saw my face, he asked, 'Sissy, are you all right?'

I nodded, tried to steady my breathing because there was no way I could express what I was feeling and explain myself. He must have assumed I was simply out of breath, because he pointed at Danny and said, 'Don't let him be lazy. Make him use his legs . . .'

I had lied to him after Bobby's jibe, and I lied again. 'I'm fine.' But I knew I did not sound fine – my voice was different, as if I had grown even in those last minutes when I had realised that now I feared rather than missed Ezekiel.

Rahul nodded, not saying anything, until he pointed at the blue car on our driveway. 'Do you have a visitor?'

'Mr Cooper,' I replied. 'The American.' I added, 'He's cooking a chicken with Mama,' and the pronouncement and the comical imagery it evoked made us both grin and I began to feel better.

Rahul laughed. 'Well, it's nice for Aunty to have some company.'

'When do you leave?' I asked. 'For university?'

'Next week. I'm a bit nervous actually.'

He met my eyes and I said, 'You'll be fine,' and he nodded. Then, 'I'm driving back into Lusaka to meet this guy who wants to buy my car.'

'That's good.'

'I never took you for that drive, did I?'

'Don't worry.'

We both fell silent.

'Well, take care of yourself, Sissy.'

'And you, Rahul. Good luck.'

I wondered if he would hold out his hand to shake mine, or even get out from his car and give me a hug or kiss my cheek, but instead we both smiled at each other awkwardly, and he drove away. Just as I had disappointed myself with my reaction at glimpsing Ezekiel, I felt disappointed that the farewell with Rahul had not stirred me in any great way.

I put Danny down and he led me back to the front door of our house, from where delicious aromas were wafting. A veritable feast was in the making and my home was unrecognisable. Here was noise: the radio on, tuned to a station that crackled and spluttered but from which some jazzy music could be heard; here was Mr Cooper humming along as he sliced some vegetables with great deliberation, a glass of red wine to his left; here was my mother smiling as she stirred and seasoned and tasted, moving gracefully around our kitchen and occasionally picking up her own glass of wine, looking very pleased with herself. Here was the table laid out as if for a banquet; I had forgotten that we had the green tablecloth, the cutlery we hardly ever used, a jug of cordial in the middle.

When we sat down to the meal, Mr Cooper drained his glass, picked up my mother's, rinsed them, and brought the sparkling wine he had stored in the fridge, poured my mother and himself two generous glasses and a dash into mine. Special occasion, he said. We talked as if Mrs Cooper and the Cooper girls, my father, were not only absent but non-existent. The ice-cream he had brought had survived our feeble freezer and provided a perfect ending to the meal. We stood up, cleared the table, Mr Cooper ignoring my mother's protests. Perhaps she was worried he would drop the plates; in the end he had finished most of the sparkling wine himself.

'No, no, I can't leave you girls to do the washing up when I invited myself over,' he said, and turned on the tap, only for it to cough and splutter, a dribble coming out and then immediately stopping.

My mother looked embarrassed. Her hands were against his arm, gently pushing him away. 'Sam, don't worry, we'll take care of this.'

He stood his ground. 'What do you mean? How are you going to wash up?'

'We'll use the water from the barrel,' she replied. Then repeated: 'Don't worry. Sissy and I will take care of it.'

'Let me help.' His voice was serious. 'Please.' And so he lifted the water out of the barrel into the bucket, and poured it into the sink, where we added some liquid soap and dunked all the plates and cutlery. Then I used a mug to pour more water over everything to rinse them. We drained the sink and after two more cycles the pots and pans were sparkling, the cutlery back in the drawers and the surfaces wiped.

He folded the tea towel he had been using and cleared his throat. 'Now listen to me, Laila,' he said quietly, and it was evident that he had been rehearsing his words in his mind. 'There's a generator and a borehole at our place. I've got water and light twenty-four hours a day. I've got empty bedrooms, and more space than I can deal with. Why don't you and the kids come and stay while the school is closed? Until everything goes back to some kind of normal?' Then his voice dropped low as he added humbly, 'I know I've had too much to drink. I wouldn't have if I'd known I'd be giving you a lift, but I'll drive at ten miles an hour, I promise, and that means I won't get us killed and I won't kill anyone else.'

In fact, he appeared to have much sobered as he stowed away the small suitcase my mother packed for us in his car. He was even whistling a little as he went around our bungalow closing and locking the windows as if he was the owner, and we were leaving for a holiday, as a family. And then, true to his word, he drove with the utmost care, as if he wanted to emphasise his awareness of the precious cargo, at no more than ten miles an hour, peering out of the windscreen with concentration, but glancing at my mother once to give her a smile, which I believe she returned, before turning to look out the window as we trundled along the road and left the campus behind us.

16

THERE was so much left behind — books on the shelves, furniture, pictures on the wall, cushions, bedsheets, plates, cutlery and glasses — as if we had usurped Mrs Cooper and her daughters. It was easy to picture them in an empty house, wondering at the family who were walking on their rugs and dusting their ornaments. No, Mr Cooper assured us, as if he had read our minds. The house had been provided fully equipped and furnished for their adventure in Zambia; they had only brought a few belongings of their own. Mrs Cooper's sister had been looking after their own house in Virginia in their absence, and the decision to return had been rather uncomplicated. Mrs Cooper had simply elected to complete her sabbatical in the comfort of their old home, with the girls slipping back into their old school and former lives, allowing Mr Cooper the liberty to answer the further demands made on him now, on account of the raid. On the telephone, Mrs Cooper expressed approval that the remaining Olikaras had been given refuge, had asked for the receiver to be passed to my mother. Much better, Laila, she had said, in that generous way of hers, so much better than being on a quiet, lonely campus surrounded only by nuns. My mother had ended the call with her cheeks flushed red and had avoided my eyes. My father, it appeared, was unavailable, and after several unsuccessful attempts to speak to him directly, she left a message, describing our new circumstances — George, all of us are staying with Sam Cooper — her voice faltering as she gave the telephone number that he should have known already. Perhaps she was unsure of how many details from our lives in Zambia he had taken back with him to India.

For me, the Coopers' house was familiar territory. But staying there now with my mother and baby brother, it felt different. The common denominator of our now-lives and our then-lives was Grace, who on seeing us arrive and on being apprised of the arrangements by Mr Cooper – Mrs Olikara and the children will be staying with us, Grace, could you make up Ally's room for her? – had clapped her hands softly. Then clasped my mother's hand between both of hers: it is good, madam, you should not be alone at this time. Words that brought tears to my mother's eyes, a reminder of Grace's warmth. And then Grace turned to me and Danny, to hug each of us, lifting Danny high and exclaiming: how big you are now. It was a warm welcome and I could see the tension leave my mother, even as she appeared timid, asking Grace rather than Mr Cooper about towels and bathing arrangements.

Mr Cooper had told us that he would be leaving early the following morning; he had promised to oversee the delivery of a relief package on the other side of the city. We spent our first day in the Coopers' house, a Sunday, speaking quietly and tiptoeing on the shiny floors; I could see my mother felt shy and awkward. When Grace appeared late morning – it was her day off, but she had wanted to make sure we were comfortable – my mother made no attempt to hide her gratitude or her relief. And then Grace insisted on making lunch, so that she could show my mother how to use the unfamiliar cooker and, even more unfamiliar, the dishwasher and washing machine. By the time Mr Cooper returned, bringing news of the red tape hindering the clear-up of the camp, it was early evening. He changed into a faded T-shirt that read 'Dartmouth Ice Hockey' and declared he had some burgers in the fridge – more goodies from the package from the consulate – that he would grill on the barbecue for everyone, which we could have with the salad Grace had prepared earlier. We ate off our laps together on the patio, all of us – Danny on Grace's knee – as if to celebrate the new domestic arrangements. When Mr Cooper stood up and excused himself as he had to finish off a few things in his study, Grace stopped my mother, who was stacking the plates, with a hand on her arm: madam, take care of the children. Leave the rest to me.

My mother looked dazed when she said good night to me later. Hard to imagine that we remained in the same city, the same country that we had lived in for so long, so different was this world from ours. We slept in our new home, cocooned and cossetted. The following morning Mr Cooper dropped me off at my school before driving on to his office, and that afternoon he sent one of the administrators from his team, a young woman with huge sunglasses, to pick me up in her car and ferry me back to the house.

It was a few mornings after that that my teacher stopped by my desk and bent down to say quietly, 'Come with me, Sissy. The head wants to see you.'

I stood up, my brain whirring. Homework was handed in, scrappily done I admitted, but completed nevertheless; my hair was neat, my uniform correct. I had not been caught chatting in class, indeed I had spent most of the recent months in near-silence, so exhausted by my thoughts and the events at home. I ticked through the checklist. Why would Sister Catherine want to see me? My teacher, an English woman who was married to a Zambian and who had lived in Lusaka for over ten years, smiled reassuringly, but I felt a twinge of concern. The office of the headmistress was not familiar territory. I had only been inside it once, with my parents, when I had enrolled in the school, and she had fixed me then with a steely gaze. She looked smaller in the office than in the school assemblies when she stood on a raised dais, behind a lectern. She was, I could see, very old, her eyes a rheumy blue. Her habit had the black veil with white trim of the Dominican order. Penguins, I had always thought when I saw them.

'Sit down, Priscilla,' she said, then smiled, revealing very small, beige teeth.

My teacher sat next to me, and I folded my hands on my lap respectfully. The headmistress stared at me for a long time, with that blue gaze, and when I could not stand it any longer I looked down at my shoes, trying not to appear furtive.

'How are things at home?' she asked.

I looked up in surprise. 'Fine,' I said, then added, too obviously as an afterthought, 'Thank you, Sister Catherine.'

'Your little brother?'

'He's fine, thank you, Sister.'

'And your parents?'

I hesitated. 'They're fine, thank you, Sister.'

She was still staring at me, and again I caved in and looked down.

Then she spoke quietly. 'We've seen you coming and going with a series of different people.'

I remained silent.

'And your mother has not returned my phone calls.'

I looked up.

'I've phoned the convent in Roma a few times. I phoned after the raid to make sure that you were all right. I left a message asking her to call me back.'

I said nothing, only found that I was staring at my shoes again.

'I'd like her to make an appointment. This is your last year in primary and we need to make applications for secondary school. I need to discuss this with her.'

I recrossed my ankles and found that my throat was dry.

'Sissy,' she said, and her voice was not frosty, only firm.

I looked up. Her brow was wrinkled but her expression was kind.

'My father had to go back to India,' I said. 'And because of the raid were staying with Mr Cooper for a while.'

'Mary-Anne's father?'

I nodded.

'How long has your father been away?'

I was stunned. I did not know. I racked my brains but I could not remember a date.

When I did not respond, she continued: 'Are you going back to India? Will you be attending secondary school here in Lusaka or in India?'

'I don't know, Sister Catherine.'

'I see.'

She looked thoughtful, began to doodle on the notepad in front of her. Then she raised her head and gave me that beige smile. 'You're not in any trouble, Sissy. I'd just like to have a meeting with your mother. Will you ask her to come and see me?'

I nodded, and she nodded in turn at my teacher, who ushered me out of the room, her arm around me as if I were a patient. She squeezed my shoulder as we walked back to the classroom.

I waited outside the school, my friends' voices a hum in my head as they chattered about a television series they had been watching, the new music teacher, the film they had all seen at the weekend, when a van, emblazoned on the side with the logo of Mr Cooper's agency, drew up, and the driver leant across, and opened the passenger door. 'Sissy? I'll be taking you home.' I winced inwardly as I slipped into the seat, willing myself not to turn around to see if any of the teachers were watching: we've seen you coming and going with a series of different people.

This man was young, with, unusually for that time, a full head of dreadlocks, tied back with a green band. He was called Tembe, he told me. He was a driver for the agency, a logistician. Was I enjoying school? How long had I lived in Zambia? He drove quickly and we arrived in no time at all. I got out at the gate and walked up the driveway as he gave a little beep of the horn in farewell. I walked around the side of the house and entered through the kitchen, which rather than being in that post-prandial quiet I had expected was abuzz with activity. Both Grace and my mother were at the counter, side by side, peeling and chopping a mound of onions and garlic.

'Ah, Sissy,' from Grace.

'Hello, mol,' from my mother.

Danny was in the far corner with a bowl of flour, another of water, and several spoons, delightedly transferring one into the other, walking up and down from one bowl to another, with proud, wobbly steps, covering himself happily with the paste, too engrossed to look up.

'We have some visitors for dinner,' my mother said. 'Mister . . .' she stopped, 'Charlie and Fee and someone else. I said I'd make chicken biriani.' She smiled sweetly, happily.

'Oh, right.'

'Are you hungry?' She pointed at the table. 'Grace made you a sandwich.'

'Thank you, Grace.' I sat down and took a bite.

'Wash your hands first.'

I stood up again and moved to the sink. When I returned to my sandwich my mother asked, 'Do you have any homework?'

'A little.'

'Have your sandwich, finish your homework, and then can you give Danny a bath?'

I nodded and watched as they continued with the chopping, then stood up again, rinsed my plate. As I turned away from the draining board, I caught Grace's eye. She was watching me thoughtfully, and she smiled but said nothing.

In the bath, later, Danny said, smacking my arm gently, 'Diddy', and my eyes filled with tears, before I realised he was not saying 'Daddy' but trying to say 'Sissy'. I felt a wave of tenderness for my baby brother. His hair was slick and wet, a black pelt covering his oversized head. His limbs had lost the rolls of babyhood; even though he was late walking he had made up for it with his energetic crawling and scooting around. I tapped his chest and said, 'Danny,' and he gave me his wondrous toothless smile, slapping his hands on the water in glee.

Grace had been invited to join the party but had declined, taking her plate of food to the granny flat that served as her lodgings. Only one plate, no lights on in the annex until she entered – no mention or sign of Ezekiel. My mother appeared, dressed in the turquoise silk sari she had worn that afternoon of the school's anniversary, with her hair falling down one shoulder in a loose ponytail. She was glowing. She appeared reinvigorated, as if the escape from the campus had injected a new energy into her, and responded to Mr Cooper's compliment – you look beautiful, Laila – with a lowering of her lashes, and I had a vision of Mrs Cooper at the table, laying down her cutlery: good God, Sam. Mr Lawrence and Miss Munroe arrived with the other guest, a journalist who was stopping by on his way to South Africa and who, it transpired, was a regular guest.

It was an attractive ensemble. The men radiated an American glamour; both my mother and Miss Munroe sparkled. I wore one of the Cooper girls' hand-me-down dresses, hoping Mr Cooper would not recognise it, with my hair free from its plaits and clipped to the side with a decorative grip, and the bracelets and anklet I had received for my birthday. Mr Cooper was an attentive host, everyone admired my mother's cooking, and she served and smiled and laughed, her bangles jangling and earrings swinging, more herself in this gathering than I had ever seen her with the Malayalees on the campus. Everyone present, I could see, appreciated her, without any scorn or cynicism. My father was a distant memory that night. Even though we had had jolly family dinners before, none had had the feeling of being under threat, as if we had dressed in our best clothes because we knew we might die tomorrow. We all ate as if this were the last meal we would enjoy, as if the helicopters would return, bombs would fall, and all that was near would burn to the ground. For we were alive, living, days after death had arrived just miles away from where we sat now; days after girls had run, terrified, to be scratched and bitten in the bush; days after governments gathered and the morality of revenge was dissected in their rhetoric. We were suspended above all this, determined to enjoy an evening of food and drink and company. And all this we could do because the land, the people, were not ours. Guests at Mr Cooper's table, guests in this land. We could tidy things away and leave, while the others would have to stay. And not even two years after we had left, Rhodesia was returned to its owners, one flag lowered, another raised. As if our presence and then our absence had played no part in the unfolding events.

These were not my thoughts that evening, though. That evening I was quiet, imbibing the view I was being offered of the adult world, watching how hands touched an arm, a glass was refilled. Mr Lawrence was seated next to me, and I had, on first taking my place, wondered if I should apologise for my brusqueness on the day of the outing to Munda Wanga. But he seemed so genuinely pleased to see me, pulling out my chair for me – oh good, you sit right here, Sissy – then smiling at me occasionally through the conversations but not dragging me into the limelight.

Miss Munroe revealed her parents wished her to return to Ireland. And will you go? Not a chance. Go back for what? For the whole town to ask me stupid questions and for me to get bored out of mind? How is Cindy doing? This from Mr Lawrence to Mr Cooper, who replied: blooming, as you'd expect. I try and call from work and she's usually out. You know she doesn't need me, Charlie. I only get in the way. My mother and Miss Munroe tutted in unison, but Mr Lawrence only smiled as he lit his cigarette and proffered his lighter to Miss Munroe, not asking after Ally and Mary-Anne. His eyes rested briefly on my mother, who had fidgeted at the mention of Mrs Cooper.

At one point, after some bottles of wine had been finished and the men and Miss Munroe had glasses of whisky in their hands, the journalist had waved his cigarette at the two women, turned to Mr Cooper and Mr Lawrence: 'You guys have quite a good thing going here.' Everyone laughed and he continued: 'I'm not sure I want to get on the plane to Jo'burg tomorrow.'

'You'll be on the sofa tonight, by the way,' Mr Cooper replied. 'Young Sissy here is in the guest room.'

At which point my mother seemed to remember me and said, 'Time for you to go to bed, I think, mol.'

I wanted to bite back, but found that, actually, it was only a fleeting reaction. I was tired of the adults. I stood up, murmuring my good nights to the gathering, preparing to leave the room, but Miss Munroe held out her arms and pulled me to her for a kiss, saying: come here, sweet, sweet girl. Her face was flushed, her make-up slightly smeared and her hands were hot on my cheeks. Mr Lawrence gave me a little wave from where he was sitting, and the journalist held out his hand, swapping his whisky glass to the other: it's been a pleasure, young lady. Mr Cooper clasped the back of my neck briefly – good night, darlin'– as I leant forward to kiss my mother, who whispered in Malayalam: get into bed and I'll come and see you.

I washed and changed into my pyjamas, tiptoeing up and down the hall from bedroom to bathroom as the voices continued and laughter erupted from the dining room. As I was brushing my teeth, I leant out of the window. I could just spy Grace's annex. It was dark.

I slipped into the bed, clicked on the bedside lamp, and settled on my side. I had read only a page when my mother entered.

'Don't read for too long,' she said, and again she spoke in Malayalam. 'It's really late and you have school tomorrow.' Then she came forward and sat down on the edge of the bed, stroked my hair. Her skin shone in the night and her eyes glittered. 'Did you enjoy the party?'

I nodded.

She leant forward so her head was on my shoulder. 'They're nice people, aren't they?'

I nodded again, and she laid her face against mine. I felt her breath on my cheek, tinged with wine, and after some minutes I thought she had fallen asleep. But she lifted her head and tucked the sheet around me. 'Sleep well.'

I watched as she turned off the bedside light, watched as she walked to the door, then stood, silhouetted in the doorway, before she left the room, shutting the door behind her. When I heard her re-enter the dining room and the door close on the noise, I switched the lamp back on, padded across the room and retrieved my notebook and pen. I scurried back to the bed and pushed the pillow up, leant the notepad against my knees.

Dear Jonah, I wrote. *How are you? I hope you are well. We are staying now with Mr Cooper until the school re-opens. Me, my mother and Danny. Tonight, my mother cooked dinner for some people and everyone enjoyed it very much.* I paused, my heart thumping, then bent forward and continued: *I hope you can visit me here. Do you know where the Coopers live? It's where Grace works now. I hope you can find the house and come and see me. If you can't, do you know where my school is in town? I know that might be quite far for you. I would like you to teach me more Portuguese. I remember how to say thank you but I'm not sure how to spell it so I won't write it down. Please try and visit me because I miss you and I want to see you.* I had written the last words in a rush, the words had tumbled from my pen. Then I steadied my breath and added: *Yours, Sissy.*

17

G RACE took the letter from me wordlessly and stared at the envelope with Jonah's name written on the front.

'Can you send this to him, please, Grace?'

She said nothing but simply looked at me.

'He's my friend,' I said, and I heard my voice tremble. 'I'd like him to know where we are but I don't know how to contact him.'

She looked at me serenely. When we had first met, if I stretched my hands up high I could place them on her shoulders. Now she was my height, which made me realise she was a small woman, with a powerful body, one she needed to bear the weight of all she endured. She could have asked me then: why did you never write to Ezekiel? Do you remember how he left? I had felt an anger at my mother when I had observed her picking and choosing; now I was doing the same. Grace stood before me: her knitted cap on her head, her dress freshly ironed, white tennis shoes on her feet. She looked wholly familiar but at the same time exotic, from a world that began when she left the house and entered her annex. I remembered her dwelling near the campus and how my father and I had visited with her medicine. It was unlikely she had relinquished the small house to the local authority; most probably that was where Ezekiel was staying. I opened my mouth, to ask after him – not because I especially wanted to know of him – only because I thought I might then curry favour and she would do my bidding. But before I said anything, before I expressed a hypocritical wish to find out if

Ezekiel was well, she spoke: 'I will give it to Constance. She works next door.'

'Does she know Jonah?'

'She is his neighbour.'

'Thank you so much, Grace.' I heard my mother's steps behind me. 'Please don't . . .'

'Sissy? The driver is ready to take you.' My mother had Danny in her arms. I turned to glance at Grace, but she had turned away herself and was at the kitchen sink. The envelope was not in sight. I walked out into the driveway with my mother. Mr Cooper had already left early in the morning to drop the journalist at the airport and from there had gone straight to his office. Tembe sat at the wheel of his pick-up and smiled his greeting.

'Have a nice day, mol,' my mother said.

'What will you do, Mama?'

'Not sure,' she said. 'I might see if I can do anything in the vegetable garden. I need to give Danny a haircut. I'll see if I can help Grace with the cooking.'

I climbed into the pick-up. My mother waved goodbye. As we drove away I realised I had not told her about the head-mistress.

There followed three days when each morning on leaving the house I remembered that I had forgotten to pass on the message, and this would then slip my mind completely until the next morning when I experienced the same flash of memory and the same stab of remorse. Mr Cooper went away for two nights. Grace slept on a roll-up bed in the kitchen the first night, Mr Lawrence came to stay the second – both arrange-ments put in place by Mr Cooper in case my mother felt anxious sleeping alone in the house. The evening when Mr Lawrence stayed, the three of us gathered in the living room after dinner. By now we were all comfortable in each other's company, like old friends. I was in my pyjamas, curled up in an armchair with a book. My mother, in her nightdress and shawl, was settled on the sofa with a magazine Miss Munroe had passed on, while Mr Lawrence tapped away on his typewriter at the desk. I wanted to ask after his project, the spiritual healers, but my mother did not know of our late-night conversation from those weeks earlier, and I felt possessive of our encounter. I watched him from over the top of my book as his fingers found the keys expertly and his typewriter clattered. He was in a T-shirt and shorts, but with his glasses and his posture and his concentration, he looked like a pianist. Or a writer. I tried to imagine myself at a desk with typewriter in front of me, glasses on my nose, but could only project an image of his unshaven chin onto an image of mine.

My mother suddenly raised her head, waited until there was a pause in his typing, then spoke: 'Charlie, I've just thought. You can sleep in Mary-Anne's room, can't you? No need for you to sleep on the sofa.'

Mr Lawrence turned around and smiled. 'That's sweet of you to worry, Laila, but I'll be fine. I'm a sofa man myself.' And then for some reason he looked embarrassed at his own words, cleared his throat and looked away, and my mother in turn averted her gaze, seemed flustered by his reaction.

Mr Cooper returned late on Friday night. I heard him unlocking the door quietly, then whispers as my mother greeted him, sounds in the kitchen after; she must have been keeping him company as he had a late supper. We were invited to lunch at Miss Munroe's friend's house on the Saturday; on the Sunday Mr Cooper took us to the cathedral in the city, even though my mother had not appeared particularly intent on attending Mass. We emerged an hour later to find him leaning against the car, parked in the shade, as if he were a chauffeur, ready to escort us to the university campus where we had another invitation to lunch, with a friend of Mr Cooper's, an American professor in the history department whose doctor wife was from Guyana.

Their twin sons were three years older than Danny, and I spent a pleasant afternoon entertaining the small boys in the garden with a hula hoop and a rubber ball. We ended the weekend rested and replenished, and on the Monday school carried on as normal, even though I no longer knew what normality meant. It seemed perfectly reasonable that we were living in the Coopers' home and among the Coopers' friends, my mother and her children displacing the American wife and her family. Perfectly unsurprising that my father should have returned to India to conduct some mysterious business and be waylaid, unable to keep in touch. Perfectly acceptable that my mother should slip into this new life with an ease that made a mockery of her ease with her previous life.

Tembe dropped me off after school and as I opened the gate I saw my mother walking on the road towards me, Danny on her hip, and propped up against the fence, Jonah's bicycle. My mother walked past it, without noticing, drew up to me smiling, her hair tousled from the breeze and held loosely by a band.

'How was school, mol?' And without waiting for an answer, bumping Danny up and down – 'He's walking so much now!' – she gestured further behind her. 'It's such a nice area, and we found a small park for Danny to run around in.' Then, pulling one of my plaits, she said, 'We'll go one evening with you.'

I muttered a reply, but I could barely hear her. The bicycle to my left seemed to emanate hot waves that burned my cheeks. We walked up the driveway and around the side of the house towards the back door, while I glanced around furtively into the orchard, the granny flat, the back lawn, but saw no sign of him, nor Grace. But when we entered the kitchen, we saw that he was sitting at the table, underneath which his long legs stretched, in work-trousers ending in work-boots, as always.

'Hello, Mrs Olikara.' He smiled, getting to his feet. 'How are you, Sissy?'

'Jonah.' My mother's voice was warm, her pleasure unmistakable, and she was smiling widely. 'How nice to see you.' She held out her hand and he took it, gave a little bow. 'How are you?'

'Well, madam, well. And you?'

'We've been staying here for some time now. I'm sorry we left without telling you.'

'No, it's not a problem, madam,' he said. 'It is good you are here.' Then he gestured to her hair loose around her, her face glowing from the fresh air, and smiled into her eyes. 'And you look well.'

My mother gave a little laugh. 'And how are your studies?'

He made a little show of looking sheepish. 'I have not looked at my books for some time, it was so busy.' Then squared his shoulders with a smile. 'But now I will start again. I have my exam in three weeks.'

'Well, I can help you again, Jonah, if you come this way.'

'I will not come this way often,' he said and then turned and caught my eye and my heart jumped into my mouth, 'but thank you.'

'We might be back in Roma soon and then you must come,' my mother said.

He shook his head. 'I'm not sure, madam. I'm not sure the school will open again very soon.'

'Oh, I see.' My mother bit her lip. 'And the camp?'

'Many dead,' he said simply, 'and many injured.'

We fell silent, all of us, and behind us Grace entered the room, said something to Jonah in Nyanja and then to my mother, 'Bwana is on the phone, madam,' adding hurriedly, as if to pre-empt any misunderstanding on my mother's part, that my father was calling us, 'Mr Cooper, madam.'

'Thank you, Grace.' My mother turned to Jonah. 'I'll just go and speak to him.'

He inclined his head, my mother smiled again and glanced at me, and I grinned back inanely. We all stood there smiling at each other, until my mother nodded. 'Nice to see you again, Jonah.'

'Madam.'

She looked at me as if she expected me to follow, but I moved to the sink and started running the water as if I had some project in mind, picked up some spoons and started arranging them randomly on the draining board. She left the room and I turned off the tap, turned around. 'Thank you for coming, Jonah.'

He was laughing, shaking his head. 'Sissy,' he spread his arms wide, 'how could I *not* come when you write to me like that?'

My face grew warm and he laughed again, his shoulders shaking, then he walked over and stood in front of me, his hands clasped, like that day when I was ill, it felt like so long ago.

'You look well,' he said.

'It was so quiet in Roma. There was hardly anyone there.' Then I remembered I had seen Ezekiel from afar, but I said nothing.

He was nodding. 'I agree. It is good you are here.'

'Would you like something to eat?'

He smiled, shook his head. 'Grace, she gave me some lunch. And how is school?'

'Fine,' I said. 'Boring.'

'No.' He looked suddenly upset. 'No, Sissy. You are lucky to go to school.'

And I remembered his mother, the story of the fish, and how she had died, how he had left with his schooling cut short. And I felt so ashamed that tears filled my eyes, and I looked down to hide them.

There was a short silence until he said, 'No, no.' His voice was gentle. He patted my arm, then bent himself forward to look up into my face. 'Do you still know how to smile?'

I felt my lips move themselves into what must have been a grimace.

'Better,' he said, smiling himself, with his white, straight teeth, and wide mouth. 'Beautiful smile from a beautiful girl.' But his eyes remained grave and he did not pinch my chin this time.

There was another silence during which I could hear Grace in the living room with Danny, my mother's voice a murmur. I did not have long, I knew, and my heart began to thump at the thought that he would leave soon. I stole a glance at him and saw that he was watching me, his expression patient.

'Shall we go outside?' I asked, and he held his arm out for me to lead the way. We moved together into the garden, and I found a shady spot in front of the orchard. He leant against a tree and folded his arms, completely comfortable and well versed in the dynamics of such a conversation whereas I could not think of another time that I had summoned someone – and a man at that – in this way and had been obeyed. I tried to stand in a nonchalant fashion, putting one foot in front of the other, then decided to clasp my hands behind my back. By now he was smiling again, no doubt amused by my machinations, but when he saw that I had noticed this, he cleared his throat and tried to look more serious, his eyes on the ground near my feet. I let my eyes move over his face, down to the open neck of his shirt; no sign of the thin gold chain.

'Tell me about the camp, Jonah,' I said quietly.

He looked up at the sound of my voice, then unfolded his arms, put them behind him so that he was mirroring my stance.

'It is men, mostly,' he said. 'There were men, nearly all of them, living without their families. Waiting for the time to fight.'

'How did they die?' I asked, and I saw him hesitate before speaking.

'There were bombs,' he said. 'And shooting also.'

'I saw one of them. One of the soldiers,' I whispered. 'From the window. He was in a helicopter. He looked at me.'

He said nothing.

'He didn't look like a bad person,' I ventured.

'What is bad and what is good?' He sounded almost angry. Now he spread his arms. 'I saw this in Mozambique when I was younger. The men around me wanted to fight the Portuguese, and some did. Now the Portuguese have gone, and they are fighting each other.' Then he shook himself and smiled. 'But why are we talking about this? Tell me what you're reading now, Sissy. You are always reading.'

'A book that Miss Munroe gave me.' I did not add that it had been for my birthday; I did not want him to think I was fishing for a gift. 'It's set during the Civil War in America.'

He laughed. 'A civil war. Like in Mozambique?'

'It was a hundred years ago, but yes.'

I wanted to continue, but then I stopped. I was not sure what he had learned when he was at school, and I was worried that I would offend him if I asked. It felt anathema to ask Jonah what he knew of slavery, of the politics and the history of a country neither of us had been to, of the world outside Lusaka. Yet he knew of the world, I reminded myself. He had lived through conflict and war, not just read stories in a book; he had only just spoken of it. He had suffered loss and it was more than likely that he had loved too. But I found myself tongue-tied, wishing to relate the tales I had read but at the same time unwilling to speak of them for fear of alienating him.

He spoke before me. 'You see, Sissy,' he was grinning, 'you see what men are like? Better if the women take care of everything.'

I smiled back, and as I had hoped he would, he chucked me under the chin, then he held his arm out again, but this time pointing towards the driveway. 'I cannot stay, Sissy. I have to go but will you walk with me to the gate?'

We left the orchard and walked down the path. I tried to take as small steps as possible, and just as on that day when we had walked together to return the tools to Moses, he slowed down to my snail's pace. My motives must have been clear, but he did not query them, just as he had not forced me to match his stride that day; a day from a different century, when my father was still with us. My heart suddenly ached when I saw ahead to where his bicycle was leaning against the fence.

'I did see someone in Roma, Jonah,' I said. 'I saw Ezekiel.'

He stopped for a moment and then carried on walking. 'You spoke with him?'

I shook my head but did not furnish him with the details of how I had willed myself to be invisible, so deep had been my horror of what would happen if Ezekiel saw me.

Jonah said, 'He came to help and then they sent him away.'

'The nuns?'

He shook his head. 'The others,' and then, 'They believe he brought bad spirits.' He turned to me and smiled weakly. 'It's not easy for Ezekiel.'

'Is Grace upset?'

'Very.'

And I thought how she did not show this on her face and in her behaviour. She had not laughed at my request: silly girl. My son is unwanted and you are asking me to play postman! But as I felt sympathy for Grace and her troubles, I also longed for some comfort, even if nothing had happened to me. I longed to put my hand in Jonah's and feel him squeeze it, but too quickly we arrived at the fence. He did not take my hand, but put his into his pocket and drew something out.

'I also came to give you this.'

It was a thin, dark leather cord on which hung a small shape carved out of a sliver of wood: a tiny hand, the twin of his own gold pendant.

'I made it for you,' he said.

My voice was somewhere in my stomach, I could not speak. He slipped it over my head, and then the cord was lying cool against my neck and the amulet was lying near my chest. I fingered the delicate hand with wonder and looked up at him, wordless.

'Do you like it?' He was smiling again.

I nodded, then managed, 'It's so beautiful.'

'Wear it and it will protect you.'

'From what, Jonah?' I croaked.

He shrugged, then grinned. 'From whatever gives you fright, Sissy.'

'Makes me frightened?'

He laughed. 'Yes, that makes you frightened.'

I fingered the pointed edges of the tiny hand. It was exquisitely made, varnished so that the wood glinted softly in the sunlight.

I found my voice. 'What scares you, Jonah? What makes you frightened?' And I looked up at him, to see that his eyes were on me.

'If I say,' he smiled, 'I worry I might make you even more.'

'So, you *do* get scared?'

'Yes, of course.' He was still smiling.

'I'm scared my father will not come back.' The words came to me suddenly, and with them a realisation that I did feel a fear, a deep fear.

His smile faded and he stayed still in front of me, his eyes running over my face as they had that day before, as if he already knew what lay ahead, that my smooth, soft skin was on borrowed time. And I let mine do the same; take in his features and the gentleness in his eyes which contrasted against his strong straightness.

'He will come back,' he said suddenly. 'He will.' Then he reached forward and tapped my nose with a finger, 'Não te preocupes. Do you remember what that means?'

'Yes.'

'Do you want to learn something else?'

I nodded, and he said, 'Adeus is goodbye.'

'I don't want to learn goodbye.'

'Okay, then what about até a próxima – until the next time?' He seemed determined to placate me and was speaking quickly as if he wished to sweep my worries away.

I felt embarrassed about what I had said and fingered the amulet again. 'It's so beautiful,' I repeated.

'It looks beautiful on you.' And now he laid the palm of his hand against my cheek, his hand so large against my face that his fingers brushed the nape of my neck. I could have turned my head and pressed my lips against his skin, but I did not. A momentary touch, and then he was walking around the gate, to his bicycle, and mounting it smoothly.

'Will you come again, Jonah?' I called out.

'I will try.'

He glided off without looking back, and I let my fingers caress the tiny hand before dropping it into my dress, so that it nestled against my heart.

18

I TOOK the necklace off before my bath, worried that the leather would spoil if it got wet, but soon after, slipped it back on so that under my pyjamas I could feel the cord lying around my neck, the amulet brushing against my chest. That night, I was already in bed when Mr Cooper arrived back from work. I listened to my mother's voice as she joined him in the kitchen, presumably to reheat his dinner, sit with him while he ate, which seemed to be becoming a routine of a kind. But I felt no inclination to take myself to the hallway, tune in to what they were talking about. Their voices were low, but I heard them both laugh at intervals; they were not like the earnest conversations I had heard between Mr and Mrs Cooper. I lay on my stomach, deliberately, then lifted my pyjama top to check whether the tiny hand had made an imprint on my skin. It had, and I watched in wonder as the makeshift tattoo faded, thinking as I saw my skin spring back that I would never, never, forget how full my heart had felt when Jonah had told me that he had made this exquisite necklace for me. I slept, clutching the tiny hand in my fist. In the morning it stroked me under my school uniform, out of sight, although I slipped my hand inside my dress at times through the day to make sure I had not imagined the whole affair, once catching the eye of a friend who stared quizzically at me. I looked away.

And then, that evening, returning from my bath, wrapped in a towel, I found my mother in the bedroom, a stack of ironed clothes in one hand and my necklace in the other. She smiled at me as I entered. 'This reminds me of something a girl in college had,' she said, holding the tiny wooden hand in her palm. 'I've never seen one made of wood before.' I said nothing, pulled my pyjama top over my head, a pair of knickers over my hips, and let the towel fall off me, suddenly feeling giddy. She was still smiling, and murmured absently, 'Hang your towel neatly, mol.' Then she put the clothes on the bed before placing the necklace back on the top of the chest of drawers where I had laid it. 'Is it one of the girls'? Ally's? Do you think she forgot to take it back with her?'

I mumbled something, my mouth dry, and watched as she left the room, catching a glimpse of her retreating form through the door as she entered the bedroom she shared with Danny. I turned away. I should have told her, I knew, but I slipped it back on over my neck, and tucked it carefully under my pyjama top, so that the leather cord was well-hidden.

The next morning, Mr Cooper took me to school, like he had so many times before, only I was more acutely aware than ever that his daughters were not in the car and that I was sitting in Ally's place, in the front seat. As if he was thinking the same, he mentioned that he had phoned the girls the previous afternoon, from work, and that they sent their love. There had been an early snowfall which they had been excited about, although their mother was less so. They were planning the Christmas holidays, less than a month away now, when he would be going back. This last piece of news reminding me that Mr Cooper was not ours, that we had our own Christmas celebration ahead to think of, but one which I could not yet picture: where it would take place, and whether it would include my father.

And so, there we were in the blue car together: Mr Cooper, a father without his daughters, and me, a daughter without her father. A swap of sorts, as if our families had been jumbled together and their members rejigged. Perhaps, I thought, my father was in Virginia, standing behind Mrs Cooper on the phone. Ask how Sissy is. Is she well? I felt a familiar shiver of fear, but at the same time I had a strength inside me as my thoughts swirled in my head, no doubt because of the tiny hand nestled against my chest. I was quiet, in my strength, but perhaps Mr Cooper regretted his earlier comment about Christmas, because he fell silent, too, and I could sense him glancing at me during the last stages of the journey. And when I opened the door to climb out, he stopped me with a hand on my arm, which he then raised to clasp the back of my head in a quick caress: have a nice day, honey.

It was Tembe who picked me up from school, deposited me outside the house, and as I walked around the side of the house I saw Grace bringing in the washing from the line. She smiled when she saw me, but made no mention of the letter, or of Jonah's visit. My mother was at the dining table, books and papers scattered around her. She told me she had gone to the bank that morning to withdraw some money – this mentioned in a casual tone that did not fool me. Perhaps she had found the account empty: he has given it all away. And she had gone back to Roma, to check on the bungalow – it was fine – to bring back some more clothes, and to talk to the Mother Superior – still no date for the re-opening. She had collected some work from the laboratory; at least she could use the time to prepare for when classes resumed. I did not repeat what Jonah had said, that he believed the school would not re-open soon, nor did I mention Mr Cooper's plans for Christmas. 'Could you take Danny into the garden, mol?' my mother asked. 'I brought back his swing, did you see?' So she had reached upwards to untie the ropes, or had she met Jonah, asked him to do it? 'Grace helped me,' she added, as if she could read my mind.

I lifted my brother into my arms, and he immediately plunged his hand into the opening of my dress, into my chest, as he always did with my mother, and before I could remove it myself, he withdrew his hand, clutching the leather cord between his fingers and then shoving it into his mouth to chew on. I tried to pull it out of his hand, but he was surprisingly strong. He tugged furiously, so that the cord was now digging into the back of my neck. I dumped him back down on the floor hoping he would then release his grip, but he pulled even more fiercely, the pendant now clamped in his fist. The tears of frustration that had gathered in my eyes meant that I could not see clearly, only hear my mother join us, then unpluck Danny's fingers one by one from the amulet. Her fingernails scraped the back of my neck as she slid the necklace over my head.

She walked silently to my bedroom, and I followed, Danny now bawling in the background. Inside the bedroom, she waited until I had entered, before closing the door and turning to face me.

'Why are you wearing this necklace, Sissy?'

I said nothing.

'Even if we are staying in their house you mustn't touch their things. It's not polite.' She frowned. 'Sissy?'

I tried to swallow but found that my tongue was over-large in my mouth. 'It's not theirs.' I heard the voice, but it could not have been me who was speaking. 'It's not Ally's or Mary-Anne's. It's mine.'

'Yours?'

'Yes, Mama.'

She looked nonplussed. 'Where did you get it from?'

For a second I thought to tell her that Bobby had made it at school, had given it to me as a birthday present. He had given me the wooden box, which lay just behind her on the chest of drawers, holding, as he had suggested, my three pairs of earrings. I would only be switching one object in lieu of another. But I found I did not want to lie on this occasion, for it would make me feel a shame over the gift I had been bestowed, make the gesture feel tawdry, when in fact it made me happier and stronger than I had ever felt before.

'Jonah gave it to me. He made it for me. It's for protection.' Now I was chattering, the words pouring out with relief. 'You see, he has one himself, from his mother, a Hand of Fatima it's called. His mother was a Muslim. She gave it to him when she died . . .'

My own mother stared at me as if I were a stranger, possessed by a strange babbling spirit, then opened the door and glanced outside. I could see Danny sitting with his back to the sofa, his thumb in his mouth, looking disgruntled but settled. She closed the door again.

'When he came the other day?'

I nodded.

She shook her head, mumbled something to herself, her eyes fixed on the floor between us. 'But he didn't say anything to me. He could have given it to me, to give to you. And how' – now she raised her head – 'how did he know where we were?'

I could have said: Grace told him, Mama. Just as I had told my father that Ezekiel had scared me that day. No. I was no longer that child. Now I found my tongue had shrunk, and it was easy to speak.

'I asked him to come and see me.'

'How did you ask him?'

'I wrote him a letter.'

'You wrote to him?'

'Yes, Mama.'

'How did he get the letter?'

'I gave it to Grace.'

She stood still, the necklace in her hand, the cord dangling from her palm.

'Shall I take Danny out to the swing now, Mama?'

I realised too late that the swing was a reminder of Jonah, of how he had reached up for her, tied the ropes around the branches for her, just as he had slipped the necklace around my neck. It looks beautiful on you. For the necklace was also a miniature echo of what he had made for my mother – the swing – and it was clear even then that he had made it for her – not Danny, nor my father.

'Mama? Shall I—'

'Wait.' Then she said nothing, just stared, not at me, but through me, until I spoke again.

'He's my friend, Mama,' I said.

But she shook her head, suddenly, savagely, her voice full of exasperation. 'I've told you before, Sissy! Grown men don't make friends with young girls!'

'I love him.'

The words fell out of my lips, and by saying them I felt an immense relief; as if my whole being had been tensed and expectant, waiting for me to make this discovery, and now every cell in my body turned to the other and nodded. Ah, *finally*, she understands. My mother stood stock still, her face pale, her eyes dark hollows. Her lips were bleached, nearly white, and I thought how pinched, how colourless she looked when I suddenly felt blazing hot, full of life.

She shook her head. 'You don't.'

'I do.'

'Sissy . . .'

'I do, Mama.'

'You don't, Sissy.' She hesitated. 'You just miss Papa.'

I stared at her, furious. 'Do *you* miss Papa?'

'Yes, of course I do.'

'And does *he* miss *us*?'

She opened her mouth, then closed it.

We fell silent, stared at each other.

'He's my friend,' I repeated.

Her eyes ran over my face. She opened her mouth, closed it. Opened it again, closed it again. Then, finally, she said, her voice barely audible, 'Has he ever touched you?'

I was silent, thinking: you should ask, did Ezekiel?

When she spoke again her voice was louder, almost harsh. 'Has Jonah ever touched you like a man touches a woman?'

I remembered the bare shoulder, I remembered the cook's hip brushing against his and I felt a yearning and a longing; the warmth of his chest as I leant against him on his bicycle, the tips of my fingers brushing against his skin as I lifted the chain from around his throat, his palm briefly lying against my cheek, his fingers extending to the nape of my neck.

'No, Mama,' I whispered, and did not say the words on the tip of my tongue: but I would like him to.

Her body slumped slightly, she stumbled, even though she had not taken a step. 'Mol . . .'

'Mama, he's my friend.'

'No.' She was shaking her head, her voice was now strong, and there was a cold, sad smile on her lips. 'No, Sissy.' She swallowed, held her elbow with one hand so that her forearm crossed her body like a shield. 'You are sweet and clever and you are a loving person. But no, Jonah cannot be your friend. He cannot.' She held out the amulet. 'I'm taking this now, and I will keep it. You don't need it. You don't need its protection. I am here and I will protect you.'

Even then, as she turned away and I balled my fists against my chest in a rage, even then I knew that she could not. And even then I knew that she would not.

Part Five

19

A ND then, only two months after my pilgrimage to Zambia, I received a phone call one evening, and a voice, at once familiar, announced himself as Sanjay Tharoor, the professor who had interviewed me in front of his fire when I was not quite eighteen years old, this now nearly fourteen years ago. It appeared that he had contacted my old supervisor in New York, who had told him of my relocation to Boston. He had waited until he was sure he could see me in person before getting in touch. And now an opportunity had arisen; he was in Boston for a few days to give a lecture.

I've been keeping track of your achievements, he said on the phone. I ordered your book for our library, *The Wild Wind*. I'm very pleased for you, Sissy, you see, I've not forgotten about you. Tell me, did you find anything more about your father?

Well, I began, caught off-guard, and he interrupted.

Forgive me for being so forward, don't answer now. I meant to invite you for dinner and we can speak more then. I have someone visiting with me whom I'd like you to meet as well.

The two months since my return from Douala–Lusaka had been disquieting and strange. The night of my return – after we had made love and were lying on top of the sheets facing each other, my fiancé stroking the small of my back, I had let the tears flow, down my cheeks, onto the pillow. For many minutes he said nothing, until: I think it was the right thing to do, Sissy. Maybe this is a catharsis, you know? Something you need to go through?

It's just – I wiped my nose which was snotty and red – it's just that I feel like it was *me* who lost the baby. Seeing the name like that, I felt it was my *child*, not my *sister*. Isn't that just so weird? Doesn't that sound so self-indulgent?

Well, you all lost something, didn't you? he replied. That's what you're mourning, isn't it? That loss, not a specific person as such.

Should I tell her? I asked, and now I laid my palm on his cheek, feeling his stubble and his warmth, and outlined his lips with my thumb, his beautifully shaped mouth, as he traced my hip bone – each of us caressing a part of our bodies that we cherished. But, as well, I wanted to touch him so he would not think I had forgotten him, or the troubles he had survived, or the fact that I loved him. His face was scratchy and familiar, his eyes looked almost black in the dim light of the bedroom. Your mom? he asked. You don't have to, you know. Or it might be something you talk about when you're feeling a bit stronger.

That other thing, I whispered. Are you sure?

And he had smiled, his fingers massaging the base of my spine: of course I'm sure. I might do a better job second time around.

We had talked about children. As we had always talked about his children, from the very first time we had gone out for a meal together. He had shown me photos in the restaurant itself, of his son playing chess in a competition, of his daughter in a school play, as if laying his cards on the table: this is what you're letting yourself in for. I had worried that the shadows of his children would dog our every move, stare at us from the corner of every restaurant and cinema and park we visited, watch us if we ended up in the bedroom. I had worried that their existence would weigh on him, curb him, inhibit him so that our love-making would feel careful and restrained and respectable: it hadn't. He was an adoring father, guilty about the break-up of his marriage to his children's mother, but he was willing and ready to plunge himself into a new life and a new future – and me. But he was all too aware that he came with a lot of baggage, discounting the fact that I did too.

Your mom is going to hate me, he said. I'm divorced, quite a bit older.

Well, *she's* divorced, I retorted. *She's* on her second marriage.

But you know what I mean, he persisted. One rule for yourself, another for your children. I mean, I wouldn't exactly be over the moon if *my* daughter brought *me* home.

You're wrapping yourself up in a web, I chided. Your kids seem happy with me, which is what counts. You really don't need to worry about my mother.

But he was nervous, that first time. We were engaged by then; high time I introduced him to my family. I took him to meet my mother and stepfather over a weekend when Danny would be home from college as well. He tried far too hard, not doing himself any justice but further endearing himself to me for caring so much.

Really, Laila, he said on shaking my mother's hand, I would never think you were Sissy's mother, you look like her sister. As my stepfather and brother exchanged a look, raised their eyebrows in perfect synchronicity, my mother replied, her tone dangerously noncommittal: well, I can assure you that I am.

But it was only like that at the very beginning. It did not take long for everyone to see how much in love I was, my mother telling me later that it was the happiest moment in her life to see me so sure of myself.

Danny hugged me before he drove back to his college: he's a nice guy, Sissy.

My stepfather held me in a tight embrace, overcome, then shook against me with laughter at the strength of his own emotions: never forget what a lucky man he is.

An all-round success. Neither of us wanted a big wedding; a simple civil service at a date which suited his children's schedules, and close family for lunch after. This the reason he surprised me with a breathtakingly intricate and elegant antique ring for our engagement – because you're missing out on all the other stuff – ignoring my protests that I would never have wanted an ostentatious ceremony anyway.

And then the trip back to Lusaka. From riding the crest of happiness, of looking forward, to scraping the detritus of the past, of days spent as if I had only recently suffered a bereavement. I called in sick for two days, something I had never done, ever, before. And just when I was emerging from the fog, another hand clawing at me, to take me back: the phone call from Professor Tharoor.

He met me outside the restaurant downtown, on the street, greyer-haired, heavier, but otherwise not much changed, and surprised me by taking my hand in both of his and kissing me on both cheeks, as if we were old friends.

Mol, uttered with great warmth and profoundly comforting. Then he repeated, forgive me, but really you don't know how pleased I am to see you again. I was so disappointed you didn't come to Haverford.

I ended up going to Penn State, and doing Italian Studies instead, I laughed.

Oh, I know, he replied. Like I said, I bought your book and enjoyed reading it very much. He looked me over, beaming. Really, I'm so pleased to see you again and you are looking so well. My friend is just waiting at the table, he said as he ushered me into the restaurant, and a man rose as we approached, late thirties I guessed, with brushed-back hair, of medium height and with strong shoulders.

I held out my hand and he took it, laughing: Sissy, it's nice to see you again.

And I couldn't help but gasp. Rahul!

Professor Tharoor was laughing as well. Forgive me, he said for the third time. I wanted it to be a surprise.

But how . . . ?

Rahul is a visiting researcher in the medical department, but a colleague found out he was a Keralite so introduced me. When he mentioned he had grown up in Zambia, I mentioned you and then, there you are!

Rahul was still holding my hand, and Professor Tharoor exclaimed: Irikku, irikku, mol! Let her sit down and recover herself, Rahul.

He switched back and forth from English to Malayalam, as he would continue to do all through the evening, and it was with surprise that I found I could still understand.

You know, the professor continued as we took our places, there is a big Keralite association here in Boston. Just tell me if you would like me to introduce you to some people. Then, noticing my hesitation, he waved his hands: of course, no matter.

He had booked a table by the window, and depending on how the light fell from the passing traffic, the reflection the glass threw back at us was either unclear or distinct. I found my eyes meeting my own in the window, often: my figure between the two men, their bodies turned to me so I was at the apex of a triangle, commanding their attention. It was an unusual experience in my life as it had become: to be one of a trio of Indians, and Malayalees, in particular.

We ordered, and as I was returning the menu to the waiter, Rahul pointed: a nice ring. I felt myself blushing.

Excellent, excellent, Sissy! from Professor Tharoor, who seemed determined to see anything I had done as an achievement of great merit.

And what does he do for a living? Rahul asked, with mock seriousness.

He's an engineer, I said, blushing further even deeper for some reason. Not a Malayalee, I added quickly.

No matter, no matter – the professor was waving my bashfulness away.

And are you married, Rahul? I asked.

He nodded. We live in Bangalore, he said, and reaching into his breast pocket he withdrew a wallet and extracted a photograph.

His wife was very attractive, with a chic haircut; she was holding a child in each hand, a boy and a girl. Rahul stood behind her, his arm around her shoulder.

You have a beautiful family.

He shrugged, but I could see he was pleased.

And have you been in Bangalore long?

For about ten years. Padma, my wife, works for the Bank of India.

And your parents?

Enjoying their retirement.

That's wonderful, I replied, remembering how his mother had rescinded the help her son could have offered my mother.

And how is your family, Professor?

Sanjay, Sanjay, please, mol. Oh fine. All grown up now.

Our food arrived and the professor fussed over us, replenishing our drinks, ordering a jug of water for the table, before returning to talk of my thesis.

You know, Sissy, he said, when I read your book, I was struck by a similar experience we share. Let me explain. When I was in fourth standard, in Kottayam where I grew up, we had to memorise a poem for a recital. It was an annual event but in those days often the school would choose Kipling or Yeats, or even a sonnet from Shakespeare. It was rare for a teacher to choose a poem in Malayalam, but my teacher did. She introduced us to Kumaran Asan. Do you know him?

We both shook our heads.

Anyway, he was a contemporary of Joyce, and he wrote the poem 'Veena Poovu'. Do you understand what that means?

And I replied tentatively, the flower fell?

The Fallen Flower, yes, excellent, Sissy. He was chuckling with delight. You see, if you go back home, your Malayalam, chaadi varum!

We all laughed, and he took a sip from his glass of wine before continuing.

Forty stanzas. Quite long for a kid to remember, but do you know I so enjoyed learning something in Malayalam, finding out about the rich literary tapestry of Kerala. But more than that, I enjoyed learning about the fellow himself. He was a revolutionary in his own right, because he swerved away from the well trodden route of religious poetry. He chose a very secular tone, with a recurring theme of our inherent humane-ness, irrespective of our origins. Which family we were born into, which religion. Exploring his words, I felt a real buzz, you know? It's my first memory of thinking that maybe that was what I wanted to do with my life. Breathe and talk and read and write about literature. And then when I read your book, I felt so affected by the narrative you wrote at the begin-ning, about why you were drawn to James Joyce.

He turned to Rahul: I will stop talking, don't worry.

Rahul waved his fork in assurance, even though he must have been bewildered.

Professor Tharoor turned back to me: you wrote about why Joyce had written the poem, didn't you? Wait a moment, I actually copied it all down.

He reached inside his jacket pocket and took out a folded sheet of paper.

Sanjay . . . I began, embarrassed, but he interrupted.

No, really, mol, let me. Like I said, I was so impressed.

Then he started reading my words out, so I could hear what I had written, coming from his lips, in his voice.

Joyce penned the two stanzas soon after watching his brother Stanislaus compete in a boat race in the city of Trieste, then still part of the Austro-Hungarian Empire. It is a beautiful late summer's day. The boatmen, on nearing the shore, start singing an aria from Puccini's 'La Faniculla del West' in which Dick Johnson, about to be executed for his crimes, wishes that his lover Minnie think that he was freed and never learn of his actual fate. The rowers' voices ring out with the optimism and passion of youth. The poet watches the young rowers, no longer young, but older and wiser. The refrain, 'return no more', can thus be interpreted as a lament for lost youth, And from his position of wisdom, with his experience of life, Joyce believes that the rowers' celebration of love is in vain: for love passes like the wind through prairie grasses, gone in a whisper, never to return. The poem is hence, as well, a lament for lost love.

He refolded the piece of paper – Rahul now staring – and shook his head as if in awe of my talent.

You wrote about how you felt that the poet was speaking to you, and about how you were reminded of the boat races your father took you to. Really, it was very touching, mol.

I said nothing, and he patted my hand.

But you know, he continued, Kumaran Asan was also so fond of those boat races! Unfortunately, that was also how he died! One of the boats capsized on the lake one year, I think in the early twenties, and nearly everyone drowned. When I read your words, for some reason, all these connections came back to me. I felt I had to see you again and tell you this about the boat races, how the lake swallowed up one of Kerala's finest poets.

He smiled, and then grinned at Rahul: eda, now she's all yours.

But Rahul was not talkative. He only asked about Danny, and followed my résumé with: I remember the night he was born. And then he smiled at me, and I remembered in turn his hands in my hair, long at that time, down to my waist, brushing it out and helping me plait it, helping me pack a snack and my bag for school. But now the years that had stretched between us seemed condensed. He would be, I calculated, about seven years younger than my fiancé, and he did not feel so much ahead of me in age or life. By the time we reached dessert – the professor insisted I choose something – I had shared my story of my sojourn in Delhi, of the failure to find any more information of my father, and the professor hummed unhappily – so difficult for you – but I did not tell of my recent return to Zambia and the ghosts I had unearthed. I was not ready for that. Rahul, it appeared, was involved with research into antiviral drugs and AIDS, was a frequent visitor back to Africa, had not long ago been to South Africa and Kenya, although not yet Zambia; that trip was in the offing. He was planning to travel to Philadelphia as well, and I mentioned that my mother and stepfather lived nearby. That's nice Aunty remarried, he said, and this comment made me remember his words, that last day: it's nice for Aunty to have some company.

The professor excused himself to use the washroom, and Rahul turned to me: you look wonderful, you know.

I fanned my fingers in front of my face. You're kidding, right?

It's not as bad as you might think it is, he said quietly. You still look lovely, Sissy – narrowing his eyes – as I'm sure your fiancé keeps telling you. Or at least, he *should* be telling you.

I grinned. You were my favourite out of all the boys, you know.

And you were my favourite girl.

I was the *only* girl!

No, you weren't. There was Reeba, remember?

Did you ever go out with her?

He shook his head: she didn't want anything to do with me.

And I laughed; charmed by him, warmed by this reminder of how much I had liked him, trusted him, and immensely moved by the thought that he had known me as a young girl.

Tell me about the others, I said. How's Aravind?

Oh, doing brilliantly, the bastard, he replied. He's in Australia. Benjy and I keep in touch with each other regularly. He's still in Zambia. He's a consultant oncologist at the hospital in Lusaka.

I was silent, thinking that if I had known I might have tried to see him on my visit, that afternoon when I had stared at that list of names. Rahul was watching me, and I tried to smile, took a sip from my drink. And Bobby?

He hesitated: Bobby died, Sissy.

His voice lowered, and he looked down at the table for some moments before speaking again.

He did so well, he became a journalist, based in Johannesburg. He reported on the first democratic elections in South Africa and he covered the Rugby World Cup for the BBC. He was working on a longer report, on the lack of new housing in the former townships. He loved it. It was his dream job, you know?

I nodded, and he continued: he was in bed in his flat in the city, when he was shot by an intruder.

The words passed through me like a chill breath, and I must have grown pale, because he touched my hand briefly. I saw the professor returning from the washroom, and then thankfully being called to the desk to take a phone call. We waited together, as a series of images played out before me: Bobby with Aravind, Bobby giving me the small wooden box and, inevitably, that afternoon, the cricket ball bruising my not-yet breast and his words sowing an iniquitous seed.

I turned to Rahul: the same kind eyes, in an older face.

Do you remember the story of the plane? I asked him. And the raid?

Of course.

I didn't really get any of it when it happened. I've read about it all since . . .

Well, you were young then.

So many people died, were hurt, Rahul. Why did nothing happen to us then?

He raised his eyebrows, gave a small smile. It wasn't our time, I guess.

I said nothing, and he took my hand.

It's so nice to see you like this, looking so well – he ignored me as I rolled my eyes – hearing of your career – and then he pressed the ring on my finger – your engagement. Everyone was so upset when we heard what happened.

Again I did not say anything.

And you haven't seen your father? he asked gently. All these years?

I shook my head, withdrew my hand, pushed my plate away.

I went back, Rahul, I said. Just a few weeks ago. I went to Roma, just for a day. Can you imagine? I flew in from Cameroon where I had some work. I kept expecting to see someone I recognised or someone who recognised me. But I didn't. The school has changed so much as well . . .

He was quiet.

You remember Moses, who used to work for you?

He nodded.

Did you know his last name?

He nodded again. Phiri.

I was speaking slowly, but the words were coming from my lips with ease, even though I had never said them before. Do you know I never knew anyone's last name? Grace, Ezekiel – I paused, stilling my heart – Jonah . . .

He said nothing, only kept watching me.

So, it feels right somehow, you know, that I lost my own last name. Olikara. I deserved it, because I never knew theirs.

Deserved it?

239

He made a face.

Sissy, you were really young, only a girl, that's why. At that age, you depend on your parents to tell you these things.

I didn't tell him that I suspected my mother, if not my father, was similarly ignorant. I asked: have you kept in touch with anyone else?

He knew what I meant without asking.

I met two Zambian guys I went to school with in Nairobi. They're also involved with the AIDS project.

From Kabulonga High?

He nodded. You see, I was nearly nineteen when I left. You were so much younger, Sissy. Which was a pity.

He took my hand again to lie between both of his, rolled my engagement ring between his fingers, cocked an eyebrow. But there was, despite the condensed ages, so much more and so many people now between us. Then he smiled, and I managed to smile back, before he continued, his face now serious: don't be too hard on yourself.

Why so sad-looking? The professor had returned. Don't make her sad, Rahul, keto? This is a celebration, a reunion!

And when, later, he offered to call me a cab, and I told him there would be no need, my fiancé was picking me up, he repeated: excellent, excellent.

20

I T was the following morning – Tembe driving the pick-up, my mother sitting beside him with Danny on her lap – that I said to her, 'The headmistress wants to see you, Mama. I forgot to tell you the other day.'

She nodded, did not reply. That morning, she had announced that she would accompany me on the school drop-off. She had hoped to leave Danny at home with Grace for she planned to meet up with Mr Cooper at his office. But, for the first morning all of us could recall, Grace did not arrive as expected. The granny flat, too, was empty. This circumstance left us uneasy, so out of character was her absence, even though Mr Cooper tried to brush it off before he left in his blue car, assuring us that she would turn up with a good explanation.

As I made my way to my classroom, I watched my mother walk down the path to the headmistress's office. She was dressed in one of the cotton saris she wore for teaching, her hair in a single plait, suddenly reminding me of the mother who had for years left the small pink bungalow, lab coat folded and tucked into her basket, my father at her side, to open the laboratory and teach chemistry to rows and rows of navy girls.

I kept one eye on the classroom window, gaining a reprimand – Sissy, pay attention! – and saw my mother walking back to the pick-up, against which Tembe was leaning. She looked no different, but an audience with the headmistress was rare. I could only imagine the conversation. My husband has left me, Sister Catherine, and my twelve-year-old daughter professes that she is in love: perhaps you could say an extra rosary this evening as an offering to halt the decline of this family? Or had she been more prosaic: no, Sister Catherine, no need to enrol Sissy into any school. She will be returning to India for her studies, as we will all be leaving Zambia to resume the lives we should have had before we left. I carried on, in my imagination: my son needs a father, my mother was saying, standing erect and proud, and pulling her sari palloo dramatically over her breasts. My daughter is lost, but my son can be redeemed.

'Sissy!'

My teacher had lost her patience, which she rarely did, and I hurriedly returned to my books, my friends tittering behind their hands.

At lunchtime, my mother again, in the pick-up, with Danny; she scanned the crowd of parents retrieving their children. Perhaps she was making sure that Jonah had not arrived to ply me with more gifts. Back at the Coopers' house, there was still no sign of Grace. My mother on the phone: hello, Sam. No, she's not here. I'll make something simple for tonight, there's still lots in the fridge. The conversation sounded cosy and domestic, my mother speaking easily. She hung up, did not pick up the phone again and dial the number in India, which I knew she had already tried several times already: other things to worry about. After lunch, she swept the kitchen and hall while I emptied the washing machine to hang the clothes in the backyard. It had become hot and sticky, mosquitoes abounded. There was talk that the rains were late and that when they arrived they would be heavy. Indeed, the weather seemed to match my feeling of foreboding: Grace disappeared, Ezekiel banished, Jonah removed, my father fading away. I slapped at my shins and remembered how my father had gripped my foot on that last encounter. But concurrently, I could feel Jonah's hand gripping my ankle, even though he never had, had he? I wiped my forehead and rested for a moment. The dizziness passed, and I walked back into the house with the empty laundry basket.

My mother and I avoided each other, and Mr Cooper seemed to sense the awkwardness. His joviality at dinner was a reminder of his earlier attempts with Mrs Cooper and Ally and Mary-Anne, so I began to feel uncomfortable, dining with their father. I asked to leave the table and I saw my mother watching me as I made my way back to the bedroom – my bedroom now. I heard her checking on Danny, and then she knocked on my door, leant against the doorway. 'Reading?'

'Yes.'

'Have an early night, okay? You slept late yesterday.'

'Okay.'

She hesitated. 'Good night, mol.'

'Good night, Mama.'

I didn't ask about the meeting with the headmistress and she did not mention it. We both knew larger things were percolating.

The next morning Danny mewled in the car, wriggling furiously on my mother's lap as Tembe drove me to school, and I felt a malicious pleasure at seeing him grab roughly at the neckline of her sari blouse – stop that, mon! Tembe jiggling a bunch of keys to distract him. Good work, Danny, I thought, climbing down from the pick-up and seeing in the distance the headmistress pausing on her way to her office to watch as it drove away, Danny now pulling at my mother's hair. But by the time I returned from school, I only felt sorry for my mother, who looked harassed, standing behind the ironing board, Danny whining on the floor beneath her. I was going to offer to make her a cup of tea when the phone rang. Mr Cooper, telling my mother that he would be bringing a Chinese takeaway home. He did not wish her to feel obliged to cook every night. She placed the phone back in its cradle. Danny was still grizzling, his fingers in his mouth.

'He's been like this all day. Maybe . . .' But she didn't complete her sentence.

I said, 'I'll finish the ironing, Mama.'

She looked up with surprise. 'Are you sure? I've done most of it . . .'

'I can do the rest.'

She smiled. 'Okay, thanks, mol. I think I'll wash my hair.'

Then she waited as if expecting a rejoinder – and the deal is that you give me back my necklace. But when I picked up the iron, she turned away, not quite hiding her relief. She left the room and I could hear the water running in the bathroom; now she was humming a song under her breath. She appeared later, fresh-skinned and sweet-smelling, with her hair damp and loose around her shoulders, in her sleeveless light green kurta and navy stirrup pants, patting at her head with a towel. 'That's better. Why don't you also have a wash, mol?'

I bathed, and was putting on my second-favourite pair of dungarees just as Mr Cooper drove up. I watched through the window as he got out of the car, brown paper bags in his arms, and then turned to watch as another car drove up: Mr Lawrence. I could hear them greet each other, then Mr Cooper – of course you can, Charlie – slapping him on the shoulder. It appeared that Mr Lawrence was at a loose end and would be staying for dinner.

The Chinese food inspired the men to become nostalgic, reminisce about their favourite take-outs from their hometowns, while they showed off their skill with their chopsticks. My mother and I had pleaded off being tutored and were allowed forks. With Danny now tucked away for the night, we made a cosy foursome at the table, and as Mr Lawrence spooned rice and noodles from the boxes onto our plates, Mr Cooper peeled the foil cap off a bottle of wine and twisted the opener into its mouth.

'Fee's gone to Victoria Falls to visit some friends who are out there working or something,' Mr Lawrence was saying.

'She didn't ask you to join her?' My mother was grinning, fluttering her eyelashes.

'Go easy on him, Laila,' Mr Cooper drawled as he pulled the cork out. 'He's just a kid.'

'Hey!'

'Although,' Mr Cooper continued, ignoring Mr Lawrence but smiling and crinkling his eyes at my mother, 'you're a spring chicken yourself, I believe.'

My mother laughed then asked, 'Can I ask how old you are, Sam?'

'You can. Forty-two.'

'And Cindy?'

'Forty-one.'

'George is forty-one.'

She spoke almost to herself, and I was not sure the men had heard. It was the first time she had mentioned my father's name in my hearing for many weeks, and as if she had evoked a charm, I had a sense that my father was behind me, his breath whispering against the back of my neck. I turned around, but saw the window was open, a breeze wafting into the room.

'Girlfriend I had in college?' Mr Cooper was saying, 'Went to *Guatemala* without telling me. Ended up hooking up with some Che Guevara lookalike . . .'

Mr Lawrence was looking sheepish and annoyed at the same time. 'I don't really mind her going . . .'

But my mother and Mr Cooper were laughing now, catching one another's eyes, and I realised that they were enjoying their shared roles. Here's to two abandoned spouses.

'Okay, okay. Well, Sissy,' Mr Lawrence turned to me, 'we'll just let them have their fun. Why don't you tell me what you've been up to?'

And as I opened my mouth, I saw my mother's expression falter, and I felt a stab of anger. Mr Lawrence, I am in love, and my mother has confiscated the necklace given to me by the object of my affections.

But I said, 'Just school and things, Mr Lawrence.'

'Well, at the weekend shall I take you swimming again someplace?' He turned to my mother. 'May I, Laila?'

'That would be nice, Charlie.'

'And you should come too. Remember, I've heard of your legendary prowess.'

'Really?' Mr Cooper looked piqued at this revelation. 'You've never . . .' he broke off.

My mother turned to him, smiling and nodding. 'Yes, it's true. I used to swim in the river near where I grew up, and the lake too. Like a fish.'

'Really?' he repeated.

But my mother did not elaborate, only fell silent. The mention of the water, the mention of my father's name, had made her pensive. Perhaps she was thinking of her childhood home, her child self, her band of brothers, the birds, the trees, and the water, warm as a bath. And the image flitted through my head of my father tossing my mother into the air, of their laughter, of my mother's wet, half-naked body wrapped around me. Perhaps she was thinking of the same, for I found that she was looking at me, her eyes solemn, a small smile playing on her lips; and then she looked away, picked at the food on her plate. We were all quiet, and then my mother put down her cutlery, laid her palm against her cheek, her elbow on the table. 'How did you and Cindy meet, Sam?'

Mr Cooper glanced at her, finished chewing his mouthful. 'I was working as a community organiser, and we brought her in one day as legal counsel.'

'And where do you live, in the States?'

'Roanoke, Virginia.' He wiped his mouth with a napkin, then picked up another piece of food. 'We knew I'd always be moving around, working on development projects. Ally was a baby, and it made sense to move back to Virginia so we could be near Cindy's family. Then she got the job at the college.' He smiled ruefully. 'When the girls were really little we went to Mexico for a year, and that was great. But it was before Cin got tenure, and the girls were more adaptable, I guess, at that age.' He raised his glass, frowned at the wine, and toasted himself. 'It was a disaster bringing them out here.'

My mother tutted, but Mr Lawrence only reached for more food from one of the boxes. No one asked the question, but as if she were returning the favour, my mother started speaking, not looking at anyone, her eyes on her bangles.

'My parents couldn't afford to send me to university, but my father's employer paid for my fees. I had finished my final exams and when I arrived back at my home with my suitcase, I saw we had a visitor.'

Both men were now watching her, listening, their chop-sticks in mid-air.

'My father had placed a matrimonial notice for me in a newspaper without telling me. It must have been very expensive to do that. Maybe his employer paid for that as well. I arrived home and there was this man sitting with my father. Very handsome, very clever.' She smiled now, glancing at me briefly before returning her gaze to her bangles. 'I was twenty-one when we married and then Sissy arrived nine months later.' She flushed before continuing: 'Then soon after we heard about the jobs in Roma.'

Now she looked up, her eyes darting around the table, at both men, 'I wonder who George would have married if he hadn't found me suitable.'

There was a silence, into which my mother gave a self-conscious laugh.

'Well, there was never any danger of that,' this from Mr Lawrence.

'I don't mean that,' my mother said, with a shake of her head. 'You see, I was very young—'

Mr Lawrence interrupted: 'You're still very young.'

She shook her head again, almost impatiently, and then pushed her chair back, her plate forgotten now, placed her forearms on the table, the bangles at her wrists tinkling, her hair framing her face and falling down to her chest. Her collarbones shone, and her bare arms and shoulders gleamed. She looked beautiful and knowledgeable of the power she wielded, my mother, sitting at this table with the two men on either side of her riveted by her words, to her.

'What I mean is, George came from a very educated family. His father was an advocate and worked at the high courts. His mother was a doctor, one of the first female doctors of her generation. They had both passed away by the time we got married, but his older brothers felt that George should have married someone from a better family. Someone who was better educated, more polished . . .'

Both men now made a sound of rebuttal, but she waved them away.

'But he married me. I think he treated it like an adoption.' She laughed, and now her eyes sparkled with sudden tears. 'He wanted to improve my life, improve *me*. He didn't ask for a dowry, he said my degree was my dowry. And he taught me so much. About politics and history. I knew nothing of the Mughals, for example, the Communists or of the kingdoms that became Kerala. He taught me about the world.'

It was only then that I realised my mother was speaking as if about a faded past, as if she knew then that she would not see my father again. I glanced at Mr Cooper, who had laid his chopsticks down and had leant back a little as if to better regard my mother. Mr Lawrence was chewing his food thoughtfully, and as I glanced at him he looked up and caught my eye, gave me a small smile. Then he cleared his throat. 'I think I might try out one of those – what did you call it, Laila, a matrimonial notice? How should I describe myself?'

'Very handsome, very clever,' said Mr Cooper, folding his arms, and we all laughed as he grinned, still leaning back in his chair, still regarding my mother.

'Adventurous,' my mother continued, smiling, and swiped at her eyes with the heel of her hand, 'and generous . . .'

'Well, I'm flattered.' Mr Lawrence bowed. Then, 'Your turn, Sissy.'

'Um. Kind and honest.'

'Don't overdo it, honey,' said Mr Cooper.

'Why, thank you, Sissy,' Mr Lawrence said at the same time, and we all laughed again.

Then Mr Lawrence turned to Mr Cooper. 'Maybe I should head off to India, Sam. Leave a message for Fee for when she gets back?'

'Gone fishin',' was Mr Cooper's lazy response.

They were bantering with each other now, the two men, so that my mother and I were suddenly on the periphery, and we took this opportunity to look at each other. I felt as if my mother had retold the story that I had heard many times before, deliberately, in a different way, one that I was now old enough to hear. We gazed at each other and I remembered her words on my birthday – I wanted more for you, mol – and while part of my heart still burned at the thought of my confiscated necklace, the other part was filled with a love for my mother, and an ache at the thought of the young woman returning with her suitcase from college. Then she broke our gaze, murmured, 'I'll just check on Danny,' while the men carried on, until Mr Lawrence turned to me. 'So, shall we say Saturday, Sissy? Do we have a swimming date?'

'Thank you, Mr Lawrence,' I said as my mother re-entered the room, and her step was so silent that, conversely, we all turned to look at her. Her lips were parted, her eyes glazed, and her face was ashen. Mr Cooper half-rose in his chair. 'Laila, what is it?'

She dropped into her seat and laid something on the table. 'I found this under the bed. Under Danny's side.'

It was a twist of materials, ring-shaped, made of twigs, giving off a strong smell as if from a scented bark. Interspersed in the mass were scraps of paper, seeds, some dried berries and human hair entwined amongst the wood: different colours of hair. Long blonde strands, like the Cooper girls had, and the wavy black strands that my mother and I shared. We all fell silent, staring at the centrepiece. I raised my eyes and looked at my mother, but she did not meet mine, did not return my gaze. Her eyes were transfixed on the object she had laid down.

Mr Cooper broke the silence. Scraping his chair back, he stood up and moved to the side cabinet. He waved the bottle at my mother, who shook her head, and then to Mr Lawrence, who gave a small nod. We listened to the sound of the liquid being poured, the glass being pushed across the table.

Then Mr Lawrence spoke. 'It looks benign,' he began and glanced at me, then back to my mother, but she said nothing. 'I mean,' Mr Lawrence continued, his voice gentle, 'it looks maternal, doesn't it? A little nest, for a mother bird to look after her eggs, you know? The other stuff,' he picked at the strands of hair, 'all this, it might not mean much. This is for protection, isn't it?'

'But why?' My mother's voice was even, her words were clipped. Not her teaching voice, another voice she used with these men. 'Why would Grace think that my son needs protection?'

Mr Cooper lowered his glass. 'We don't know that it hasn't been there a while, Laila. She could have put it there when Ally was sleeping in the bed—'

But my mother swatted his words away, biting her lip. 'No,' she whispered. 'No. Grace knows.' And then she looked up at me and her eyes were my eyes, and as if the nest had the facility to transport me into my mother's body, I felt that gnawing, aching sadness that she must have had lodged inside her, so real that I made a sound – a gasp or a rasp – and she said quickly, in Malayalam, 'Manassilakunnuthe?' Do you understand?

I nodded.

The silence was heavy and the two men watched us, not asking for a translation, and while Mr Cooper's eyes were fixed on my mother, Mr Lawrence turned his from my mother to me, from me to her.

'There was another child,' my mother suddenly said. 'A baby girl.'

Both men were quiet, their hands unmoving on the table, watching as tears gathered in my mother's eyes, spilled out and ran down her cheeks, fell off her chin and onto the table.

'She died inside me, and we lost her,' she whispered, and perhaps it was the use of the word 'we', a reminder of my father, but she stopped speaking, pressed her lips together.

Mr Cooper reached forward, and I thought he would take her hand, but he grasped her upper arm, his fingers almost inside her armpit, his thumb pressing into her flesh, and I looked away, to see Mr Lawrence watching me. I stared at the table, for a long time, then back up, at the nest, and in the corner of my eye I could see Mr Cooper release my mother's arm. Then she was standing up, her face flushed, her hands smoothing down her kurta. Come, Sissy, help me clear the plates. The men stood up as well, and we all took the crockery and glasses into the kitchen.

And later I heard him speaking to Mr Lawrence by the gate, where the younger man stood in a half-slouch, looking uncomfortable, his car door open, and one foot inside the vehicle. But he was still talking, even though it was clear that Mr Lawrence wanted to leave. His voice carried up the path and into my window: it's a mess, Charlie. The whole thing is a goddamn fucking mess.

21

THE talk from town was that there would be other strikes, other raids, more retribution for the fallen bird of a plane – an eye for an eye, a tooth for a tooth – but not necessarily in Lusaka. The curfew had not been reinstated because few believed that the Rhodesians would target Nkomo's camp and risk such a deep infiltration into a country's airspace again. Indeed, reports had been heard of a similar raid on a camp in Mozambique a few days ago, where Mugabe's men were stationed. The Rhodesians were flailing, lashing out without discernment at any perceived threat.

My latest purveyor of news was not a circle of Malayalees, or a group of Americans, but Tembe, who drove me to school without my mother's guardianship the following morning. Danny was out of sorts, and she was worried he would be sick in the car. While Tembe apprised me of the developments in the world around us, I tried to dim the hope that was blossoming in my heart. Today, the day that mother was not my gatekeeper, today Jonah would come to meet me at school. I was willing to brazen out the curious stares from my peers and the coterie of nuns and teachers. I was willing to risk my mother learning of a clandestine encounter. I was willing to lie and reprise my skill as teller of tales to explain or disguise what would be the only thing I wished for. But when I arrived at the school gates, there was no sign of him, and at the end of the school day Tembe arrived, alone, in the pick-up. No one stepped out from a group calling, Sissy, how are you? There was no sign of Jonah.

'For you, from your mother,' Tembe said as he passed me a note. I looked up at him, and he said, 'Don't worry, I don't think it's serious.' His words were echoed in the message my mother had written: *We are taking Danny to the hospital. I don't think it's anything serious so don't worry. But I want him to have a check-up. I will phone you later.* She did not sign off 'love, Mama', 'yours, Mama', or even just 'Mama' – we were unused to writing to each other. I stared at the word 'we'. But while I contemplated her use of this pronoun, I also felt a deep misgiving slide into me, alongside a vision of the bark and matted hair lying on the dining table just the evening before, and the thought of how it had idled below my brother as he slept, without any of us knowing, whispering into his ear at night. 'Will you be all right?' Tembe asked before speeding off.

I walked around the house to enter through the back door for which, since Grace's disappearance, I had a key, and stepped into a kitchen and a house which was empty and quiet. There was the faint aroma of pine-scented cleaning fluid; my mother must have washed the floors. I ate a biscuit while standing by the window, not bothering with a plate, then brushed up the crumbs guiltily. It was hot; my head hurt. I touched my forehead and was surprised to find it sticky. I went back to my room and threw my satchel on the floor, pulled off my uniform and slipped into the striped T-shirt and blue shorts outfit that had become my go-to daywear. Then I knelt on the floor and looked under the bed, wondering as I did so if my mother had done the same earlier in the day. It was empty, save for a small ball of fluff which I did not remove, as if it were a talisman of good fortune.

I was about to lie on the bed and open my book when I found myself leaving the room, my feet pulling me forward as if by a magnetic field, through to Ally's old room where my mother and Danny now slept. The bed was made, with the blanket that covered Danny at night placed on top of the bedcover. It was larger than a single bed, probably a queen-size, but my mother was clearly worried about him falling off when she was not in it with him, and she had pushed the bed up against the wall, and arranged some cushions to pen him in.

I opened the wardrobe and saw a row of empty hangers, next to the few which held my mother's nightdresses, and two kurtas. A pile of saris lay neatly folded at the bottom. I opened the top drawer of the chest and saw my mother's sari blouses and underwear, a collection of hair slides in a bag. The next drawer was empty, save for her hairbrush and face creams; she seemed not to want to display her toiletries on the top of the chest. I looked around the room and saw the suitcase we had arrived with, pushed under a chair. In the inside zipped compartment, alongside some documents in an envelope – our passports and what looked like a contract of employment – I found, stuffed into a corner, the leather cord holding the tiny wooden hand.

I drew it out, pressed it to my mouth, where it slid like silk over my lips. I let my teeth bite on the leather cord, and then watched as the teeth marks slowly faded away as if I had written a message in the sand that would survive only a finite amount of time before being washed away by the sea. Then I looked at the amulet, lying in my palm, for an age, as time swirled around me, taking me forward, to womanhood when I could stand opposite Jonah not as a child. I was wearing one of my mother's saris, my midriff and navel discernible through the thin material, a cleft where my spine dissected my back, a waist that spanned out into a hip, and my hair falling down my shoulder.

The phone rang in the other room, and I jumped to my feet, catching sight of my face – childish, abashed – in the mirror on top of the chest of drawers. I quickly stuffed the necklace back into its pocket, zipped the compartment, pushed the suitcase back under the chair, and hurried to the hall, where one of the handsets lay on a small table. I picked it up, held it to my ear, ready with a suitable lie for my mother to explain my delay in answering – I was outside, I was just clearing up in the kitchen, I was in the bathroom – but a burst of music greeted me. A horn, a crescendo of notes, the plucking of a sitar, and in the background the percussive beat of a tabla. Papa? I whispered, then cleared my throat so that I could speak louder. Papa? I repeated.

The music continued, a high-pitched woman's voice arrived, and the notes behind her voice soared upward.

'Papa?' And then the music disappeared, to be replaced by the dialling tone.

My hand was trembling, and I held the phone to my ear for many minutes, expecting the burr to be replaced by a song again, expecting the door of the house to be opened and someone tall and dark to walk inside. My throat felt dry and my head swam. The hollow of my neck was damp when I placed the receiver in its holder and touched my throat.

And then the phone rang again. I was standing so close to it and the ring was so shrill I knocked over the table in fright, then clutched at the handset again.

'Sissy?'

My mother.

When I did not reply, she repeated: 'Sissy?'

'Mama.'

'We're leaving the hospital soon. The doctor thinks it's just indigestion.'

'Oh, good,' I whispered.

'Could you bring the washing inside from the line? They're predicting a storm. And look in the freezer. There's some soup we can have for dinner. Can you take it out to defrost?'

'Yes, Mama.'

'We'll be back soon.'

I put the phone down and went outside, desperate suddenly for fresh air, and it was as if the landscape had changed as much as I had in those few minutes that had elapsed. The sky was covered in grey clouds, the light was in turns honeyed and harsh, and there was a wind: a swirling unquiet wind. It blew hot and damp. Not a pleasant breeze, but one that lifted the clothes we wore to expose our frail blemished bodies. Stirred the people buried in the ground so that they turned over from one side to the other, fingers splayed against their coffins. I shook the macabre vision from my head and struggled to bring the clothes back into the house. My mother's sari kept whipping around me, clothing me like a shroud, as if readying me for burial, returning my thoughts to the images I was trying to discard, as if the wind was indeed ushering me to my death. After it had insistently wrapped itself around me several times, I decided to walk back to the kitchen door as I was, to unravel myself inside the house. But as I neared the door, which I could make out through the thin material, I saw another figure enter my vision. Tall and dark, and then a hand reached towards me and I screamed.

'Sissy? It's me.'

His voice had started with amusement, but then became concerned when he realised that I was paralysed with fear. He patted me down, trying to find the end of the sari which clung to me, my nose, my chin, and lifted it off me with a tug.

'Jonah.'

He was smiling now, folding the sari under his arm, and then he asked, 'Are you all right?'

I was embarrassed. I must have been a spectacle, wrapped in my mother's cream-coloured sari like a ghost, and then squealing like a piglet. 'I'm fine.'

'Are you sure? You look . . .' He reached forward and touched my forehead with the back of his hand.

'I'm fine.'

He nodded, but his eyes remained concerned.

'Did you come to see me, Jonah?'

'Of course.' He smiled. 'How is school?'

I hesitated. 'It's fine.'

'What did you learn today?'

'I had to write an essay . . .' He waited. 'And we had geography today as well.'

'That's good. And how is your mother?' He glanced towards the house.

'She's not here.'

'I see,' then he patted the bag he had over his shoulder. 'I also came to collect some things for Grace.'

'Grace?'

He shook his head, was quiet for a few moments. 'It is not right, what she did, Sissy. To just leave without telling. But she asked me to help and she has helped me so much, so I must.' He gestured to her lodgings. 'She wants me to bring back some things.'

'Is she well, Jonah?'

'I think not, Sissy,' he said gravely. 'Her body is well. But here,' he placed his hand on his heart, then his head, 'and here, not so well.'

We were both silent, as if paying our respects to the small woman who had helped us both and who had a heart so large and strong it was easy to forget that she could feel pain and falter and ache. Then he said, 'I will just leave this,' gesturing to my mother's sari. I watched as he walked into the kitchen and placed the sari in a heap on the table, then came out and moved to Grace's annex, to open the door.

'She left something under one of the beds,' I said, following him. But I did not continue because there was an odour in the small building: two rooms, a bed with a stove to one side, a bathroom to the other side. The stench was at odds with the quaint prettiness of the room — with the pastel-coloured quilt, the floral curtains on the large windows — and it was strong. Stale, foreign, something living and dead at the same time, and

I wondered if I was imagining it, if it was an extension of the images of coffins and corpses. But Jonah was opening all the windows, and had left the door wide open, as if he had taken note of it too. He moved quickly, picking objects and throwing them into the bag, collecting a pile of folded chitenges from the small trunk in the corner. I wanted to put my hand over my mouth to stop the poisonous air from entering my nostrils, entering me, but I was worried that it would appear rude, and so I stepped further into the room.

'She left something,' I repeated, and Jonah turned to look at me. And then I felt his gaze wash over me, lift my feet, so I was lying horizontal in the air, and above me was my father's face, his features blurred as if disintegrating, staring at me, and I was saying, turn it down, turn the music down, it's too loud, but he took one of his hands and placed it on my stomach and pressed, until it felt like his whole weight was pressing me down, to stop me from floating up into the sky. But it was not my father's hand, I realised, that was trying to tether me to the earth. It was someone else's.

'Sissy?'

I opened my eyes, and it was Jonah I saw, with his high wide cheekbones, and his full lips, his square jaw. His face was full of concern, which he then tried to disguise with a small smile, as I felt his fingers brush my cheek. I was lying down, but not in Grace's annex, even though the smell was still in my nose and mouth. I was on the sofa in the living room, in the Coopers' house, the same place I had sat with Mr Lawrence looking at maps on the table. I turned my head, no maps on the table. I heard his voice – I'm a sofa man – and then remembered his awkwardness following this remark to my mother, and how I had known that there was something I had not understood. I reached my hand to my forehead to feel a damp cloth cooling my skin.

'How are you feeling, Sissy?'

Jonah's voice was a balm.

'Funny,' I said.

He nodded, touched my forehead. 'Does it hurt?'

'Not really.'

He waited, and I began to feel a warmth returning to my limbs and the tips of my fingers, as if I was creeping back inside myself.

'Why am I here?'

'I carried you,' he said. Then, smiling: 'You are not heavy.'

The thought that I had been in Jonah's arms sent a thrill through me, borne simultaneously on a ripple of self-consciousness; since my early years, I had only ever been carried by my father. The question of whether Jonah had carried me in a fireman's lift, like that day by the lake when my father had swooped under my mother, or like a bride over the threshold, as I had seen in the cinema, distracted me for many minutes. I looked down now at my bare legs, and noticed that fine hairs had appeared on my thighs and calves; this metamorphosis no doubt heralded, as was everything else, by my father's departure. Jonah would have noticed the down on my legs as well, and I could feel my cheeks burning. He might have taken note of my striped T-shirt, maybe even the shape of my not-yet breasts, and I glanced down at myself again, involuntarily. My feet were crossed at the ankles, and my T-shirt and shorts were arranged neatly over my body, as if I had been laid out for inspection.

'Don't worry,' he said suddenly, as if reading my mind. 'It was only a few minutes.'

I placed my hands on either side of me and pushed myself up to a sitting position. The cloth fell off my forehead onto my lap, and he picked it up and laid it on the coffee table.

'Can you drink this?' He held out a glass of water, and I felt his hand at the back of my head as I took a sip. I drank thirstily, and felt a little better.

'Have you eaten?' he asked.

'Not really.'

'Are you hungry?'

'I'm still thirsty.'

'Shall we go to the kitchen? Can you walk?'

'What was wrong in Grace's house, Jonah?' I was loth to use the word 'smell'. It felt so incongruous to be associated with a woman like Grace, who was always neatly turned out.

But he understood what I meant, because he shook his head. 'I don't know,' and then he added, 'I don't want to know, Sissy.'

'Is it about Ezekiel?'

And again, he understood my oblique reference, nodded. 'It's possible.' Then, 'It's not easy for Grace.'

I fell silent, and must have been silent for some time because he prodded my arm. 'Sissy? Can you stand?'

I pulled my knees to my chest, so I could swing my legs past him on the sofa, and got to my feet, just as he stood up himself. I felt steady and stronger, and looked up to see him smiling.

'Good.'

'Would you like a cup of tea, Jonah?'

He smiled again. 'Thank you, Sissy.'

I learned that he took his tea strong with lots of milk and two sugars, a fact that surprised and delighted me, and that he sipped it slowly. I poured some cordial for myself. And having him near me made me feel warm and whole again; the strange telephone call and the image of my father falling down a shaft on the other side of the world was easy to push to one side. When I offered Jonah the biscuits I had arranged on a plate, he took one and ate it whole, which also delighted me, and when I pressed him to take another, he did so with the little bow he used with my mother. He asked me more about school and told me about the work he was doing, and I wanted to ask him whether he could come and meet me at the school gates one day. But I laid the palm of my hand against my cheek, my elbow on the table as my mother had done the night before, and asked him, 'Where did you meet the lady I saw you with at the anniversary?'

'Juliette?'

'Where did you meet her?'

'Where you usually meet a cook. In the kitchens.'

'And she's your wife?'

He shook his head. 'I'm not married.'

'Your girlfriend then?'

He laughed. 'I don't think *she* thinks she is my girlfriend.'

'But was it her' – I could not stop now – 'was she with you that night I came to your house?'

He said nothing at first, then nodded. 'Her husband died last year. And she has a son living with her mother in the village and she misses him.'

'And will you marry her?'

'I don't know,' then, 'maybe I should ask,' before grinning widely, briefly.

'Would you marry me,' I asked, 'if I was older?'

The flicker of surprise in his eyes lasted only a second and he stopped for only a fraction of a beat. 'No question.'

'Would you really?'

'Yes, yes. Without doubt.' His face solemn, as he placed his hands in front of him on the table.

'I'm being serious, Jonah.'

He burst out laughing. 'Sissy' – he shook his head, smiling – 'you can marry a better man than me when you are older.'

His words hurt me, more than he could have imagined, and my eyes filled with tears, which I tried to brush away before he saw, but he did, and I saw the expression in his eyes soften. But I did not want his pity or his tenderness. The tears kept coming. My heart was aching, my throat tight with all I could not tell him: that I loved him and that I wanted him to love me back. My nose was running and my cheeks were wet, but

Jonah did not reach out to comfort me, lay an arm around my shoulders. My fingers found my mother's sari, lying on the table next to me, and I buried my face in it, to absorb my tears and muffle the sobs I was unable to hold inside. Eventually my tears subsided and then we were quiet for many minutes. I felt a total humiliation and I had no wish to look at him.

'You need to study hard and finish your school first, Sissy,' I heard him say softly, and I managed to raise my head, my heart heavy, my eyes no doubt swollen and red.

'Like your mother did?'

He smiled suddenly, his eyes widening slightly. 'You remember?'

'I thought it was a beautiful story.'

He nodded, his eyes running over my face. 'It is.'

'Is your father lonely now?'

He tilted his head. 'Maybe. But he has not taken another wife.'

'I think my mother is lonely,' I said. 'And I think I'm lonely.'

He heard my words silently, and we sat like this, looking at each other across the table, as if we were in a café, a restaurant, enacting the rituals of romance; this comparison elicited from the future I had sketched. Then he reached towards me and I thought he would pinch my chin or tap my nose. But he hooked a finger into the neckline of my T-shirt and traced its outline, as if drawing a circle on the skin around my throat, before I felt his hand open out to clasp my neck, his thumb stroking my throat. I stared back at him, the feel of his fingers against my skin silencing me – has he ever touched you? – until he returned his hand to his mug of tea.

He said, 'You are not wearing your hamsa, Sissy. The Hand of Fatima that I gave you.'

I swallowed, found my breath. 'I lost it.' My voice faltered as I said the words; it was not as easy to lie to Jonah as it was to my mother.

He did not react, nor appear to believe what I said. He watched me for some time, his eyes not scanning my face as they had done before, but this time holding my eyes, and looking at me with a different gaze which made my heart stop.

'Then,' he said, raising his hands to meet at the back of his neck, and drawing them forward, the gold chain now twined between his fingers, 'wear this until you find it. Or until I can make you another.'

He leant forward to clasp it behind my neck, his face now near mine. His breath reminded me of rain, and his skin of trees. I could see into his shirt, his chest, his throat, and the line of his jaw. I wanted to kiss him but had no idea how to begin so I laid both my hands on his shoulders, and he smiled at me. 'Don't lose this one.'

I shook my head, and then he seemed to wait, holding his position patiently, for me to have my fill of feeling his warmth beneath my fingers. I dropped my hands and he straightened up. 'I will stay,' he said, 'until your mother comes.'

And this brought me back suddenly to where we were. 'You need to go!' I had barked the words, and he looked surprised at my tone.

'I will stay—'

'No, you must go now.'

'I cannot leave you when—'

'Mama won't like it, Jonah. You need to go.'

My words fell into a silence, and my heart thudded. He tilted his head as if waiting for me to explain but I said nothing; I felt faint and strong at the same time. 'They'll be back soon, they phoned,' I said. 'I'll be fine and you mustn't be here.'

'Sissy—'

'Please, Jonah. Mama will be really cross.'

He gazed at me solemnly.

'She found my hamsa,' I whispered.

He said nothing, only continued to hold my eyes. And I told her I loved you because I love you, Jonah – but, of course, these words only stayed in my heart.

'And she doesn't think you should be my friend.'

He raised his eyebrows.

'She said,' I hesitated, 'that grown men don't make friends with young girls.'

His teeth flashed in a sudden grin, before he became serious in the same instant, and nodded. He did not look angered by what I had said, or even offended. He seemed to be mulling over something, and I wondered whether this expression was an attempt to hide a deep hurt he might have felt at my mother's words.

'That is true,' he said suddenly. 'Your mother is correct, Sissy, and you should obey her.'

'She doesn't understand . . .'

'You must obey your mother, Sissy,' he repeated, and he stood up, as if to show me that he was convinced himself by my mother's directive. 'I will leave,' he said, 'because I don't want to make trouble for you.' And I remembered he had said the same words to my mother, that night he had brought me back, when I had leant against his chest on his bicycle. 'But you have a fever, Sissy. You must tell your mother. Will you do that?'

I went to the door, but when we saw the wind whipping up the dust and the trees leaning sideways as if in prayer, he turned and said, 'Stay inside, Sissy. And be well.' And then he was gone, the bag bumping against his back as he jogged to the front of the house. I ran to my bedroom window and just caught sight of his bicycle disappearing at the end of the road. I stayed there for a few more minutes until the blue car swung into the driveway, my mother next to Mr Cooper and, just visible, my brother on her lap.

22

I HAD forgotten to take the soup out to defrost, but my mother did not scold me; her sari lay in a crumpled heap on the table, but she did not seem to notice. She was bright-eyed, her cheeks somewhat flushed. She looked eager yet restless, as if released from her worries over Danny. My brother went down to sleep in a docile fashion, sucking his thumb greedily, and over the soup Mr Cooper mumbled about the storm coming, but neither adult spoke much. In fact, they seemed to be avoiding each other's eyes as if they were suddenly ill at ease in each other's presence. Now I worried that they had had an argument earlier in the day. Perhaps Mr Cooper's goodwill was being depleted, we were an extra burden. But I was tired, too tired to speculate on these matters, and too tired to tell my mother about the strange episode of the film music that had emanated from the phone line.

When I undressed in my room for my bath, I looked at myself in the small mirror propped up on the chest of drawers. The gold necklace, the exquisite tiny hand, blended with the tones of my skin, whereas against Jonah's it had stood out in contrast, like a filigree. I fingered the hand, let it nestle where it reached, against my diaphragm, the chain forming a V between my two not-yet breasts. It was beautiful. But if I was wearing it, then what protection did Jonah have? This pendant did not belong to me: I had one, carved for me, with that exact purpose, in the room where my mother slept. I knew then that I would disobey her. If I waited a few days, she might well forget its existence and not notice its absence. And where she had kept it was not a place that she was likely to be checking frequently. She had chosen it precisely so she could forget about it. If I reclaimed my pendant then I could return the gold chain to Jonah. I looked in the mirror. I raised my hands to the back of my neck and imitated his actions. I would unclasp it as he had done, lean forward and place it around his neck. And I would kiss him then, I knew.

I had never seen anyone kiss on the lips. The films we watched in India avoided the act with elaborately contrived scenarios; there was much cheek-to-cheek pressing but no mouth-to-mouth contact. The British and American television programmes and films which constituted the diet here in Zambia were similarly censored, with sudden leaps and bounds in the plot so the protagonists would be on the beach one minute staring into each other's eyes and then in a car the next minute, hurtling through a tunnel. My father had kissed my mother's cheek often, snuggled his face into her hair and neck, but I had never seen them touch their lips to each other. I could only thus assume that, despite knowing that those muffled sounds I used to hear were evidence that they made love, they must have done so without kissing. Mrs Cooper had once greeted Mr Cooper at the door when he had arrived from work, and he had made a sound of appreciation, as if he was tasting something delicious, before asking: does this mean I'm in your good books again? Don't count your chickens, Sam, Mrs Cooper had said, and he had replied, I wouldn't dare, Cin, I wouldn't dare. And then there had been a sucking sound not dissimilar to when Danny plugged in his thumb. But I had not seen anything, only Mrs Cooper's back, with Mr Cooper's hand sliding around to her hip. The closest, I realised, I had come to seeing a kiss was when Jonah had leant close to the young cook, Juliette, his body pinning her into place, her face upturned to his, poised at the ready. He had kissed the cook, I was sure, when Danny and I had removed ourselves, and while

I knew I was no match for a woman of her experience, I hoped I would not fare very badly.

Now, I bent forward and pressed my lips to the surface of the chest of drawers, the cool wood reminding me of how Jonah smelled as fresh and natural as a tree. The girls at school had mentioned closing eyes and tongues, but how to orchestrate all these effects in one practised move was beyond me. I heard my mother returning from the bathroom, calling out – your turn, mol – and I straightened up guiltily. I spent my bathtime plotting about not only when I would retrieve my rightful possession – my pendant – but when I would present Jonah with his, sealing my thanks with a kiss on his mouth.

I slipped into bed, opened my book and there was a knock on the door. My mother came inside and sat down on the covers beside me.

'I'm glad Danny's all right,' I said.

'I know.' She smiled. 'He just made me worried. He's usually not so grumpy, is he?'

She picked up the book on my bedside table, turned it over and looked at the blurb. 'This is the one Fee gave you?'

I nodded.

'What's it about?'

'This family of sisters and their mother. The dad is away in the American Civil War.'

I remembered talking about the same book with Jonah, and wondering whether he knew of the war. I found myself wondering the same about my mother, whom I had never seen reading a book – magazines, often – but never a book.

As if she could read my mind, she said, 'Between the North and the South?'

I nodded.

'Abraham Lincoln, wasn't it?'

I nodded again, and she started laughing. 'You're surprised I know, mol, aren't you?'

I started to protest, but she tapped the book on my nose and said, 'You know more about these things than I do, Sissy. You're like Papa in that way. He was the one who told me about it all.'

I found I was amazed by the mention of my father. I had begun to believe she would never speak of him again after talking about him in that way, at the table with the two American men on either side of her, listening to her.

I said nothing, and she continued smiling, opened the book. 'Maybe I should read it.'

I shifted onto my side. 'I'd recommend it.'

I watched as her eyes skirted over the first page, before she turned to the next. It was true what she had said of my father. There had always been a book on his side of the bed. He borrowed constantly from the school library. He had ploughed through Dostoevksy's *Crime and Punishment* a while ago, not something he found an easy read. When he had caught me looking through it once, he had laughed, saying: I'm looking forward to when you can read it and explain it to me.

Now my mother put the book on her lap. 'And this one?' She tapped the novel in my hand.

'A Nancy Drew,' I replied. 'Ally left it behind. She must have finished with it.'

'That's fine,' she said quickly, as if remembering that she had told me not touch their things.

I watched my mother as she smoothed the cover of the book on her lap with her palm. I needn't have worried about my mother's awkwardness at dinner in Mr Cooper's presence. She was wearing her night-time wear – her cream-coloured sleeve-less nightdress, her hair loose around her, a shawl over her shoulders – even though I knew it was too early for her to go to bed, as if to prove how at home she felt by now in the Coopers' house. The shawl was one I remember her cousin had given her, when Danny was born: in soft cashmere, a blue so dark as to appear black with a spray of gold leaves. I fingered it, and she smiled. 'You can borrow this whenever you want.'

'How is Thresiammaaunty?'

'Oh, fine. She wrote a few months ago.'

I had seen the aerogramme, I wanted to tell her; it had fallen onto my face like a sheet, the same day that Jonah had presented us with the swing. How easy it was, I thought, to collect my own memories, my own stash of treasured moments, beyond her knowledge.

She stroked my hair. 'Anything you want to talk about?' she asked. Her tone was light but her eyes were soft. Too late, I thought. By now we had each gathered too many things that should have been brought into the open. On her side, she had still not mentioned the letter from my father. On mine, well, there was a list: Jonah's visit today, the music at the end of the phone line, the gold chain lying under my pyjama top.

I shook my head.

'Sleep well, mol,' she said, and bent forward to kiss my cheek. Then she leant against me, forehead to forehead. It was a reconciliation, I understood that much. Perhaps the twist of bark and hair had scared her so that now she worried about my wellbeing as much as Danny's. And then, a sudden memory, perhaps elicited by the feel of her skin on mine: that same day, we were swimming in the lake, my father was watching us from the bank. My mother was swimming ahead and I was following, with that mixture of doggy paddle and breast stroke that had been my speciality, and she had turned around, ducked under and then appeared in front of me. Not too far out, mol, she had said. Sometimes there are weeds that can trap you, and she had slipped my arms around her neck, so I was riding on her back. We swam back towards my father like this, like dolphins, together through the water, I was giggling. I was small then; now I was not far off her height and she would not be able to do the same so easily.

She stood up and left the room and I could hear her enter the living room, not her bedroom. Perhaps she would make herself comfortable on the sofa I had lain on not long ago with the borrowed novel; Mr Cooper would finish his paperwork at the same desk where Mr Lawrence set up his typewriter. A companionable evening spent in the golden light of the lamps. I turned the pages of the book in my hand, but the story no longer interested me. My eyes felt heavy and I felt shivery. I turned off my lamp and turned over to my other side, my hand inside my top, clutching Jonah's amulet, which felt warm against me. I fell asleep and then woke again, as I had done on the night of the raid. I had gone then to check if my mother had left us, I remembered, and found her sleeping on my father's side of the bed. It felt like a different lifetime, our circumstances seemed much altered.

My chest was wet with perspiration, and outside the rain had come and was falling in sheets of heavy water, smacking against the windowpanes. And just as on the night of the raid, I had a similar urge to leave the bed, enter the bedroom she slept in. But this time I was not concerned about her. I was concerned for Jonah, who was sleeping somewhere without his gold chain, and I felt a pull, a tug, urging me to retrieve what was mine, which had been given to me in good faith, without any sinister ulterior motives, and which I had every right to reclaim. Before I had fully dissected the merits or not of thwarting my mother, I found I was already out of my bed, moving down the hall, and pushing open the door to her bedroom.

I felt my way through the gloom, my fingers touching the edge of the door, the bedstead, then the chest of drawers, and the chair standing near it, all the while my eyes adjusting to the light, so that by the time I looked under the chair and pulled out the suitcase, I could see my hands opening the zip, ferreting in its depths. I did not turn around, did not risk making eye contact with my mother in case she opened her eyes drowsily, avoided that meeting of eyes just as one does with a snake, just as I had done with Ezekiel that day on the campus. I slipped the leather cord out of the compartment and over my head. The tiny hand slipped down my chest to rest just above its gold twin so there was a hand with its fingertips brushing against another hand. I felt my heartbeat slow down as if the talisman had calmed me. I risked breathing out. There was nothing to fear. This was right, the pendant belonged with me and it did not feel like disobedience to claim it back. I was ready, in fact anticipating my mother's ire, so that I could speak eloquently and make my case. It was only after I had straightened up, pushed the suitcase back into position with my foot, and perhaps because the double hamsa had given me double courage, that I glanced at the bed to see the mound made by my brother's small body under his blanket, his fortress of cushions. And next to it, nothing.

So, she had left after all. I stood still for many minutes. My mother was slender, and would not be cumbersome in the bed, but nothing could rationalise what I saw. Her side of the bed was not even open; she was not at this minute making a night-time visit to the bathroom. She had not disturbed the covers because she had not got into the bed this evening. She was gone, like my father was gone, perhaps to join him in some universe made of memory, some lustreless past where parents went when they tired of their children.

I stared at Danny's sleeping form, clueless, unconsulted. I could not shake my brother, waken him, interrogate him: Danny, where did she go? Did you see when she left? What did she take with her? After some minutes of not moving, hardly breathing, I turned, left the room. I moved slowly as if in a dream, down the hall to Mr Cooper's bedroom. And it was only then, as I stood breathless outside the door, my knuckles raised to knock – to raise the alarm, to call a search party to comb the area as we had done for the missing girls – breathless, even though I had only walked, not run, and only covered a distance of a few yards no more, it was only then that I realised that my mother was on the other side, with him.

Some part of the bed – the headboard, or one of the legs – was banging against the wall behind it. For a moment, I wondered if he was hurting my mother, for there was a violence to the sounds, a frightening persistence, as if he was pushing her again and again against something – her will or her memory of my father or an image of his wife – as if to break it. But then there was a pause and I heard his voice, filled with desire not anger – Laila, Christ – and my mother's response – don't stop, don't stop – both breathing into each other, and the bed began its hypnotic rhythm again, but now from a different place, with a slower tempo, as if they had melted into each other's arms.

I turned and fled, my hand on the pendants, my heart pounding. This time I knew I could not run to find my mother. She was finding herself, behind that door. Finding herself with the man with whom she would spend the rest of her life, who would one day sign a paper so that Sissy Olikara disappeared. I knew I could run to only one person, I only wanted to be with one another person, and that person was Jonah.

23

THE rain lashed down, quickly filling the shoes I had slipped on my feet, and when I reached the end of the drive I thought to turn back and retrieve a raincoat, for I had fled in my pyjamas. But I had not taken anything with me, not a bag, not a key, and I had no wish to knock on the door. I wanted never to return to that house again. I walked with my arms wrapped around me as if to stop my insides from blowing away in the swirling gusts around me, to keep my mind from sailing out of my body in fright at what I had heard. And just as I had mined the memories I had of my interactions with Ezekiel, pored over them to see if I could identify a moment, an instance that should have alerted me, I tried to sift through all the scenes which held my mother and Mr Cooper, searching for a clue that would lead me to an understanding of what was happening on the other side of that bedroom door. But my mind kept returning to another day, that afternoon, when my father and Mr Cooper had leant against my father's green car, a memory which played out in bright sunshine as if to underline how untouched and innocent we all were then. What had they been talking about? There was the mention of Ezekiel, then the witchdoctor. I could recall how they had appeared. Both of an age, both with arms folded, completely at ease with each other, neither man dominating the other. Equals, clearly enjoying each other's company. They had mentioned my mother, too, I was sure of it. The image disintegrated, as if on a faulty projector, to be replaced by a blackness and the sound still echoing in my ears of the bed thudding against the wall.

And now in front of me was a vision of the room in my great-uncle Monuchayan's house in India, in which we all slept when we stayed. My father and I were opening the door, we were arriving late, just off the train from the boat races in Alleppey. It was dark outside, but inside the room there was a dim light coming from the lamp on the bedside table. My mother was lying on her side on the bed that she, my father and Danny shared – I slept on a mattress on the floor – and as often in moments of repose, all she wore was her sari-blouse and the underskirt. Her blouse was undone, and Danny was on one breast, his fist tucked under the flap of silk on her other breast. This, I knew, had been a point of much contention. The women in the household were suspicious of breast-feeding and berated my mother for not feeding him formula; this the reason, they claimed, that at a year old, he showed no interest in walking. My mother whispered her welcome, and asked to see my sketches, so I lay on the bed, facing her, Danny between us, and opened my book to show her; my father stretched out behind her, one hand stroking her waist. The bed was our boat, we were sailing a wave, the four of us – the only movement the gentle rocking motion when my father shifted his weight and the only sound, now that Danny had fallen asleep at my mother's breast, the creak of the mattress. A gentle sound, not like that which I had heard just minutes before. I had not thought a bed could act in that way.

Now, I clapped my hand over my mouth, because I realised I was making a sound like an animal, a low howl, a keening, and so I tried to empty my mind and think of something beautiful and precious and good: Jonah. That walk in the rain, in the dark, my instincts leading me, sustaining me, and guiding me. The wind wild around me, whipping my hair into my face as if it were heavy wet ropes, my skin trembling from the cold and my throat raw, an open wound. It was only years later that

I understood. Lost love, lost youth. I was walking away from my youth and my innocence. And even as I believed I was approaching him, I was walking away from my love.

I reached the cluster of tin-roofed houses, incredibly, without having met anyone, fallen over, taken the wrong turning, with water streaming down my face, my hair a wet sheet around my head and down my back, as if I had just dived into a lake, fully clothed, to swim in the water. And as before, just as I could make out where I had arrived, two hands grabbed my shoulders. Child, child. The same old woman, in the same place, who now seemed unsurprised to see me, even chuckled, showing yellow teeth. Despite the plastic sheeting she wore around her, a grotesque parody of a cloak giving her the air of a witch, I felt a surge of relief. I had arrived: Jonah was near. She grasped my arm, tightly, still chuckling, peered into my face as she had done before, but this time there was something else on her breath, and I had to stop myself from jerking my head back in revulsion. Can you take me to Jonah, please? She made a sound from her belly, like a growl, and I could see her eyes were bleary, but her yellow smile was still visible. Come, child. She gripped my shoulder, leaning her weight on me, the plastic sheeting whipping against my legs as she led me down the hill, past the houses, invisible this night through the rain, and then opened a door, not red, and steered me into the interior.

It was blessedly warm inside, and dry, even as the rain thundered on the corrugated-iron roof. There was a rich golden light from the paraffin lamps that encircled the room and from the small fire in the centre, on the earthen floor. The air was pungent, filled with an acridity that stung my eyes. The man who was sitting cross-legged at the centre was feeding the fire with seeds and sticks and leaves, and while the flames were not high they seemed to lick greedily at the offerings. I saw Grace, sitting on the floor, watching the man. She was not wearing her knitted cap, and her hair was uncombed, dull. Her eyes were unfocused and her head lolled in a way that reminded me of a broken doll. And she did look broken, not the Grace I had known for so many years, while sitting next to her, his legs drawn to his chest, his arms folded and balanced on his knees, with a frame like a skeleton so that his shirt hung off him, so that I could better see the dark, bruise-coloured marks on his neck and chest, was Ezekiel.

But of the people gathered in the room, his eyes were the brightest, the most alert, and when they turned to see me, his alone were vivid with an expression: dismay. Sissy, how are you? His voice, too, was warm, concerned, as if he was fully cognisant and had instantly read the situation. Perhaps because he could see how my teeth chattered and my face was wet from the rain, as well as the fear in my eyes at this gathering I had stumbled across, he had shaken his head slightly, gestured to the gathering: don't worry, this will finish soon. And then he smiled to buoy my spirits, his distinctive crooked smile, but I saw his teeth were white and clean and straight as they had always been.

I remembered, and a warm feeling flooded into me. A memory of how Ezekiel had been my companion those long, dull and lonely afternoons, when I was so much younger, even though only a few months had passed by. A reminder of how I had been disloyal to him, finding him become ugly, fearful that his thoughts and intentions to me were impure. And I felt ashamed of how I had curved away from him, just as I felt relief that I had finally learned that I had not been wrong, not misjudged him, to count him as a friend.

Why are you out in this weather, Sissy? he asked. Where is your mother? I could not answer but only shook my head. When this is finished – and he gestured again to the centre – I will take you back to her. His words were punctuated now by the man in the centre, who was beating a stick against the earth, and I remembered the rhythm I had heard, of the bed against the wall. I shook my head again. Could you take me to Jonah? I asked, but my voice was drowned out by the high-pitched moan rising and rising from the man sitting by the fire. He called out, and Grace and the old woman ululated in response, and he did this again and again, each time eliciting a terrible groan from the women's lips, of mangled words and an animal's growl – a terrifying call and response, like a Mass that had been blackened – become unholy.

Ezekiel pursed his lips and raised his eyebrows, a furrow appearing on his brow, and I could see he was trying to mask his exasperation, just as Jonah had done that night in the face of the same old woman's admonishments, and this almost made me laugh with relief that I could feel affection for Ezekiel again, despite the fear of how this evening would end. My throat was aching, and I knew that I had a fever: Jonah had been correct. Ezekiel, I don't feel well, I whispered, but the noise in the hut was too loud now: the noise, however, only coming from the two women and the man, because, merci-fully, it appeared the rain had abated to a steady drizzle. The wind, however, continued to blow. I felt the heaviness of my eyelids and the ache in my bones. My pyjamas clung to me but I felt no self-consciousness, only safety from the storm, and I could feel the two tiny hands, the cord and the chain, against my chest. I slid my hand into my top and moved the tiny hands from where they had rested just above my belly and placed them where I could feel my heart beating.

I must have dozed off because I found that I was back in India, on my father's shoulders, his hands grasping my ankles, massaging them. Look there, he was pointing to the great lake, see the boats, Sissy. And I turned and looked at the flat grey expanse, and realised there was no need for me to be on his shoulders because there was no one around us, no crowds, no spectators. Just my father and me, tall as a totem pole. With the lake before us, with the boats, the beautiful black streaks, the men with their oars, silhouetted against water that was as clear as a mirror. But my father was jumping up and down now, shrieking, while I bumped against his head, clutching at his face, stop it, Papa. He was crying out – look at the boats, Sissy – and I saw what was upsetting him. One was sinking, slowly, in an exquisitely tender and graceful motion, surrendering to the water, so that all the men inside fell off one by one, like ants off a leaf, into the lake, and my father was weeping: look, look, Sissy. My chin bumped against my chest and I woke up, in the small dwelling, which was still warm, which still held the same occupants.

They were eating something now, something dark and fibrous, which dripped with a liquid that made my stomach turn, and I wished I had not woken to witness this. I wanted to close my eyes against the sight but found I could only stare, fascinated. I watched as they chewed, swallowed, as their lips were dirtied by the wetness. But when Grace offered a lump to Ezekiel, he refused. She offered it to him again, and again he refused, his head half-turned away. Her eyes blazed, and she struck him across the face. Once, and then again, and as she snarled at him, unrecognisable, the same body but within it a different spirit from the gentle, clean woman I had known, Ezekiel took the soft, fibrous matter and his hand moved closer to his mouth.

But I do not know if he ate or not, or if, just before he died, he was finally cured of his illnesses and his ill luck – the epilepsy and the vicious virus that would have taken his life anyway before the year would end. For the wind was finally victorious. The door of the small hut flew open, the latch broken by a gust, and it slammed against the head of the old woman, who let out a scream, her teeth bloodied by what she had been eating. Before anyone could tend to her, the lamps balanced on the beam around the hut toppled, one after the other, so the paraffin sprayed over us, bathing the interior like holy water from a priest's incense pot, allowing the fire in the centre, that had until then been contained but already titillated, aroused by the small offerings, to leap upward with a release and an exhale of breath that reminded me of my mother's voice – don't stop, don't stop.

The flames did not stop, and within seconds we were coated with a golden heat that warmed me from my fever, so for a brief glorious moment I felt an intense pleasure at the cold ache in my bones being alleviated. And then the pain arrived, on my neck and on one side of my face and in my hair, a pain so intense that it felt like an epiphany. I could not see clearly, could just make out Ezekiel rising to his feet, the fire on his back and around his head like a halo, as he lunged towards me. The expression on his face was monstrous, terrifying me so much that I could hear myself screaming just as I could not even then use my voice. I felt his hands grip me, and with a strength that belied his skeletal frame, he picked me off my feet and threw me out the door, out of the hut, so I landed on the wet grass outside, snapping my wrist as I tried to break my fall, then lay on the earth, unmoving, as it shook and thundered beneath me with the stamps and screams of the people running towards us. But the small hut succumbed under the weight of the fire, disintegrated into ash. The interior and the people who remained inside – the old woman and the man, the person who had been Grace, and Ezekiel – purified at last by the flames, to join the soil, join the earth.

So, how are you reborn? You are thrown up into the air, and you float above the world with your arms outstretched, your legs akimbo, as if you are lying on a cloud. Around you the air is sweet and cool and caresses your skin, which is shining, vital. Your eyes are open and brilliant, your lips are parted, as you breathe and breathe, feeling the air fill your lungs and flood into your heart, your stomach, through your limbs and into your fingertips and the ends of your toes. You see the universe ahead of you and the stars, and you smile and smile because now you understand. That you are wonderful and beautiful. A creation of such intricacy and excellence and innovation that you laugh out loud at your perfection. Your voice rings out like a bell, as melodious a sound as you have ever heard.

And then you look down to the earth and you see gathered below you, and looking up, all the people you know and love and fear and dislike and envy. And swirling around them like black smoke are all the thoughts and deeds that you regret and feel shame for, all the words you said in anger, all the lies you told to save yourself. And as you grasp at the cloud it begins to shred and fray and you realise that you were foolish, so foolish, to believe that so fragile a bed could have ever supported you. You start falling, and you fall fast, and as you plummet towards the earth, you know you are leaving behind everything you knew before. And when you find that you have survived the descent, that you are still alive, with your feet now planted on the ground, you hold yourself erect and survey the world you have returned to. But everyone around you sees you with different eyes, just as you see yourself with different eyes. You are two faces: a before and after, a now and then. You have left your home and your people. And you belong, now, to a different tribe.

24

O F the events that followed the fire, there are some things I cannot separate from the many dreams that merged with my reality, so that the past, the present and the future, fictional or not, became one. I am certain, for example, absolutely certain, that I saw my father, the man who made me, sitting beside me in the hospital, while next to him was Ezekiel, the man who saved me. I know my heart broke and that I wept, for Ezekiel and Grace both dead, even for the old woman and the man, for who would wish for such an end? But I also know that I was unaware of their lot for a long time, would only have heard of the full extent of the tragedy much later, when I had gained enough consciousness to understand what was being said to me. Early on, in one of the days when reality and dreams were particularly intertwined, I saw my mother sitting by my side, in the chair she slept in through the nights. I want to say something, mol. She was whispering in Malayalam and I was not sure if she thought I was awake or asleep. Her eyes were huge and bright. That night, I know you wanted to see Jonah and I know what made you run away. One day, perhaps, you will understand. And whether this was in a dream or if this was indeed real and true, I could not respond, but only watched as her hands twisted in the folds of her sari.

Some things I know for certain. That the men in the settlement fought the fire valiantly, endangering their own lives trying to rescue the four who remained inside but succeeding only in containing the blaze to the one hut. That one of the women had run in the dark to the convent, woken one of the nuns, who had then driven me, wrapped in the wet chitenges the other women had swaddled me in, and in Jonah's arms, to the hospital, where my mother and Mr Cooper arrived, having received a deathly phone call that erased all their pleasure and joy from that night. I know that Charlie Lawrence and Fee Munroe harnessed the aid of Rahul's father to contact my great-uncle Monuchayan, who promised he would do his utmost to get a message to my father of my injuries; this promise itself was dispiriting, in that it was clear that my father was not easily to hand, and would have to be unearthed. When my mother finally heard from him, she had already made her decision: to leave my father and take sole custody of myself and Danny. I know that Sam Cooper was at my bedside as much as my mother was, his face as stricken by my fate and as determined to right it as if he were my father himself. I know that he moved heaven and earth for us. But not without the assistance of his then-wife Cindy who, when given both the news of the fire and my injuries, and the declaration from her husband that he had fallen in love with my mother, had from some inner strength and a deep well of integrity and goodness chosen to process and react to the latter only after she helped stage-manage our arrival in America a few months later. She would grant my stepfather a divorce, without acrimony, and pave the way for my mother's second marriage. It did not happen immediately, but over time we became a large, if not quite blended then untidily knitted family so that when it was time for graduations and house-warmings, the turn of the daughters to get married, everyone attended everyone's celebration. My stepfather walked both Ally and me down the church aisle and town-hall aisle respectively; Mary-Anne and her husband got married on a beach, no aisle in sight. Cindy never remarried, but as testament to the deep respect and love they had always had for each other, and the love they both had for Ally and Mary-Anne, she and Sam Cooper remained close. While my stepfather was imprinted as 'Mr Cooper' in my mind – I even jokingly referred to him as that and he signed my birthday cards as such – Danny had never known another father. He was always 'Dad' to Danny, and eventually I followed my baby brother's example and called him the same.

I know that Jonah came to me both in my dreams and in reality. I know the dream, and I know it was a dream because I could see both of us, as if I were watching myself on a film. And I had no bandages on my face, and my skin was smooth, and my hair lay around my shoulders and framed my face, and I was smiling as he held my hand with one of his, and in the other, on his palm, lay the two tiny hands, the gold chain and the leather cord intertwined. This was not true; I know that my clothes were cut from me at the University Teaching Hospital in Lusaka, and the wooden hand and leather cord disappeared in the charged adrenaline of the emergency room in the hospital, the gold chain removed and bagged. My mother told me later that she had shown it to Jonah, asked if it was his. Whether she had clasped it around his neck as I had wished to, I did not ask. All I know is that he told her that it was from his mother, as if in apology and an explanation for why he would reclaim it, not leave it in my possession. At least, then, part of my mission that night when I had walked to him in the rain was accomplished.

I heard his voice. He spoke to me, but I cannot remember what he said, only that his voice was deep and soothing and his tone persuasive, like it had been when he spoke to the cook, Juliette. I don't know how long he was allowed to stay by my side, or how many times he visited, but I do know he was there and often, and that this was not a dream, because my mother told me of this. And that he kissed me – on the top of my head, above the bandages, when he said his farewell – and this news had given me comfort; that he had not been repulsed by my shaven scalp. He might have kissed my mother, too, but she did not tell me, only that she felt, when he had left, that she would miss him. He had told her that he had not attended the exams he had been due to take and he had not yet decided if he would try to sit them again in the new year. He was returning to the Copperbelt where he would join his father and brother and look for work. He had no wish to remain in Lusaka or at Roma, even though my stepfather offered to help him find different employment.

And both my mother and I, when she gave this news to me, weeks later, when I was well enough to listen, having had to recover not only from the fire that burned me from without but from the pneumonia that burned me from within, both of us felt something profound and powerful: a bond with Jonah that would connect us inextricably, more than the memory of my father ever would. A bond that would survive the anger I felt towards her for many years, and the guilt she bore for all her life since. That she remained her undamaged self while her daughter was maimed; that she had found love, again, and was loved, again, while her daughter for so long believed herself to be unlovable. We were bound irrevocably by our shared hope that Jonah would stay safe and find happiness.

Not long afterwards, when I was sitting up, sipping a drink through a straw without assistance, when we knew that we would be leaving Zambia to begin a new life across the ocean, even further from my father, my mother presented me with the envelope.

'This is for you, mol.'

I turned it over in my hands. It said simply: *For Sissy.*

'From Jonah,' she said.

I looked up in wonder, and she continued: 'He left it with me to give to you when you were better.' Her face crumpled at the words because we both knew that I was a long way from any kind of recovery. 'He left it when he said goodbye to you, that last time.'

My whole body felt as if it were caught in a moment of time that would never find its end. 'Did he say if he was coming back, Mama?'

The question was clear in my head, but I had to repeat myself many times because my words were still not clear, my facial muscles and vocal cords not yet fully functioning. When she finally understood she shook her head, stroked my cheek, laid her palm against my face, my bandages – no, mol – and for a second I was not sure if we were referring to my father or Jonah. She stood up then, and she turned to leave me with the envelope, before we realised that I was trembling so much I could not open it. But after she had helped me slide out the folded sheet from its sheath, she left the room so that I could read it alone.

It was short, but on clean, stiff paper, of the type you would find in a high-quality stationer's; it would have been hard to find something like that at that time in Lusaka. I had never seen Jonah's handwriting before and I found it exquisite: sloping and even, the capitals extending high, and then tapering down. He began the letter with *Dear Sissy*, and when I read those words I had to close my eyes; only one eye could cry, but my whole body could ache. He continued: *When you read this I hope you will be feeling better. I am so sorry for what happened, but I know this will make you more strong, more beautiful and more kind. Nothing can change how special you are inside. Adeus, Jonah.*

No mention of the tiny hands that had failed, no mention of friendship, of marriage, or of love, or that we would never see each other again. But I knew the words were steeped with these sentiments, and I felt his presence so strongly that I had to put a hand on my chest to stop my heart from breaking. When my mother re-entered the room, she did not ask to read the letter, but helped me fold it carefully and place it back in the envelope, where it still lies – an everlasting memento of, and a farewell to, that night, that man and my childhood.

Epilogue

W HEN my stepfather died aged seventy-two, after a merci-
fully brief period of illness, my brother and I arrived at
the house in Philadelphia for a consultation with my mother.
She refused to move in with either of us. Yes, the house was
large, but she wished to remain where she was for as long as she
felt able to look after herself. Her words only brought into
relief how she appeared suddenly much more fragile and debil-
itated, as if she had held the ageing process at bay only until she
found herself alone. But she was insistent and could not be
swayed; she wished not to be a burden to us.

While driving to the airport to catch the flight back to
Boston, I said to Danny: maybe it's time to go back.

To where? my brother asked.

Back to India, to Kerala. We could go together and see if we
can find him.

Danny's hands on the steering wheel slid right down to the
lowest curve, and he was quiet for some time before he said:
find the old man? Do you even know where to start?

Monuchayan, I said. I'm sure he will have seen Papa, at least
when he first returned. He's still alive, Monuchayan, that is.
I've been in touch with Sanjay Tharoor, who's found out
where he lives now.

My brother did not probe, but he will have known this was
a timely request. He knew I had been unsure if he would
accompany me while my stepfather was still alive. Eventually
he nodded, his eyes fixed on the road ahead.

Just the two of us? I asked.

Sure, he said. If that's the way you want it.

I had rehearsed the conversation; it was not made on a whim. I had pondered whether I wanted to make the journey with my husband and my seven-year-old daughter. I had wondered what I would say if Danny wanted to bring his girlfriend. But my baby brother, while finding success as the host of a frivolous radio talk show, was no fool. And when, a few months later, I watched as he kissed his girlfriend on the lips in goodbye, I felt a wave of guilt. Perhaps I was imposing my own desires on my brother who, now in his thirties, had never shown any wish for such a quest. But when we were alone on the plane and in transit, when I was rediscovering how much I enjoyed his company, he said that he had visited my mother a few days ago, to find her listening to an old vinyl album, playing it on my stepfather's treasured old record player.

Malayalam songs, he said. I'd not heard them before.

I remembered those afternoons when she had barricaded herself in the bedroom in the small pink bungalow, with me and Danny, then not yet two, left outside, listening through the closed door to words I did not even then fully understand. I looked at my brother. He appeared pensive, unlike his usual, more ebullient self. He was not tall, not like my father had been, and he resembled my mother, as did I. It was as if we had decided as a trio to erase my father, given his decision to abandon us.

Maybe, he said suddenly, maybe because Dad has died, she's letting herself think of Papa a bit more.

He rarely used that term to refer to my father. In fact he, all of us, rarely spoke of him at all.

I wonder why she cut herself off so completely, I said. I mean I'm sure her family were horrible to her at first, but years and years, Dan. So many years have passed.

He nodded. I know what you mean.

Was it because of me? I gestured to my face. Did she think that no one would ever forgive her? That they'd blame her?

I don't know, he said.

Years and years, I repeated.

And then he said hurriedly, I wouldn't want to judge her.

He had always been quick to defend her. She had not, as she had promised, disappeared.

We landed. It was hot and humid. Danny looked around in a daze. That evening we walked up and down the promenade, just a few streets away from our hotel, taking in the atmosphere, the breeze, the sounds of Malayalam, the smells. Waves of memory washed over me, and crashed against my head and my heart, but I realised for Danny it would all be a new and a not insignificant experience, to see it all finally with his own eyes.

Stop staring at my sister, he groaned under his breath at one point, as I stifled my giggles at the, in turns, sheer brazenness or casual cruelty of the attention I was gathering.

God, look at that guy checking you out, he muttered.

I know, I said, I mean how dare he when I'm middle-aged and hideous to boot. But he did not laugh, only looked upset by my attempt at humour. Hey. I squeezed his arm, and he tried to smile. He was, I could see, more vulnerable to this return than I had imagined.

The following morning we presented ourselves at the house, the address of which Sanjay Tharoor had procured for us, to be greeted by several cousins and second cousins, uncles and aunts, all of whom had gathered together to welcome the two prodigal Americans, who greeted us with warmth and genuine pleasure in seeing us and hearing of our lives. And lying on a cot, wizened and aged, but recognisably the great-uncle whose hand I used to hold, was Monuchayan, who had, he related in Malayalam, not seen my father since he had reappeared briefly to inform everyone of the fire which I had survived and my mother's decision to divorce him. That no one had heard from him, as all around us people nodded to confirm this piece of news and lament the situation and sigh in sympathy.

My brother was silent on the way back to our hotel, late that evening. We had not been allowed to leave until we had been plied with food and had promised to attend several gatherings organised in our honour over the next few days. But when I was sitting on my bed in our twin room, having made a quick call to my husband, with Danny in the shower, I suddenly heard a bang, then a thump, from the bathroom, that repeated itself three or four times. I stood uncertainly outside the door, fearful of what would happen next.

Dan? You okay in there?

He said something indistinct, but at least I heard his voice. When he emerged, his fist was swollen and his eyes were red.

We had those few more days in Ernakulam, and then we extricated ourselves from my father's family to take a bus up into the hills, for I had planned one last salvo, a swim in the river. I had not attempted to make contact with my mother's family; that was her preserve. But the bird sanctuary remained, and the river and the lake too; none of these had been affected by my father's disappearance and my mother's exile. We took an autorickshaw from Kothamangalam to the gates of the bird sanctuary, and then wandered down a path to the river, where we laid down our bags. My brother was down to his shorts in seconds, but we soon realised I would be a spectacle. I accepted the T-shirt, Danny's, that he silently handed to me to pull over my swimming two-piece, so that the small crowd of children who had gathered on the riverbank and the small group of hot-eyed young men further up would have less to see. We ducked and dived like children, the water calming and cleansing us, and only here did I allow my heart to open, to be soothed by the river. Only here did I feel my father's presence, and my mother's, her golden, slender form arcing over us as she was thrown into the water, my parents' laughter echoing around us like ghosts. And then my brother and I sat on the riverbank, let the warm air dry our skin and curl our hair, sat so still and so quietly that the onlookers lost interest and left us alone. So that by the time we made our way back to the bus station in Kothamangalam, we had left a whisper in the river, to be carried in the current to where our father was: we wish you well, Papa.

That evening, on arriving at the resort on the coast that we had booked for our final two days, we ordered a beer each to accompany our meals, watched the families and couples around us, soaking in the scent of the air and its warmth.

I look across the table at my baby brother, his eyes are full of something. Here's to us, Danny, I say, unable to stop the tears in my eyes from sliding down my cheeks, into my lips, and he taps his bottle against mine, then reaches across and takes my hand. Here's to us.

Clearing out a cupboard in my mother's house with my daughter, I come across a small shoebox. Inside it is a photograph of my mother with her college roommates, which I have not seen for over thirty years: four young women in matching saris, bought for their photo shoot, their eyes rimmed with kohl, bangles at their wrists and large gold hoops in their earlobes.

Wow, is that Grandma?

She was effortlessly graceful. Her large eyes, and the delicacy of her face, the slender body in the dark silk sari. Among her roommates she stood out, a glowing beauty. I want to cry seeing that photograph, she has changed so much. Not just the usual marks of age – at seventy, she has in fact aged well – only now there is a gluey, wet look in her eyes. She does not focus, and those long eyelashes that cast feathery shadows on her cheeks seem to weigh her eyelids down. I hand it to my daughter, to stare at, and start pulling out the other boxes stacked on top of each other in the cupboard.

Each holds a pile of magazines, an eclectic collection – *Reader's Digest, Femina, Good Housekeeping* – some from as far back as the seventies. She hid her hoarding instincts well, I think, just as I see, tucked at the back, not a box but a manila envelope, no address or label, sealed with a rubber band. I open the envelope and they spill out, a stack of blue aerogrammes, the kind that you needed to open along one edge, to unfold the words folded into themselves. There are, in total, perhaps twenty-five such aerogrammes, all addressed to my mother at the house we are standing in, in Philadelphia. And the sender of all of them is the same: my long-lost father, George Olikara.

What is it, Mama? my daughter asks, then comes over, and placing a hand on my shoulder, leans against me. What are these?

Letters, I whisper.

She opens one, and frowns. It's a different language.

Malayalam, I whisper again.

Are they to Grandma? Who are they from?

They're from my father.

She must have said something, under her breath, but I hear nothing for many minutes, only the sound of my heart, holding papers that my father would have held himself.

Did you know, Mama?

I shake my head. No, mol, she never told me.

My daughter is gathering them, laying them out, sorting them, in rows of four across, ever the pragmatist – her bedroom is as organised as a monk's.

There's no return address, and he hasn't dated them himself, she is muttering, but I can just about read the postmarks.

I watch as my daughter arranges them, chronologically.

One a year, pretty much, she is saying, and then she leans back on her haunches: last one here was seven years ago.

Seven years ago. My stepfather was still alive, my mother had not slipped into the universe she now occupies, with a memory that has become a fleeting gossamer-thin fabric floating just out of her reach. It was the following year that my brother and I had gone to India on our failed quest.

Do you want to have a look, Mama?

I recognise the first one. It was the aerogramme I had found myself, that afternoon in Roma, when I was slightly younger than the age my daughter is now. It fills three-quarters of the space, beginning with *My dearest Laila*, ending *Yours, George.* I see the words *Sissy* and *Danny* in the same place. The other letters all begin with *Dear Laila*, and end simply *George.* In all of them, we can discern the words *Sissy* and *Danny* close to the top. In none can we see any mention of Sam Cooper.

Can you understand what he's written?

No, I can't.

I never learned to read Malayalam. I have translated countless texts, novels, poems, manuals, instructions, medical pamphlets, fashion articles, government manifestos, translated them all into Italian, but with Malayalam I cannot make a start. I stare at the curls and swirls which say nothing to me. Send these to someone to decipher? I know I will not. I am holding, in my hands, a tale which my mother has not wished to be told.

Do you think Grandma wrote back?

I don't know, mol.

She is scrutinising the letters, then places her finger on one in the middle. Look, Mama!

In English, nestled among the Malayalam, we can make out *The Wild Wind.* I raise my eyes, hold my daughter's; her mouth is open, her cheeks flushed.

What does that mean? she whispers.

My book, my useless endeavour, a folly, but still a source of pride, and which has its pride of place in my study at home. I had not understood when I was writing it what I understand now – that while I did not make a systematic, sustained effort to find my father, that all the while I was delving into words and sentiments and inflections I was searching for him and his thoughts and feelings and fears, wishing I could have given him something that he could clutch in his hand and from which to gain an inner strength. I stare at the words, my words, but written in his hand: *The Wild Wind*. For him to know of this, he will have needed to do more than wait somewhere for news of us to drift his way. He may have never lost his love for reading, even if he might have lost his love for the life he had. He may never have lived far away from a bookshop or a library. He might have bought it, or borrowed it, opened it to the first page. He might have read there what I had decided to include only after much painful deliberation. Perhaps, then, I had not been so unconscious of my motives; I might have wished to leave something on this earth that could be excavated as proof that my father had existed.

I cannot claim James Joyce as a countryman or a life-long inspiration. I was in my twenties when I first read any of his works, novels or poems. But I discovered 'Watching the Needleboats at San Sabba' when I needed to understand something about something – which must be why we write and read literature. The poem spoke directly to me, striking chord after chord, just as if the poet could see into my heart. My father used to take me to watch the boat races when I was a child. Not in Trieste, the location for Joyce's poem, but in the state of Kerala, in South India. 'Watching the Snakeboats in Alleppey' is the poem I have never written, and do not have the talent to write. But if I did, I would dedicate it to my father and those happy memories.

My daughter is watching me and repeats: what does that mean?

But I only shake my head, I don't know.

She returns now, energised, peering eagerly at each letter and picking out the English words, not many, but each a clue of what my father discovered of us. There is only one phrase connected with Danny – radio station – and I ache for my baby brother who never knew his father. Each letter becomes shorter and the last, written in a spidery, trembling hand, is a single paragraph. Her eyes are darting over and over the light blue rectangles. Then she picks up an aerogramme, perhaps the third along from the top.

What does this say, Mama?

She points with her finger, and I squint, then my breath is gone: Jonah.

It is years since I have said the name, heard it spoken, and it transports me, to the scrape of the bark of a tree branch under my bare legs, to a sari being pulled over my head in a wind, to the feel of a tiny hand nestling on my chest. To a strength that did not leave me but stayed with me. Nothing can change how special you are inside. I turn the aerogramme over to check the postmark: 1981. My mother was remarried, we had relocated. Why *then* and not before would my father mention his name?

And I remember how we stood together, him and me, that afternoon, watching Jonah and my mother, Danny between them, as Jonah reached his arms high, looped the ropes over the branch, the wooden swing hanging down below, just as later he would loop a leather cord around my neck, a tiny wooden hand at its end. Perhaps that was the day, that was the moment, when my father realised that both my mother and I would look beyond our immediate reach, stretch ourselves and tap against the fragile cocoon of his love and protection, make a small cranny, peel it open and climb out of it. Perhaps even then, my father had discerned something – a spark in my mother in my stepfather's presence, even in Jonah's. Perhaps I am holding in my hand an explanation, a request for, if not forgiveness, for some kind of understanding: I watched you with Jonah, that day he brought the swing, and realised I was holding in my hands a beautiful bird, like those you grew up among, that would fly away one day. And so I decided to fly away first, Laila.

I let the aerogramme flutter forward, watch it slip out of my fingers, swimming away in a tease in a lake. But there are reasons to be happy. Many reasons. My daughter is waiting patiently for the right moment, then she asks: who was Jonah, Mama?

She has her father's smile, but her eyes are mine. I stroke her face, so smooth, so untouched. I know I will share everything with her later. Because there lies the difference between myself and my mother. One of us is a storyteller, and the other not.

Author's note

The shooting down of the civilian aircraft and the retaliatory raid on the camp in Lusaka are both real events. Roma Girls' Secondary School is also real, although it was not closed for an extended period after the raid. The Olikaras share many similarities with my family, the Kalayils, but the differences are plentiful: not least that my father did not leave us. The dynamics and demographics of the people who lived and worked in Lusaka are true for that period of time. The layout of the school and the staff bungalows are all true to my memory and any errors are mine alone.

Acknowledgements

Thank you to my agent Stan for pushing me on, and to my editor Alison Rae for her calm wisdom and excellent eye. Thank you to Jan Rutherford, Kristian Kerr, Lucy Merketis, Edward Crossan, Jamie Harris and all the team in finance, production, publicity and design at Birlinn for all your faith, work and efforts.

My gratitude to my parents, who gave me my siblings and my education, and to my ever-supportive sisters-in-law, my wonderfully loving friends and readers.

Thank you to my playmates in Roma and at St Mary's in Lusaka, now scattered all over the world, to the Devasias family for lending their name, and the Lowthers for their unforgettable patience and generosity.

I am grateful to Sara Sullam for her discussions on Joyce's poetry in translation, and to Yulisa Dube, Thabo Kunene and Ian Pringle for their reports and accounts of the cross-border raids into Zambia and Mozambique.

Thank you immensely, James, for keeping my spirits up as I delved into my past. And finally, to my precious daughters: thank you from my heart for reminding me of my wonderful present.